'I kissed you ███████ irresistible, b███████████ have offended you, Miss Horne.

'It was wrong of me to take advantage of you.' Her eyes widened, their colour the hue of a mountain pool, clear and green, touched by sunshine. And then she smiled. 'You have robbed your action of any offence, sir. Nor can I pretend that I found it distasteful, for I did not—though I beg that you will not do it again without my permission.'

Drew laughed, for she was a breath of fresh air. It was her frankness, her open manner that fascinated him as much as her beauty. He had met women in society who might perhaps come near to her in looks, but none had made this direct appeal to his senses. At that moment he would have liked to take her down to the soft earth and lose himself in the sweetness of her flesh. Yet if he did that she would hate him, and he would be beyond redemption.

Author Note

Marianne's story is the first of a trilogy dealing with the lives and loves of three sisters. Marianne, Jo and Lucy are the Reverend Horne's daughters, and their papa, now sadly deceased, has been a big influence in their lives. Now things must change, for their mama has very little money and is at the mercy of her sister's charity. When Marianne is asked to stay with an ailing great-aunt, she cannot guess that she will be involved with dangerous smugglers, or that she will find love and change her life for ever.

I hope, dear reader, that you will enjoy following Marianne's story and that of her sisters as they struggle against and overcome the difficulties fate throws at them.

MARIANNE AND THE MARQUIS

Anne Herries

First published in Great Britain 2007
Harlequin Mills & Boon Limited,
Eton House, 18-24 Paradise Road, Richmond, Surrey TW9 1SR

© Anne Herries 2007

ISBN: 978 0 263 85189 2

Set in Times Roman 10½ on 13 pt.
04-0807-87655

Printed and bound in Spain
by Litografia Rosés S.A., Barcelona

Anne Herries, winner of the Romantic Novelists' Association ROMANCE PRIZE 2004, lives in Cambridgeshire. She is fond of watching wildlife, and spoils the birds and squirrels that are frequent visitors to her garden. Anne loves to write about the beauty of nature, and sometimes puts a little into her books, although they are mostly about love and romance. She writes for her own enjoyment, and to give pleasure to her readers.

Recent novels by the same author:

A DAMNABLE ROGUE*
RANSOM BRIDE

Winner of the Romantic Novelists' Association ROMANCE PRIZE

and in the Regency series *The Steepwood Scandal*:

LORD RAVENSDEN'S MARRIAGE
COUNTERFEIT EARL

and in *The Banewulf Dynasty*:

A PERFECT KNIGHT
A KNIGHT OF HONOUR
HER KNIGHT PROTECTOR

and in *The Hellfire Mysteries*:

AN IMPROPER COMPANION
A WEALTHY WIDOW
A WORTHY GENTLEMAN

Chapter One

London—1813

'They are a particularly nasty lot,' Captain Jack Harcourt said to his friend when they met at their sporting club that August afternoon. They had enjoyed a bout in the ring under the tuition of the master pugilist, Gentleman Jackson, and, stripped to the waist, their bodies gleamed with sweat. Jack's opponent was a little taller and more muscular, but they were evenly matched. 'If you take this on, you must understand that you risk your life if you are caught.'

Andrew, Lord Beck, Marquis of Marlbeck, doused himself under the pump in the yard and grinned at his friend of many years. They were alike in so many ways that they might have been blood kin, but in fact there was no relationship other than the bond they had forged fighting together in Portugal and Spain.

'If I were fool enough to get caught, I should deserve my fate,' he said, his eyes bright with mockery. 'Do not fear, Jack. I shan't let you down. I may have been forced to sell my commission, but I haven't gone soft. If this spy is to be found where you say, I am your man.'

'I didn't imagine you had lost your nerve for a moment. I rely on you to get to the bottom of this,' Jack told him. 'Because of him, seven of our friends died, Drew—and there were the men that served with us. At least twenty died needlessly that day, and who knows how many more? I want revenge for them, as I know you do. I would investigate this tale myself, but I have been seconded to special duties for Wellington.'

'You believe the spy was one of our own?' Drew looked at him through narrowed eyes. 'Someone we fought with, ate with…' He frowned, tasting the bitterness he had tried so hard to put behind him these past months. 'I like not the thought of that, Jack.'

The memory of all that they and their comrades had shared out there, of the pain, fear and grief at seeing the men they knew and cared for die in agony, was sharp in his mind.

'It makes me sick to my stomach,' Jack replied. 'If I could think otherwise, I should be a happier man—but everything leads me to believe that we were betrayed that day by an Englishman—and that even now he is working for Bonaparte.'

'My God!' Drew's eyes glinted with anger. He could never forget that day in Spain when he and a small detachment of his men had been sent on what was supposed to be a surprise sortie against the French. The enemy had somehow known of their coming and, though Jack, two others and Drew had escaped with their lives, seven of their comrades had been cut down as well as a number of the men that followed them. 'If I find him, he should say his last prayers!'

'No, that is not the way,' Jack warned him. 'He must hang

for his sins, Drew. If you take summary justice you are no better than he and his accomplices.'

'You think there was more than one involved?'

'One Englishman—the others are undoubtedly French.'

'And you think that they are now running this smuggling gang?'

'The smuggling is a cover for their other activities,' Jack said. 'I am sure that the spy comes and goes with the French ship, which brings in brandy, silks and laces under cover of darkness. But the Englishman is able to mix with people like us and use what he learns against our army. In short, he is a gentleman, or what passes for one. We are far from done with this war, Drew. It will come to a showdown in the end, and Wellington wants this spy caught and hung before he can betray more of our secrets.'

'The devil he does!' Drew frowned, his eyes glinting with blue fire, which burned cold, black ice at its centre. 'Well, I shall do my best to bring the traitor to heel.' He clapped his friend on the shoulder. 'It was good to have this time with you, Jack. I miss the old days…'

Drew had been called home when his uncle died—the Marlbeck estate was an important one, and, as his uncle's heir, he had been expected to sell his commission. It was his duty to care for the land, but with no other family, except a cousin some twenty years his senior, he sometimes found it a lonely task, missing the comradeship he had known in the army.

'You are sure you wish to become involved in this?' Jack asked. 'When Old Hooky suggested you, I thought you would turn it down. I confess I am surprised that you feel able to take something like this on. You must have enough to do with Marlbeck?'

'Duty becomes boring at times,' Drew said wryly. 'Wait until you are forced to settle down, my friend. You may long for adventure.'

'Adventure?' Jack frowned and wondered. He loved Drew as a friend and a brother, but there had been times when his wildness and temper had led him astray. 'This is serious business, Drew. You would be well advised not to forget it.'

'Do not look so doubtful,' Drew told him. 'I assure you that I am over all that…the nightmares hardly trouble me now. And even if they did, I should not let them interfere with my duty. You have asked me to discover the identity of the man who betrayed us—a spy working for the French and using a smuggling gang to cover his activities. I give you my word that I shall do everything I can to bring him to justice.'

'Then Wellington was right,' Jack said. 'You are the man for the work—and here's my hand on it.'

Drew clasped his hand firmly. No need to tell his friend that if he ever caught the spy, and knew him to be the traitor who had betrayed so many good men, he would kill him.

'Your aunt is coming to tea this afternoon, Marianne,' Mrs Horne announced as the family sat in their handsome parlour. The Vicarage was a large, substantial house filled with the personal treasures accumulated over the last twenty-five years since Mrs Horne had first come there as a bride. It had a slightly shabby air—money had not been plentiful—but until the last few months that had not bothered the family one whit. However, today there was a slightly apprehensive look in her soft blue eyes, for Cynthia Horne had always been in awe of her sister, and the feeling had grown more overpowering since the tragic death of the Reverend Horne some months earlier.

'Her note says that she has something she wishes to discuss with us.'

'Do you think she is going to ask us to live with her?' Jo asked, pulling a face. She had been cutting out a fashion plate from a magazine given her by some friends, which she intended to make into a doll for one of the poor children in the village. It was an attractive illustration; pasted on to a piece of board, it would make a toy for one of her worthy causes. Jo was always willing to help and had spent the morning visiting a poor family in the village. 'I think I would rather not be her guest, Mama.'

'You know we cannot stay here for much longer,' Marianne reminded her sister. At nineteen she was the eldest of the three Horne sisters and generally accounted a beauty, with her honey-blond hair and eyes that were a greenish-blue and often reflected her moods. She had a soft, very appealing mouth and was known for her equable disposition. 'It is only because the living is in Lord Wainwright's gift that we have been allowed this special favour—and we cannot expect it to continue for ever. We ought by rights to have left within a month of Papa's loss.'

The Reverend Horne's death had been such a shock to his family, for he had always seemed hale and filled with energy, forever working for his parishioners or in his long back garden, where he thought it no shame to grow food for his table and that of others.

'We need not despair,' Mrs Horne said, trying to rally herself as much as her daughters, because any mention of the Reverend's death was enough to have them all in tears. He was much missed by his family and parishioners alike. 'There is always the cottage that belonged to your grandfather. It is mine, though it has been let for years and provides me with a small income of my own. However, we could live in it if we had to. I know it means moving to Cambridgeshire, but I think I might prefer that to living on Agatha's charity, which would not be comfortable for any of us.'

'Please, do not say we must live with Lady Wainwright,' Lucy cried. Her blue eyes filled with tears. 'If only darling Papa had not died. He was such a good person, always helping others. Why did he have to get pneumonia and die? I think God was cruel to take him from us.' The youngest of the three sisters, she was her family's darling. She burst into tears and was comforted by her eldest sister, who put an arm around her and hushed her.

'Don't cry, dearest,' Marianne said, stroking Lucy's soft hair, which was like pale silk, shimmering in a ray of sunshine that pierced the long windows overlooking the back garden. Just now the garden was a mass of roses and sweet-smelling flowers, a peaceful haven for the birds and droning bees. 'We all wish that Papa was still with us, but tears will not change things. We have to decide what to do for the best. Uncle Wainwright has been good enough to let us stay here until we have had time to come to terms with our loss, but he needs to provide a proper house for the new vicar—and this is his property.'

Lord Wainwright was a generous man, and Marianne knew that her family had reason to be grateful to him, but his wife, her mama's sister, lost no opportunity to make them aware of the fact that they were living on her husband's charity. Lady Wainwright was very conscious of her position in society and had always let her sister know that she was very much below her in the social scale as the wife of a poor parson.

'But it is our home,' Jo said. 'It is unfair that we should

have to move. Why can the new vicar not live somewhere else? Lord Wainwright has plenty of houses. He could let us stay here if he wished.'

'Because this is the Vicarage,' Marianne said. Jo was the fiery member of the family. She had hair the colour of flame and eyes that were sometimes as green as the emerald in Mama's wedding ring. 'Uncle Wainwright may let us live in one of his other properties, but we must leave this house soon. It is the way things are, Jo, and there is nothing we can do but be grateful that we shall still have a home.'

'Can you not talk to him, Mama?' Jo demanded, unwilling to be pacified by her sister. 'He likes you. I sometimes think he likes you more than he does Aunt Agatha.'

'Jo!' Mrs Horne was startled. She was well aware that her sister's husband had feelings for her, but she was careful never to presume on them. 'You must not say such things. It is quite untrue, my dear. Besides—' She broke off as they heard the rattle of carriage wheels at the front of the house. 'Your aunt is here. Please, my darlings, no more of this talk. Remember that for the moment we are living on your uncle's charity.'

Jo subsided, though she looked stubborn. Of the three girls, she possibly found it the hardest to hide her resentment of the problems that had beset them since the Reverend Horne's untimely death. She had a bright, quick mind like her father, and she had taken his loss hard. Marianne and Lucy grieved for Papa, as Mama did, of course, but it was Jo who was angry at the unfairness of their situation. The discovery that Papa's trust fund, as a younger son, had ceased on his death, had thrown the family into a precarious situation financially.

Marianne smiled at her sister encouragingly. She understood what Jo was feeling, because she had never been particularly fond of her aunt. Lady Wainwright had a dominant personality and her marriage had given her an inflated idea of her own importance. A woman of some temper, she tended to look down on Mrs Horne because she had married for love a gentleman of good birth but little fortune—and perhaps, the perceptive Marianne thought, because she was aware that her sister had been truly loved.

Marianne rose to her feet as the imperious figure of her aunt swept into the room. Lady Wainwright was tall and thin, her features often giving the impression that she found life sour. She surveyed her sister's family as they curtsied politely, nodding as if she expected no less. They were beneath her in rank, and must be made aware of what they owed to their benefactor.

'Cynthia,' she said and kissed the air as Mrs Horne presented her cheek. 'You look tired. I suppose it is no wonder with all your troubles. Well, I have good news. Wainwright says you may have the Lodge. It is smaller than this house, but adequate, I dare say, for you cannot afford to entertain as you did. You will move as soon as it can be arranged.'

'That is good of him…' Mrs Horne was flustered, relieved that she was being offered a home, though there were only three bedrooms at the Lodge, which would mean that two of the girls must share, and their maid Lily would have to sleep in the kitchen on a truckle bed. 'It is very kind of him, I'm sure.'

'Yes, for he need not have done anything,' Lady Wainwright said, 'and would not but for the fact that you are my sister.' She smiled in a satisfied way as she saw her sister fade back into her chair. 'But that is not all my news. I must tell you that my physician has decided I need to take the waters in Bath.' She put a hand to her ample bosom, just now clad in crimson silk. 'Wainwright insists that I overdid things when we were in London. It was Annette's coming out, as you know, and now that she is safely married I have time for your daughters, Cynthia.'

Marianne and Jo exchanged glances across the room, their expressions registering shock and dismay. Neither of them wished to be the centre of Lady Wainwright's attention, but they knew that it must be one of them, for Lucy was too young to come out yet.

'But we…' Mrs Horne subsided under her sister's frightful eye. 'Of course we should be grateful for the house, but—'

'You did not look for anything more,' Lady Wainwright finished for her. 'And why should you? The tenancy of the Lodge is extremely generous of Wainwright—but this is to fall on my shoulders. I have decided that I shall take Marianne to Bath with me. I believe she will have plenty of chances to find a good match there, for she could not normally expect to look higher than a younger son, though as my niece she may gain some credit. I might have taken her to London with Annette, but I thought it a waste of money and time. Annette is an heiress and received several excellent offers, as you know—but Marianne must settle for something less. I hope that she may catch a baronet if she is fortunate, but, if not, a gentleman of some reasonable fortune will do well enough.' She looked at Marianne expectantly. 'There, miss, what have you to say to your aunt? Is that not more than you could ever have hoped for?'

'Yes, indeed,' Marianne answered. She clasped her
hands in front of her, because it would not do to speak as
she felt. Every sensibility cried out at her aunt's words,
making her embarrassed and angry. Had Lady Wainwright
couched her invitation in another way, she might have been
grateful for the opportunity, but as it was she could hardly
keep from letting her anger show. 'It was kind of you to
think of me…'

Mrs Horne saw her daughter struggling and understood her
resentment. Fortunately, a knock at the door heralded the
arrival of Lily with the tea tray, and for a few minutes they
were occupied by the pouring and serving of tea, tiny cakes
and biscuits, all freshly made by the girl that morning under
Mrs Horne's expert eye.

'That gel is well mannered and she makes a decent cake,'
Lady Wainwright said as she ate three of the almond comfits
one after the other and then sipped her tea. 'If she ever leaves
your employ, I should be happy to take her.'

'I am sure she would be gratified to know that,' Mrs Horne
told her, 'but I simply couldn't manage without her, Agatha.
She has been invaluable and offered to work just for her bed
and board when she knew how we are situated. Of course I
pay her what I can, but I am afraid it isn't much.'

'Lily knows you would give her more if you could,' Jo
said. She had watched her aunt's hand reach for the last of
the almond comfits, which were her favourites, and felt
cheated, because she hadn't managed to save one for herself.
'Besides, she loves being with us. I am sure she would rather
live with us than at the Hall.'

'You are very outspoken, Josephine,' Lady Wainwright
said. 'I wonder that your mother allows you to speak your

mind so openly—but I dare say it is all of a piece. Cynthia never was a disciplinarian.'

Jo opened her mouth, but shut it again at a warning look from her elder sister. She got up and went over to glance out of the window. Seeing the curate walking towards the house, she excused herself to her mother and ran out through the French doors to greet him.

'Well, really,' Lady Wainwright exclaimed. 'You must teach that girl better manners, Cynthia. Otherwise she will never marry.'

'I am not sure that Jo wishes to marry,' her mother said with a fond look at her second daughter as she stood talking to the curate. 'She is rather a bluestocking, I am afraid, though where that came from I do not know. I suppose her father, for it is not from me. I was never much given to study.'

'You were always something of a featherbrain in your youth,' Lady Wainwright said. Marianne made a movement of protest for it was not the truth, but her mother's expression prevented her from speaking out. 'However, we shall not draw comparisons. Marianne is decidedly the beauty of the family, and she does get that from you, for you were a beauty in your day, Cynthia.'

'How kind of you to say so,' Cynthia said and smiled faintly. 'I believe I was admired once upon a time.'

'You are still very handsome,' Marianne said, rushing to her defence. 'No one could think otherwise.'

'Yes, I agree,' Lady Wainwright said, surprising them. 'I think you might make another match if you set your mind to it, Cynthia, which would be much the best for you if it could be achieved—that is why Marianne must make a good

marriage. She will then be able to introduce her sisters
her circle and perhaps you, too, may meet someone suitab

'Oh, no, I do not think—' Once again Mrs Horne
saved by the arrival of her maid, this time bearing a le
'Yes, Lily, is that for me?'

'Yes, it is, ma'am,' Lily said and beamed at her. 'It
come all the way from Cornwall and the post rider says
he is to return for your reply in the morning—unless you v
to give it now?'

'That sounds urgent,' Cynthia said and took the letter.
broke the seal in an agitated manner, because she kne
must be from Lady Edgeworthy, her Aunt Bertha.
scanned the lines swiftly and then closed her eyes f
moment. 'Oh, dear, it seems that my Aunt Bertha has l
ill, Marianne, and she begs that you go to her at once, fo
needs a companion.'

'Marianne is to come to Bath with me,' Lady Wainw
cried. 'You must write and tell Lady Edgeworthy that it i
possible—or send one of the other girls.'

Cynthia sat up straight in her chair, because she was ca
on the horns of a dilemma, but for once she was not prep
to give in to her sister. 'I am sorry, Agatha,' she
'Marianne is Bertha's godchild and I think, in this insta
I must deny your request. Bertha is elderly and possibly
I know that she loves Marianne dearly, and I think she
take precedence this time.'

Lady Wainwright gave her an awful look. It was on th
of her tongue to say that she would withdraw her favours
the family, but she knew that it was not in her power to
them the Lodge. Wainwright had been most insistent th
wanted to give them a home of their own, and had

inclined towards letting them stay at the Vicarage. His wife had persuaded him that it would look odd if he did, so he had substituted the Lodge, though he had told his wife that he might look out for a larger establishment for them in time.

'Well, I suppose if she has been ill…' Lady Wainwright rose to her feet. 'I shall have to think about this again, Cynthia. I am not sure whether or not Josephine is ready to go out into society, but I will let you know my decision in a few days.'

Marianne smiled and went to kiss her aunt's cheek. 'It was very kind of you to think of me, Aunt,' she said. 'But I am sure my great-aunt needs me or she would not have sent all this way and paid for a reply.'

'No, perhaps not.' Lady Wainwright nodded. 'You are a good girl to give up pleasure for yourself in favour of Lady Edgeworthy. I shall consider whether I think Josephine is ready to accompany me to Bath, but I must confess I should have been happier with you.'

Marianne made no answer, but went to the door to see her aunt off. She returned to find the parlour in turmoil. Jo had returned to the room and was venting her frustration at not being able to tell Lady Wainwright what she thought of her invitation, and Mrs Horne was trying to soothe her.

'You never know, she may decide that you are not good mannered enough to accompany her,' Marianne said with a sparkle in her eyes. She dodged the cushion Jo threw at her. 'Well, you do not exactly put on your best manner when she is near, Jo—do you?'

'Perhaps not,' her sister said, her cheeks pink. 'But she is so—so smug!'

'Yes, she is,' Marianne agreed. 'And some of the things she says to Mama make me want to strike her, but we must be

careful. Politeness keeps us from saying too much—and
husband has done a great deal to help us these past mont[

'Indeed he has,' Mrs Horne said. 'I do not know how
should have managed without him. Besides, you will m
others like your aunt in company, Jo. You have to learn to [
your tongue, my dear. It will not do to be churlish or
mannered, for you would soon find yourself unwelcome

'I know,' Jo said and looked slightly ashamed. 'But
does try my patience so. If she asks me to accompany he
Bath, I need not go—please say I may refuse her, Mama

'I cannot compel you to go,' Mrs Horne said and loo
distressed. 'But it will make things so difficult, Jo, my d
You know your aunt as well as I—and, besides, it migh
a good thing for you. She is sure to buy you some new clot[
and you may meet someone nice.'

'I am not sure that I wish to marry,' Jo reminded her. '
a pity that I am not Aunt Bertha's godchild—I would w
ingly exchange places with Marianne.'

'You might enjoy yourself in Bath,' Marianne reasor
'You are always saying that there are never enough book
the library in Mallham, Jo. I dare say there will be many n
in Bath, for it is a fashionable spa.'

Mallham was the small neighbouring village, and [
nearest town was Huntingdon, a drive of some fifteen m[
While the Reverend Horne had lived, they had manage
visit the town every few weeks to purchase or borrow bo
but now, without the carriage that they could no longer aff
it was impossible.

'Yes, I suppose there is that,' Jo agreed, looking thou
ful. 'And there may be some literary circles I might joir
the time we are there.'

'There is also the matter of Lucy's future,' Mrs Horne said. 'I know she is young yet, but she will wish to marry one day, and I shall never be in a position to give her a Season in town. Your godmother may do something for you, Marianne, and Jo may find a husband in Bath…if she wishes—but what of Lucy?'

The sisters turned to look at Lucy. She was sitting by the window, looking out, her head full of dreams, hardly aware of the discussion going on behind her, but she turned to look at them and smiled.

'Did someone speak my name? I was dreaming again…of a knight on a white horse who came and rescued me from the castle of the wicked witch. He took me to his home in a land where the sun always shines, and then I sent for all of you to come and live with me. And we were all happy ever after.'

'Oh, Lucy,' Mrs Horne said and shook her head, smiling because, though she tried very hard not to favour her, Lucy was her baby and her darling. 'You read too many fairy stories, my love. I fear that you will be disappointed one day when you discover that the knights you dream of are only fables.'

'Oh, I know that,' Lucy replied, uncurling from her seat in the window and coming towards them. She was perhaps potentially prettier than either of her sisters with hair that floated like white gold about her face and made her look like one of the princesses she dreamed of, her eyes a deep-sea blue that seemed as mysterious as the ocean. 'I just like to dream because everything is so awful. I did hear what my aunt said, but neither Marianne or Jo want to go with her. Do they have to, Mama?'

'I am not certain that I shall refuse after all,' Jo said and put an affectionate arm about Lucy's waist. 'It will be : perience, and an author must experience life to write it…' She waited expectantly for their questions.

'Jo?' her mother asked anxiously. 'Just what are y to?'

'I have decided to write a book,' Jo said and laughed mother looked shocked. 'It is not so very wicked, M Other ladies do it and I think I should like to try, thou course I cannot afford to have it published, and I d imagine a publisher would pay me. However, for my pleasure and that of my sisters, I shall write my story.'

'How exciting,' Lucy said. 'Will it have knights and cesses in towers, Jo?'

'No, I don't think so,' she said. 'It will be a love Lucy, though it may not end as your fairy stories do everyone living happily ever after.'

'I shall look forward to hearing you read little bits Marianne said, 'though we may have to wait for a because I think I should go down to Aunt Bertha almc mediately, do you not, Mama?'

'Oh yes,' her mother said and clapped her hand mouth. 'Do you suppose that poor boy is still waiting answer?'

'I asked him to return in the morning when I went door with my aunt, Mama. I knew you would wish to cc your reply. He will be here at seven of the clock ton so that your letter may catch the mail coach at ha seven.'

'How thoughtful you are, dearest,' her mother said, her a look of approval. 'I hope that you did not mind up the visit to Bath in favour of your godmother?'

'You must know that I did not,' Marianne said. 'It is always a pleasure to see Aunt Bertha, and I could not do otherwise when she wrote and asked for me especially. I expect she feels lonely, though I know she has a companion.'

'I thought you would feel as you ought,' her mother said with a smile. 'We must go through your clothes, Marianne. Fortunately, you had a new evening dress last year, which you have hardly worn, but we must see if we can manage something further—I would not have you go there in rags.'

'I am not yet reduced to that,' Marianne said and laughed. 'Indeed, several of my gowns will be perfectly suitable with a little refurbishment.'

'You must have at least one new gown,' her mother said with a fond smile. 'I had been saving my shillings for your birthdays, but I think Marianne's gown should come first—do you all agree?'

'Yes, of course,' Jo said. 'Aunt Wainwright will not have me shame her so she is bound to have some dresses made for me. You don't mind, do you, Lucy?'

'Of course not,' Lucy said, though her birthday was in a few weeks' time. 'Marianne must have some new clothes.'

'We shall go into Huntingdon and buy them,' Mrs Horne said. 'There is no time to waste, Marianne. We shall take the mail coach in the morning—all of us. It will be a treat and we surely deserve it after these past few months.'

The girls looked at each other in delight. Jo thought of the books she might subscribe from the library, Lucy thought of the adventure it would be to ride in the mail coach, and Marianne was wondering how much ribbon and trifles she could buy with five shillings, which was all the money she possessed in the world.

* * *

However, Mama had been hoarding her shillings for s[o]
time and she actually had ten pounds in her purse when
descended from the coach the following day.

There was but one shop in the small town that sold go[wns]
already made up, and they set off immediately, becaus[e]
wanted to help her sister choose her new clothes be[fore]
visiting the library.

In the event, Mrs Herrington had three gowns in stock
would fit Marianne: a pale blue silk with a high waist
little puff sleeves that would do for an evening party, a
blue walking gown and a yellow afternoon dress. All t[hree]
looked well on Marianne, needing only a few tucks here
there, which she could easily do herself. After some d[elib]
eration she decided that she would need the evening gow[n]
most, but the seamstress saw their difficulty and told
Horne that she could make a good price for all three.

'Oh, no, Mama, that would be much too expensive. I
easily refurbish some of my others with new ribbons
some silk flowers,' Marianne protested.

'How much for the three?' Mrs Horne asked bravely.
kept her smile in place when she was told that the eve[ning]
gown was five guineas, but twelve would buy all three go[wns]

'Oh, dear, I am afraid that is beyond me,' Mrs Horne
and frowned. 'It is very reasonable, madam, but too muc[h for]
me. We shall take the evening gown, but must say no t[o the]
others.'

The seamstress looked disappointed. 'They were m[ade]
for a customer who did not pay her bills,' the seams[tress]
replied. 'I am letting them go at cost to recover some o[f my]
money.'

'I wish we might take all three,' Mrs Horne said. 'But it cannot be done. If you would be kind enough to have it delivered to the posting inn, madam. We have some more shopping to do.' She smiled at Marianne. 'You will need slippers, too, my love—and a bonnet if we can manage it.'

'It is a beautiful dress, Mama,' Marianne said as they left the shop afterwards. 'But expensive.'

'I should have liked to purchase all three,' Mrs Horne said. 'But we shall buy some material from the market and you and Jo can make at least one afternoon dress before you leave if you each do some of the sewing.'

'I'll help, too,' Lucy said and then laughed, for she was not yet as clever a seamstress as her sisters, being inclined to fall into a dream over her work.

'Yes, you can help, dearest,' Marianne said and smiled at her. 'Besides, I have several dresses that can be refurbished with new sashes and some fresh lace.'

'I have some lace put by,' her mama said. 'Yes, I dare say it will be enough, Marianne—and who knows, your aunt might give you something.'

'You do not mean Aunt Wainwright?' Marianne frowned. 'I had rather not, Mama.'

'I meant my aunt Bertha,' Mrs Horne said and smiled. 'Now, let us see what else we can buy…'

Two pairs of slippers and a pair of boots were bought next, but the bonnets proved too expensive. Marianne purchased some ribbons to refurbish her old ones, and a bunch of silk flowers. Both she and Jo were good at making and trimming their hats, and it was something they enjoyed doing together.

Jo had slipped away to the library while they were pur-

chasing some small items from Mama's remaining shi▮
and returned with an armful of books for herself and ▮
Her young sister was delighted with the illustrated cc▮
fables and thanked her sister with a hug and a kiss.

After partaking of some bread and honey and tea ▮
inn, they collected their parcels and climbed wearily in▮
coach heading home.

'Well, that was a splendid day,' Mrs Horne said. '▮
save my money again for some months and then we m▮
it again—perhaps for Lucy next time, because I am su▮
Agatha will give you a generous sum to purchase ▮
clothes, Jo. She would not allow you to appear with ▮
Bath looking dowdy.'

'Yes, I dare say,' Jo replied. She already had her no▮
book and was lost in a world of her own.

Mrs Horne gave her a rueful look. Jo was the least e▮
manage of her daughters and she dreaded to think what ▮
happen if she accompanied her aunt to Bath.

When they arrived back at the Vicarage, it w▮
discover that a letter had come from Lord Wainwri▮
it, he said that he would be sending Marianne to Co▮
in one of his own carriages. She might therefore ▮
refund on the public coach ticket that her godmoth▮
purchased for her, and he had sent a small purse o▮
sovereigns, which, once opened and counted, amour▮
twenty pounds.

'Oh, Mama,' Marianne said in awe. 'It is far too mu▮
must send it back. I could not take all that from my u▮

'Nonsense,' Mrs Horne said and smiled. 'It is g▮
him, to be sure, and I did not expect it—but he wo▮

offended if we returned it. You must write him a letter, my dear, and thank him for his kindness.'

'I am very willing to do so,' Marianne said, 'if you think we may accept such generosity?'

'Yes, of course. You will need some money in your purse and I was wondering whether I might sell my pearls…but now I can give them to you to wear, for you have nothing but your silver locket.'

'Oh, Mama…' Marianne glowed. 'I shall keep them safe and give them back to you when I return. And I want you to take the ten pounds you spent for my clothes today, if you please. Ten pounds is more than enough for me.'

'I shall take five, if you wish,' Mrs Horne said. 'Perhaps Lucy and I will have a day in Huntingdon when you two are away.'

'Please take the ten pounds,' Marianne said. 'I felt very guilty to be spending all your money, Mama. You may need it and I shall be quite content with what I have.'

'Had we known he intended to give you something we might have purchased all three of those pretty gowns, my love,' Mrs Horne said, looking regretful.

'I am very pleased with the material we bought, and that roll of blue velvet from the market was so cheap that there is enough for both Jo and Lucy to have something as well.'

'You have such a generous nature,' Mrs Horne said. 'Your papa told me so often that you would make all our fortunes, because you were bound to marry well. He was sure that one day you would meet a young aristocrat at your uncle's house—or a guest of the Marquis of Marlbeck…'

'I have never met anyone I liked particularly at one of Aunt Wainwright's dinners,' Marianne said. 'All her friends seem

so proud and disagreeable, Mama. And you know tha
were never invited to dine at Marlbeck, though of cours
went to the open day in the garden as all the marquis's ne
bours did.'

'Well, he has died, poor man,' Mrs Horne said and si
'As yet no one has met his heir. I have heard that he spends
of his time in London, but I do not know how true that may

'Even if he lived here, it would change nothing,' Mari
said and smiled at her mother. 'He is probably very pro
like his uncle—and I am sure he would not wish to marr
daughter of a parson, even one as beautiful as Lucy.'

'Well, it does not matter,' her mother said. 'All I wa
for you to be happy, dearest. If it pleases you to marry a
man with no fortune, I shall not blame you.'

'Oh, Mama,' Marianne said, smiling at her through
misted with tears. 'We were all so fortunate to have de
Papa. I am sure that none of us would consider marry
man who did not match up to him.'

Alone in her room later that night, Marianne sat a
window and looked out at the night sky. The garden v
shadow—the moon had gone behind clouds and there
no stars to be seen. She had opened her window
because it was a warm night and she did not feel
sleeping. Her thoughts were busy with the visit to her
aunt and her hopes for the future. Marriage had been a d
possibility until recently, because she had known that th
of a dowry might hamper her chances, even if friend
family universally acclaimed her as a beauty. Her fa
curate, Thomas Rowan, liked her very much, po:
enough to ask her to marry him, but he could not affe

take a wife just yet and Marianne was not certain of her answer if he did ask her.

However, she was relieved that she had been spared the visit to Bath with Lady Wainwright, for she would not have cared to be paraded on the marriage mart. Her only true experience of high society had been met with in her aunt's house, and it had led her to have a dislike of aristocrats. She much preferred the company of ordinary, good-natured folk like her papa and the neighbours she was accustomed to meeting.

She was not surprised when she heard a knock at her door and then Jo came in, dressed in a white nightgown with pink embroidery about the high neck. She smiled when she saw that Marianne was not in bed, perching on the side of it and tucking her feet underneath her.

'I saw that you had not blown out your candle,' she said. 'I could not sleep for thinking of Lady Wainwright. If she does ask I must go, if only for Lucy's sake. I am sure I shall not meet anyone who wishes to marry me—and I shall not care for that—but if I do not show willing, Lucy may never get her chance.' Both sisters were extremely fond of their young sibling and thought her perfect in every way.

'If Aunt Bertha had kept her house open in London, she might have invited us all there,' Marianne said with a little frown. 'I know Mama visited London with her once, and had hopes that we might be invited again. I do not mind for myself, Jo, because I would as soon not marry a man of high birth— but Lucy ought to have her chance.'

'You are the beauty,' Jo said and looked at her elder sister fondly. 'Lucy may match you in a year or two—but I am cursed with this!' She scrunched up her red hair, which curled into ringlets naturally and was the bane of her life. 'But I know you do not wish for a grand marriage. Perhaps you will meet a pleasant gentleman…someone like Papa…'

'Yes, that would be the most fortunate thing,' Marianne said and smiled at her, in perfect agreement. 'But I am not sure that another such could be found…'

Jo nodded—their father had been the best of men and they both still mourned him sincerely. 'Well, I suppose it would be unfair to compare other men to his image,' she said. 'But it would suit you to be married to a clergyman, I think.'

'Yes, perhaps,' Marianne agreed. 'Though I should like to be loved and to love…'

'Romantic love.' Jo laughed a little scornfully. 'I think Mama and Papa cared for each other, but I am not sure that I believe in true love the way Lucy does.'

'No?' Marianne smiled at her sister. 'I think if one is lucky it does happen, dearest—but undoubtedly many marriages are for reasons other than love.'

'Such as the marriage Aunt Wainwright would have had you make?' Jo looked angry. 'As if you were not far more beautiful than Annette could ever be! She is nothing beside you.'

'Jo dearest,' Marianne reproved with a loving look that robbed her words of their sting, 'you must learn to curb your tongue. It just will not do to say such things in company.'

'Well, my aunt need not take me if she is afraid I may shame her,' Jo said defiantly. 'I am happier at home and would tell her so, except that it might rebound on Lucy—and you also if Great-aunt Bertha sends you home with nothing.'

'I am going to visit her because I care about her,' Marianne said. 'I do not think of a reward, despite Mama's hopes. I know she worries for us, but I do not particularly mind being poor, Jo. I just wish Papa were still alive. I miss him.'

'We all miss him,' Jo said. 'As for Aunt Wainwright suggesting that Mama might marry again—and Papa hardly cold in his grave!'

'Yes, it was thoughtless of her,' Marianne agreed. 'But I dare say she does not realise how loving Mama and Papa were together.'

Jo nodded and yawned. 'Well, I suppose talking will not change things. I shall go to bed and allow you to sleep. We must be up early if we are to have that new afternoon gown ready for you in time…'

'Goodnight, dearest.' Marianne kissed her cheek.

After her sister left, she got into bed and blew out the candle. However, she lay awake, thinking for some time before she drifted into a peaceful sleep.

Drew stood in the library of Marlbeck Manor, glancing around him, his eye passing over row upon row of leather-bound books that gave the room its immaculate appearance. Not a book out of place, most of them as untouched as they had been the day his uncle had bought them, by the yard in all probability, and few of them worth reading.

His boots rang on the marble floor as he strode into the hall, echoing in the emptiness of what felt like a huge mausoleum. The house was a magnificent piece of architecture, furnished to the highest standards and stuffed with valuable objects from gold snuff boxes to Chinese vases and oil paintings that had been perfected by a master long ago, and he hated it. It was not a home, had never been home to him. For two pins he would sell it or tear it down and build something more comfortable, and yet that would be sacrilege. And he knew that it didn't belong to him; he was merely

the custodian, and he must pass it on one day to so
more deserving.

Perhaps it wasn't the house that he hated, Drew
as he stared at a reflection of himself in a magnifice
framed mirror. Maybe it was his life—himself. Since
been forced to resign from the army and come home
his responsibilities as the eleventh Marquis of Marlb
had become aware that he was almost as empty as t
house—empty of anything worthwhile.

He frequented the clubs when he was in town, dra
other young gentlemen, drove his horses and sparred
himself fit—but where was the point of it all? At leas
he was out there in the thick of battle, not knowing fr
to day whether he would survive, he had known who
and what he wanted of life. Now there was nothing
prospect of the lonely years stretching ahead.

But at last there was something he could do—so
that might ease the anger he had held inside him si
friends were killed…betrayed by a traitor who had
their lives for gold. If he could bring that man to
would at least give some purpose to his life.

His eyes gleamed, self-mockery driving away his
blue devils as he shouted for his manservant.
promised Jack he would do what he could, and now
duty was done here for the moment, he would keep h
Suddenly, he felt better than he had since he came
would be a mad adventure, perhaps his last before he
he knew to be his duty and settled down to finding a
order to provide an heir for the estate.

But where would he find a wife that he could bea
with for more than a month? Most of the young lac

were paraded under his nose every time he attended a social affair would drive him to distraction within hours. He needed...wanted...he did not know. At times there was a yearning need in him, but he had no idea what it was that he needed...

Suddenly he laughed out loud, the sound of it echoing in the vast hall. What a damned fool! He was like a wounded dog, howling at the moon for no other reason than a feeling of deep loneliness inside.

Chapter Two

~~~~~~~~~~~~~~~~~~~~~~~~~~~~~~~~

Marianne glanced at the woman sitting opposite her in her uncle's comfortable carriage. Lord Wainwright employed Sally as the housekeeper's assistant, and he had insisted on sending her with his niece, because she was five and twenty and a capable young woman.

'You will need to break your journey for at least two nights, and if there should be an accident to the coach you might be marooned at an inn for a day or so while the repairs are done. I should be anxious if I thought you alone, Marianne. You are still young and innocent, though I know you are very sensible. However, I should feel easier in my mind if you had Sally Jones to accompany you, because she will look out for you, my dear.'

'Then I shall be very happy to have Sally as my companion for the journey,' Marianne told him. 'You have been so considerate, Uncle, and I cannot thank you enough.'

'You are a good girl and deserve every consideration,' he had told her and kissed her cheek.

So far her uncle's fears for her journey had proved unfounded, but it had passed the hours more pleasantly having someone to talk to—though Sally had been sleeping for the past hour or so. Marianne might have followed her example, except that she enjoyed looking out of the window. Her thoughts were already with her great-aunt. It was some years since she had seen Aunt Bertha and she was wondering if she might find her much changed.

Suddenly, the coach halted amidst a jangling of brasses and some juddering that shook Sally awake, making her rub her eyes and look at Marianne in bewilderment.

'What has happened, miss?'

'We have stopped for some reason,' Marianne said. She looked out of the window. 'I think there has been an accident to a coach ahead of us…yes, it appears that several men are helping to push it to the side of the road.' She opened her door and got down, looking at Lord Wainwright's groom as he came up to her.

'I had to stop, Miss Horne. I'll give them a hand and then we'll soon be on our way again.'

'Yes, of course, George,' Marianne said. She followed the groom along the narrow country road towards the damaged coach, because she had seen two ladies standing at the edge of the road. They looked upset, as they might well do, the younger almost in tears. 'I am so sorry for your misfortune,' Marianne said. 'It could be some time before your wheel is repaired—may we take you up with us as far as the next inn?'

The older lady looked at her for a moment and then nodded. 'How kind of you,' she said. 'We should be glad of that, should we not, Henriette? My grooms may fetch help and follow us with the coach as soon as they are able.'

'Oh…yes, Mama,' the girl said, but she was not looking at her mother. Her eyes were on one of the gentlemen helping with the carriage. Marianne glanced in the direction of the girl's gaze, seeing a man with fashionably cropped black hair. He had taken off his coat, his shirt sleeves rolled up to the elbows. He looked to be very strong and was directing the operations, but as he did not glance their way, Marianne could not see his face. The two ladies followed her to the coach and climbed inside.

'I should introduce myself,' the older of the two said. 'I am Lady Forester and this is my daughter Henriette. We are on our way to stay with friends in Devon.'

'I am Marianne Horne, and I am visiting my great-aunt. She has been unwell and needs some company.'

'Ah, yes, illness always makes one so low,' Lady Forester said.

'Yes…' Marianne glanced out of the window as she heard a shout. 'They have moved your carriage, Lady Forester. We should be on our way at any moment now.'

As she spoke, the man who had been directing operations turned in their direction and looked towards their coach. Marianne could see his face now. He was attractive with a strong, determined face and eyes that looked a very dark blue. He was such a striking man that she was not surprised that Henriette had been more interested in watching him than listening to her mama. For a moment his eyes seemed to dwell on Marianne's face and she was aware of a peculiar flutter in her stomach. He was so…very masculine, so very different to every other man she had met in her sheltered life. Her cheeks felt a little warm and she looked down. When she dared to look again, he had turned away and was about to mount his horse.

'It was kind of that gentleman to help us, was it not, Mama?' Henriette said.

'Yes,' her mama agreed. 'But no more than any decent man would do, I dare say.' She spoke dismissively, as if the gentleman were of no consequence to her mind, though her daughter's face reflected rather different feelings towards their gallant rescuer.

As their carriage drew level with him, the man glanced towards it once more. For a moment Marianne gazed into eyes that were so blue and bright that she felt suddenly breathless. Something about him made her heart race for no reason at all that she could think of. He looked directly at her, his eyes bold and challenging. He did not drop his gaze, continuing to stare at her until they had passed him. It was unsettling to be looked at in that way, and she decided that he was not a gentleman, for surely a gentleman would never have looked at any lady in that way, particularly one he did not know. Meeting Henriette's gaze across the carriage, she saw the slightly wistful expression and smiled, understanding that the girl had been smitten. She was very young, not much above Lucy's age, and the incident must have seemed like something out of a fairy tale perhaps…a handsome prince riding to their rescue.

'Tell me, Miss Forester,' she said. 'Do you read much?'

'Oh yes,' the girl replied, her face lighting up. 'I love the romantic poets, do I not, Mama?'

Her mother agreed that she did and the conversation turned towards various poets they all admired. In this way the time passed pleasantly enough until Marianne was able to set them down at the next inn.

'Well, that was an adventure,' Sally said, once they were on their way again. 'It is a pity they were not going to Cornwall, miss. The young lady would have been a nice friend for you.'

'Yes, perhaps,' Marianne said. 'She was charming, her mother, too—but I dare say we shall not meet again.'

She eased against the cushions, feeling thankful that her uncle had provided her with such a comfortable mode of transport. They would probably be on the road for at least another two days. For a moment she sighed, wishing that she might have travelled on horseback like the man who had seemed in command when the damaged coach was moved from the road. He would get wherever he was going much faster. For a moment she envied his freedom, thinking how pleasant it would be to be riding on a day like this, and then she shook her head and smiled. How shocking of her to be thinking that she would like to be riding with a man she did not know and never would.

Drew yawned as he leaned his head against the high back of his chair. It was now well past midnight and nothing had happened. Earlier that evening, he had carried his chair to the window, giving himself a clear view of the cove below. He had been lucky to find a suitable property, but it belonged to the Edgeworthy estate and had once been home to a cousin of the elderly lady who owned it now. His agent had negotiated the lease for him, telling him that the lady's man of business had been very willing to rent it to Drew for a few months. He had found the local man eager to be of service when they arrived the previous day.

He had given Drew the key, saying, 'You will find it a solid house, though nothing has been done to it for years, Mr Beck. The last occupier fell to his death from the cliff path and Lady Edgeworthy thought it best to shut the place down. However, she will be happy to rent it to you for as long as you wish.'

'That is most kind of her,' Drew said. 'As I told you, I am here for my health…' He gave a little cough behind his hand. 'Sea air and exercise will benefit me greatly, and I like to watch the gulls as they circle over the cliffs.'

'Well, if you feel it will suit you. I've had the house cleaned, of course—shall I hire a woman to cook and clean for you every day?'

'Thank you for having the house cleaned,' Drew said, 'but I have brought my manservant—he will care for me as he always does.'

Drew was smiling to himself as that servant entered the room, carrying a decanter of brandy and a glass on a small tray, which he set down on a table nearby.

'Will you be wanting me again this evening, sir?'

'No, thank you, Robbie. If I were you, I should get some sleep. You will have enough to do in the next few weeks— and I may need you one of these nights.'

'Right you are, Captain.'

'It's just Mr Beck for the moment,' Drew reminded him gently. Robbie had been his batman in Spain, and had returned to the estate with him when he sold out, caring for his personal needs much as he had while they were both soldiers. He knew that some of his neighbours, and indeed the other servants at the Manor, found it an odd arrangement, for Robbie was no picture-book hero with his scarred face and black patch over one eye. 'We want to appear as ordinary as possible. I am recovering from illness and you are my faithful manservant.'

'Yes, sir,' Robbie replied. 'It might be better if you called me Harris—some might find Robbie a mite familiar. You can get away with it as Marlbeck, but not as Mr Beck, I believe.'

'Yes, perhaps you are right,' Drew acknowledged. 'But when we are alone it does not matter, Robbie.'

'Right you are, Captain.'

Drew grinned as his servant left the room. Robbie never missed a trick, and perhaps it was his intelligence and his dry humour that had forged the bond between them. Robbie had patched Drew's wounded shoulder with the same dexterity as he repaired his uniform, his manner usually polite but direct, though it had sometimes bordered on insolence when he considered that his officer was stepping out of line. And there had been times during his wild days when the only man who could steady him with a word or a look had been his faithful batman. Drew had been damned lucky to find such a loyal friend to serve him!

He had chosen to bring Robbie as his confidant in this mad adventure, for it was as such he saw it, knowing that he could rely on the man to keep his mouth shut and do whatever he asked of him. The agent had provisioned the house before they came down, and for the past two days they had lived in splendid isolation, eating their way through the generous hamper his chef at Marlbeck had prepared. When that was finished, it would be plain rations, because Robbie's cooking was not his best asset.

Drew hoped they would not receive many visitors up here, which was one of the reasons he had chosen the house, but he knew that he ought out of politeness to pay at least one social call. He must visit Lady Edgeworthy, if only to introduce himself.

He looked out of the window again. The moon was full and the sky clear of clouds. It was unlikely the smugglers would risk landing this night, because they would be too easily seen. He might as well follow his own advice, and go to bed.

For a moment the picture of a woman's face came into his mind. She had taken up the stranded passengers from the damaged coach he had helped to manoeuvre from the road the previous day. Something about her face had made him stare, possibly too long and too intently, for as her carriage passed him he had seen a spark of anger in her eyes. He smiled at the memory, suspecting that she was as spirited as she was beautiful, though undoubtedly a lady. And not at all the meek woman he had envisaged as making his wife one day in the hope of an heir. She was far too good for a man such as he, for he knew that he would break the heart of an innocent girl. Far better to find a widow who would tolerate his restless nature for the sake of a comfortable life.

Besides, it was unlikely that he would ever see the beauty again.

'Marianne, my dear,' Great-aunt Bertha said and kissed the girl's soft cheek as she entered the parlour that afternoon. 'I am so pleased that you could come. I was afraid that the journey would be too tiresome for you, but I see that your Uncle Wainwright was good enough to send you in his carriage, and that was kind of him.'

'Yes, very kind,' Marianne said. 'We were more than three days on the road and it was tiring, though we had no accidents ourselves. Also, it meant that I was able to get a refund on the ticket you purchased for me, Aunt. I have the money in my purse and shall give it to you later.'

'I would not dream of accepting it,' Lady Edgeworthy said. She was a small, thin lady with wiry grey hair hidden beneath a lace cap and bright eyes. 'Keep the money, Marianne. I intend to make you an allowance and that may be a part of it. You must have some money in your pocket, my dear.'

'Even after I gave Sally a guinea before she left for her kindness to me on the journey here, I have ten pounds of my own and the fifty shillings I was refunded. I assure you that I have never been half as rich in my life.'

'Well, I am pleased to hear it,' Lady Edgeworthy said, her soft mouth curving in a smile. 'However, you will need things for yourself, my dear. I am hoping that you will stay with me for a long visit. You are young and naturally you will marry one day. It is my intention to set up a trust fund for you, which will become your dowry when you are wed. You are my god-daughter and I have always intended to do something for you, and now it is done we may forget it.'

'You are too generous,' Marianne said and blushed. 'I am sure I did not expect it.'

'We shall say no more of the business,' Lady Edgeworthy told her. 'I just wanted you to know that you will not be penniless, Marianne. I may do something for your mama, too, but that is for the future.' She smiled at her great-niece. 'Do you think you can be happy here with me?'

'Yes, of course,' Marianne replied without hesitation. 'I never realised it was so beautiful here, Aunt Bertha. I shall enjoy walking on the cliffs, and perhaps on the beaches, too.'

'Most of them are quite safe,' her great-aunt told her. 'But the cove can quickly become a trap if the tide turns. The water sweeps in there very swiftly and it is difficult to climb the steep path, unless you know it well.'

'I shall remember,' Marianne said and thanked her. 'But I have not asked how you are. Your letter said that you have been ill?'

'Oh, I had a chill and it left me feeling low,' Lady Edge-worthy said. 'You must not think me an invalid. I still entertain now and then, and occasionally I visit friends, though most of them are kind enough to call on me these days.'

'You gave up the London house, I think?'

'I have lent it to a distant cousin of my late husband's,' Lady Edgeworthy said with a slight frown. 'You know that I have no children of my own, Marianne. My son died in infancy and I was not blessed with a daughter. Had I had grandchildren, I should have kept it free for them, but as it is…I have no use for it. I do not care to racket about town myself, and Joshua asked if he might rent it from me. I told him that he may use it for as long as he wishes, though he says that in time he intends to settle down in the country.'

'I do not believe I have met your husband's cousin?'

'Joshua Hambleton,' Lady Edgeworthy said and looked thoughtful. 'In truth I do not know him well, for he had never visited me until a little under a year ago. He is a very quiet, unassuming man, Marianne. He comes down regularly now, and he stays with me then, but his visits are normally no longer than a few days. I dare say you may meet him while you are residing with me.'

'I shall look forward to it,' Marianne said and looked round as the door opened and a lady came in. She was neither young nor old, but in her middle years; tall and slender, she had light brown hair and eyes. She was dressed plainly, but Marianne thought that she might have looked more attractive if she had dressed her hair in a softer style. She stood up and went forward to greet her great-aunt's companion. 'How are you, Miss Trevor?'

'I am very well, Miss Horne. It will be nice for Lady

Edgeworthy having you to stay. I think sometimes we are too quiet here and she feels the lack of company.'

'You do yourself no justice, Jane,' Lady Edgeworthy told her with a slight frown. 'I am content with your company most of the time—but I have been wanting to see my great-niece for ages. I believe you were no more than fifteen when I last visited your home, Marianne?'

'The same age as Lucy is now,' Marianne told her. 'She is so pretty, Aunt. Jo made her a redingote of blue velvet just before I left home, and it suited her so well. We trimmed her best bonnet with matching ribbons and a bunch of blue forget-me-nots.'

'How charming,' Jane Trevor said, taking her seat. 'It must be nice to have sisters to share one's pleasures with, Miss Horne. I had a brother, but I have not seen him since he ran away to sea as a boy.'

'Mama and Papa longed for a boy, but instead they had three girls to plague them,' Marianne said and laughed, because it always made her happy to think of her family. 'Jo wishes she were a boy, but I'm afraid that she must be bound by the rules of society as we all are. If she had been the son Papa wanted, I think she might have been a lawyer or a surgeon for she is very clever.'

'Ah, yes, that reminds me,' Lady Edgeworthy said and looked at her companion. 'I must ask Doctor Thompson for some more of that peppermint cordial he so kindly made up for me. It certainly helps my digestion.'

'I shall make a note of it and ask him when he calls on Friday.'

'I thought you were better now?' Marianne asked.

'Oh, Doctor Thompson comes to tea each Friday,' Lady

Edgeworthy told her placidly. She glanced at her companion. 'We have known each other many years, and he is a pleasant gentleman—is he not, Jane?'

'Oh…yes, I suppose so,' Miss Trevor said and blushed. 'He was very good to you when you were ill this spring, and I think his remedies have helped you considerably.'

'Yes, well, I dare say they have,' Lady Edgeworthy said and sighed. 'I do not feel quite as I ought…' She shook her head and looked at Marianne. 'But I am sure I shall improve now that you have come to stay, my dear.'

'I do hope so,' Marianne said, though privately she thought that perhaps loneliness rather than illness had caused her great-aunt's low spirits. She had retired to this isolated estate in Cornwall, cutting herself off from many of her friends and acquaintances, which was a little sad. In London, she might still have gone into company had she wished.

'Take Marianne upstairs, Jane,' Lady Edgeworthy said. 'We should all change for dinner soon, though it will be just the three of us this evening—but that is no excuse for lowering standards, is it?'

'No, indeed,' Marianne agreed. She stood up and accompanied the companion from the room, glancing at her curiously once they had left the pretty parlour where her great-aunt still sat. 'Was Lady Edgeworthy very ill?'

'It was a nasty chill,' Jane Trevor said and looked thoughtful. 'I think she is much better in herself, but she has not recovered her spirits. I do not know why. She thinks a lot of her life as it was years ago and it makes her unhappy.'

'Does she not go out in company?'

'Very seldom,' Jane replied. 'I do not think she has left the house, other than to walk in the gardens, since last Christmas.

Her friends and neighbours call to see her now and then, and she did have a dinner party last time Mr Hambleton was staying, but that was two months ago.'

'It is hardly surprising if she is in low spirits,' Marianne said. 'We must see what we can do to cheer her, Miss Trevor.'

'Please call me Jane...if you wish...' Jane's face went pink.

'Yes, of course. There is no reason why we should be formal with each other,' Marianne said. 'I should be happy to do so if you will call me by my name?'

'Thank you,' Jane said and looked pleased. 'It will be nice to have young company in the house.'

Marianne nodded, for she wished to be on good terms with her great-aunt's companion. 'You must tell me the best place for walking here, Jane. Aunt Bertha warned me that the cove can sometimes be dangerous.'

'Oh, yes, I should stay well clear of that if I were you,' Jane told her, a flash of alarm in her eyes. 'It is very dangerous— and there are plenty of beaches just round the corner from there where you may walk safely. If you would care for it, I shall show you how to reach the safe beach in the morning— but there are pretty walks on the estate. We have some lovely rhododendrons, though of course they are over for this year— but you may find it more pleasant to walk on the cliffs, for the views are spectacular on a clear day.'

'Yes, I dare say I may, for sand always gets into one's shoes, does it not?'

They had reached Marianne's room and parted as she went inside. It was a large bedchamber, furnished in shades of green and blue with a hint of white here and there. The silk bedspread was made of green quilted silk and very handsome, as were the drapes at the windows, the sofa and stool covered in a deeper shade of blue. Matching chests stood at either side of the bed, and a dressing table with an oval mirror standing on top were placed in front of the window to the right, while a small writing table occupied the similar space before the window to the left. Because of the two windows, it was light and airy.

Marianne's few possessions had been unpacked, her combs, brushes and scent bottles placed on the dressing table. However, there were silver trinkets littering the tops of occasional tables and some handsome Chinese vases filled with dried flowers helped give the room an air of richness and comfort. Her dresses had been unpacked and were carefully laid on the shelves of the armoire.

Marianne chose one of her older gowns, thinking she would save her new ones for when they had company. She had begun to change when a knock at the door heralded one of Lady Edgeworthy's maids, who inquired if she could help her dress.

'Thank you, but this dress buttons at the front,' Marianne told her. 'I may need help another evening if we are entertaining, for my best gown is fastened at the back.'

'Would you like me to dress your hair, miss?'

'Thank you, Ruby,' Marianne said. 'I should like to put it up on top, if you please.'

She took her seat at the dressing table, allowing the maid to dress her hair in a smooth double knot at the back of her head, smiling and thanking her when she was finished.

After the girl had left, Marianne glanced at the little silver watch that she wore from a pin on her gown. Papa had given it to her for her seventeenth birthday and she treasured it. It was now ten minutes to six and she went to gaze out of the window before going downstairs. Her view was mostly of the gardens, but in the distance she could see the cliffs—and a house outlined against the sky. It was completely alone, as if it had been built for the use of someone who needed to be near the sea—perhaps the captain of a ship? She imagined the sea captain's wife standing at her window, looking for the sails of her husband's ship, and then laughed at herself. More likely it was the coastguard's house. She knew that on occasion smuggling went on along this Cornish coast, and the house would be ideal for a Revenue officer, though of course her aunt would not permit smuggling in her cove.

She had far too much imagination for her own good! Which was undoubtedly why she had found the gentleman with the intensely blue eyes creeping into her thoughts at the oddest of times.

Hearing a gong sounding within the house, Marianne went downstairs. She found that Aunt Bertha and Jane had already gathered in the drawing room, and dinner was about to be served in the small dining parlour.

Rising early the next morning, Marianne went out to explore the countryside surrounding her great-aunt's estate. It was warm and still that day, the sea calm, almost flat as Marianne walked along the edge of the cliffs. She stood for a few minutes, looking out towards the sea, watching as some gulls landed on a protrusion of rock a little way from the shore. In rough weather the rocks would be surrounded by foaming water and probably invisible from a ship. It was not surprising that so many ships foundered in these waters.

Something caught her eye in the cove below. A man had

appeared from nowhere and was walking towards a small boat that had come inshore. She was too far away to be able to distinguish the man's features as he waded out to it, but there was something about his appearance that she found odd. He was clearly a seaman, and that in itself was not surprising, but it was the cap he was wearing on his head...the style of it was unusual. It seemed to be made of some material that fitted snugly to his head, hanging down in a sort of tail at the back—and it was red...

It was the style of cap often worn by the French revolutionaries! Marianne recalled the sketches she had seen in one of her father's newspapers. He had showed it to her because there was a long article about the rights of man and the French revolution.

The man had got into the boat and was being rowed away from the shore. Marianne stood watching as it pulled away. Now that she looked, she could see that a sailing ship was moored out in the bay, clearly waiting to pick up the man she had just seen. Where had he come from—and who was he?

Marianne frowned as she turned away. She did not think the man was a Cornish fisherman, nor that his ship was a small fishing vessel. She thought that both the man and his ship looked French, though she had only her instinct to guide her. She had seldom been to the seaside and had seen very few ocean-going ships, but she had seen pictures in her father's books and journals.

What was a French ship doing in the bay at this hour? It was early in the morning, but if it were an enemy ship it ran the risk of being discovered by the Revenue men. It was almost sure to be a smuggling vessel if it were French, she thought, wondering why it had not sailed under cover of darkness. Of course, it might be perfectly innocent...

Glancing to her right, she saw that she was not alone in watching the ship. Another man was standing near the house she had seen from her bedroom window, and he was looking out to sea through his spyglass. At that moment he turned his head to look at her. From something in his manner, she felt that he was annoyed to see her there, but he made no move to approach her or to speak to her. And, as she watched, he shut the glass and moved away, clearly intending to climb down the rocky face of the cliffs to the cove below. Recalling her great-aunt's warnings, she called out to him.

'Be careful, sir. The cliff is unstable and the cove can be treacherous.'

He glanced at her and shook his head, frowning as he saw her, but he did not speak, making a gesture that she took to mean he did not wish her to speak or follow him. Marianne felt a spurt of annoyance. She had merely been trying to help him.

Going to the spot where the steep path was just about passable, she watched as the man descended safely to the beach below. His face was hidden from her, her view only of the top of his head as he climbed down the dangerous cliff face. At the moment only a thin line of sand was visible, and she wondered if that was the reason that the ship had risked being seen in daylight. Perhaps it was only possible to take someone off when the tide was in?

Suddenly, the man with the spyglass disappeared. He was there and a second later he had gone…completely disappeared from her view. For a moment she was puzzled, and then she realised that there must be a cave somewhere in the cove. The French seaman had come from it, and the man with the spyglass had disappeared into it!

Turning away, back to the house, Marianne was thoughtful. Something was going on in her aunt's cove, but what ought she to do about it? If smugglers were landing contraband there, she ought to report it to the Revenue—but was her great-aunt aware of what was happening?

She knew that many people who lived in the area did know about the smugglers, and some of them turned a blind eye in return for a barrel of brandy left in their barns. She did not imagine that Aunt Bertha would be one of them, for her husband had been a Justice of the Peace, but she could not be sure.

She would ask about the occupant of the house on the cliffs, because if he were a Revenue officer he would not want interference from her—and for the moment she would say nothing of what she had seen to anyone but her great-aunt. But one day, when the tide was out and it was safe, she might go down to the cove and see if she could discover the cave for herself.

It was only as she reached her aunt's home that it occurred to her that the man she had seen on the cliffs that morning might just have been the same man that had helped to push Lady Forester's coach from the road. How strange that would be, she thought—but of course she had not seen him clearly and she could have been mistaken. She smiled as she wondered if her imagination were playing tricks on her. For some reason the small incident had lingered in her mind, though she had no idea why it should.

'Did you enjoy your walk this morning?' Lady Edgeworthy asked when they were alone later that day. 'I used to walk quite often when I was younger, but I do not care for it since my cousin died… Cedric fell from the cliffs, you know. He was such a lovely young man, and he knew them so well…' She sighed. 'He lived in Cliff House, but I shut the house afterwards. It was empty for over a year, but I have recently let it to a gentleman. Mr Beck has been ill and the sea air may help him. He called on me yesterday, as it happens. Had you arrived an hour sooner you might have met him.'

'How strange. I was about to ask who lived there,' Marianne said. 'I saw someone this morning. He was using a spyglass and looking out to sea.'

'He will have been watching the gulls then,' Lady Edgeworthy said with a smile. 'He told me that he is a keen bird-watcher, and he is enjoying the peace and quiet here. I asked him to dine with us, but he asked if he might leave it for another time, as he is still not himself and he wishes to be alone. I think he must have been very ill indeed.'

'Poor man,' Marianne said, but wondered if the man she had seen had been her great-aunt's tenant, for he had seemed to climb the cliff very confidently and did not appear to be ill. Indeed, when he had directed the disposal of Lady Forester's coach he had looked very strong—if it had been the same man. She might have been mistaken, of course. 'Aunt Bertha…'

'I must tell you something,' her great-aunt said suddenly. 'It must remain our secret, Marianne, for I do not wish to upset Jane—but I think someone is trying to kill me…'

'I beg your pardon?' Marianne was so startled that her own questions were forgotten in an instant. 'Did you say that someone was trying to kill you?'

'Yes, I think at least one attempt has been made on my life and perhaps more are planned.' Aunt Bertha looked upset, as well she might. 'I know this must come as a shock, my dear, and I hate to burden you with it, but I have been in fear for some weeks now.'

'What do you mean? What has happened to make you think it?'

'It was when I was ill,' Lady Edgeworthy said. 'I had taken some of the sleeping draught that my doctor had left for me, but for some reason it had not worked as it ought. I was only half-awake, but I heard someone creeping about in my room. It was the chink of glass that woke me and I cried out. Whoever it was fled and I sat up, lighting my candle.'

'That is very strange,' Marianne said. 'But what makes you think that that person was trying to harm you?'

'Because the stopper had been taken from the laudanum,' Lady Edgeworthy said. 'It had been a full bottle that evening, but someone had poured half of it into the flask containing my peppermint cordial. If I had not been woken, I should not have known anything was amiss. Had I taken my medicine as usual, I might have died—as you may know, laudanum can kill if used to excess.'

Marianne looked at her in silence. Lady Edgeworthy was not given to flights of fancy as far as she knew, and she realised that this must have been very distressing for her. It would be for anyone, but her great-aunt was vulnerable having few relations to care for her, and none living nearby.

'Do you know who entered your room that night? Was it a man or a woman?'

'It was too dark to see, for I was still drowsy and cried out before I opened my eyes. I saw only a dark shadow. I think it may have been a man, for the shape was tall and slender... but I cannot be certain.'

'Has anything more happened since then?'

'I have taken to locking my door at night,' Lady Edgeworthy said. 'And I have placed my medicines in a locked cabinet…but there was the other thing…' She hesitated, then, 'Someone tried to break into the house two weeks ago. One of the servants was downstairs, because she had the toothache, and she raised the alarm. She said that she looked out of the window after she screamed and saw a man dressed in dark clothes running away.'

'And you think it may have been the same person… breaking in to make another attempt on your life?' Marianne was startled and anxious; the matter was very serious if it were true, and her aunt would not lie.

'I know it sounds foolish, and indeed I have told myself that I imagined the whole thing,' Lady Edgeworthy said. 'I have wished that it might be a dream, but in my heart I know that it happened.'

'Who was in the house that night?'

'Only the servants, Miss Rudge, myself—and Jane, of course.' Miss Rudge was Lady Edgeworthy's personal maid, and of a similar age to her mistress.

'You do not think it was either Jane or Miss Rudge?'

'No, of course not—and I do not think any of my servants would wish to harm me either.' She shook her head. 'I must have imagined it, must I not? Do you think that my illness disturbed the balance of my mind?' She looked upset and confused, making Marianne instantly concerned.

'No, Aunt, I do not,' Marianne said. 'If someone tried to get into the house…it must have been an intruder that night, Aunt Bertha. And yet I cannot imagine who would want to harm you.'

'I am a wealthy woman,' Lady Edgeworthy said. 'I have some valuable jewellery actually in the house and money invested, besides this estate and the London house. Yet I cannot think…' She shook her head. 'I changed my will after Cedric died, leaving a proportion of it to your mama and the rest to…' She sighed again. 'I cannot believe that Joshua would wish to kill me. He has the London house for nothing and, besides, he is always so charming and kind.'

'But you said he was not here when someone entered your room and interfered with the laudanum, Aunt,' Marianne said. 'If he resides in London, it is hardly likely that he came down just to put something in your medicine…'

'Yes, I know, it sounds foolish. I have considered the possibility for he is the main heir, but I cannot think it. Jane has a small bequest, of course, and Dr Thompson.'

Marianne looked at her thoughtfully. 'What would happen to this house and the estate if you should die? Forgive me, but it seems I must ask.'

'It might be sold, perhaps,' Lady Edgeworthy replied. 'Why do you ask that?'

Marianne took a deep breath, then, 'I saw something this morning in the cove and I wondered if it might be used for smuggling… I am fairly certain there was a French ship in the bay.'

'I do not understand, my dear.' Lady Edgeworthy frowned and then nodded. 'Oh, yes, I dare say it might be inconvenient for them—if one of us should see them bringing the goods ashore…'

'It supplies a reason why someone other than your husband's cousin or your companion might want you out of the way, does it not?'

'Yes, it does,' Lady Edgeworthy said and looked relieved. 'Do you know, that makes me feel much better. I am glad that I told you, though it was not fair of me to lay such a burden on young shoulders.'

'It is one I am well able to bear,' Marianne said. 'Now that I am here, I shall keep my eyes and ears open, Aunt. If I discover that someone is planning to harm you, I shall consult you at once about what we ought to do to see that you are protected.'

'You are a good girl,' Lady Edgeworthy said, giving her an affectionate look. 'I confess it has been playing on my mind these past weeks, for I should hate to think that Joshua or Jane… No, I cannot think it of either of them.'

'It could not have been one of the maids?' Marianne looked thoughtful. 'The girl who was suffering from tooth-ache…she could not have come into the room hoping to borrow some laudanum?'

'Bessie is not a thief,' Lady Edgeworthy said. 'I am perfectly certain that she would have asked had she needed it for herself. I should have told her that Jensen has his own supplies for the maids' use…but I am sure that she knows that and would have gone to him in the first place had she wanted it.'

Marianne nodded, for in a house like this it was up to the butler and housekeeper to care for the needs of their assistants, and only a very reckless maidservant would risk taking medicine that belonged to her mistress. Yet it was an area that must be explored, if only for the purpose of elimination.

'Perhaps she did not wish to disturb him. You know that the laudanum bottle was half-empty, but can you be sure it had been poured into your peppermint cordial?'

'No, I cannot be certain. I assumed that it had and threw

it away,' Lady Edgeworthy said and frowned. 'I suppose it might have been one of the servants…' She looked unconvinced. 'I did not think so at the time, but it could have been, of course, though I believe I almost prefer the idea that someone outside this house wants me out of the way.'

'Yes, well, I think we must both be alert, but do not let it distress you too much, Aunt. If no further attempt has been made, it might just have been one of the maids looking to borrow your laudanum.' Marianne sought to comfort her aunt, even though she thought it unlikely.

'No, I shall not give way to melancholy,' Lady Edgeworthy said stoutly. 'I feel much more comfortable now that you are here, Marianne.'

'Good. I am glad to be here with you,' Marianne told her.

She was thoughtful as she went upstairs to change for the evening. She did not imagine that a thief had broken into her aunt's house to steal laudanum. It would be for some other reason, possibly something more menacing, she imagined. It might have been one of the servants, as she had suggested. And it *was* possible that it might suit the smugglers if the house were empty. However, a new master might be more suspicious about their activities than an elderly lady living alone. To Marianne's mind, Miss Rudge was above reproach and that meant there were possibly three candidates for her suspicion at the moment, though she had tried to convince her aunt otherwise.

It was difficult to think ill of Miss Trevor, who seemed a meek and loyal companion to Lady Edgeworthy, and she could think of no reason why her great-aunt's doctor should wish to kill her—which meant that Mr Joshua Hambleton *was* the most likely of all. Unless the intruder *had* simply been a maid with the toothache, of course.

It was a mystery, but Marianne was determined that she would get to the bottom of it, even if only to set her great-aunt's mind at rest.

The next two days passed pleasantly, for Marianne had settled into a routine. She went for walks in the mornings or performed small tasks, like picking and arranging flowers. Some of the soft fruit was ready for harvest, and one morning, she helped the maids in the task, picking redcurrants that would be made into jelly, and some raspberries for bottling and jam. In the afternoons Jane, Lady Edgeworthy and Marianne sat together, talking while they sewed or played cards, and sometimes Jane would read to them.

Marianne studied Jane Trevor for any sign that she was resentful of her employer, but as far as she could tell Jane genuinely liked and respected Lady Edgeworthy. It was only on the third day, when Dr Thompson came to tea, that she noticed a slight agitation in the companion's manner.

Jane blushed as she passed him his tea and a plate of sweet biscuits, avoiding his eyes. When she sat down, she chose a chair near her employer and studiously avoided looking in his direction.

'I trust that you have not been too busy of late, sir?' Lady Edgeworthy asked the doctor. 'There are not so many fevers and chills at this time of the year, I believe?'

'No, perhaps not,' he agreed. 'But there was an unfortunate disaster at Wheal Mary the other day, and I was called to attend the injuries of five miners who were hurt. Two others were killed by the fall and beyond my help, I fear.'

'I am sorry to hear that,' Lady Edgeworthy said. 'I believe that particular mine has more than its fair share of accidents?'

'Yes, indeed. I have spoken about safety to Sir Henry Milburn,' the doctor said. 'I am afraid that he refuses to listen. Until there is a law to protect workers in the mines, I fear there will continue to be accidents.'

'Unfortunately there is little other work for the men in these parts,' Lady Edgeworthy replied. 'They must either face the dangers of the sea or the mines—unless they are lucky enough to be put to a trade when they are young.'

'That costs money,' the doctor said and glanced at Marianne. 'It takes every penny a man earns to feed and clothe his family and it is seldom that they can afford to apprentice a son for seven years, when he could be working in the mine and contributing to the family income. You will not know of the conditions in this part of the world, Miss Horne. The land is not as fertile as you have in the east of the country, I think?'

'I did not realise that life was so hard here,' Marianne said and looked at him with interest. 'Mama always offered charity to any who called at the Vicarage, but most of the people we knew worked on the land and were at least well fed and housed.'

Doctor Thompson frowned. 'I see several people each week that suffer from malnutrition or scurvy. I can help them, but what they truly need is a good diet and a decent house. The wages they earn provide them with neither.'

'You must find that very frustrating, sir?'

'Yes, I do,' he replied and then recalled himself. 'Forgive me, this is hardly the kind of conversation for a lady's parlour.'

'Please do not apologise. I found it interesting. Mama has always tried to help others when she can.'

'You are very quiet today, Jane,' Lady Edgeworthy

remarked, glancing at her companion, who had taken no part in the discussion. 'Are you feeling quite the thing, Jane? If you are unwell, you must ask Dr Thompson for a few moments of his time before he leaves. You may be private in the small parlour.'

They were using the larger front parlour that afternoon, as they always did when they had guests. The doctor was of course the first guest that Marianne had encountered, and she had worn her new blue gown, which she and Jo had made together, in his honour. It was stylish and suited her well, trimmed only with a wide sash at the waist, and a little lace at the neck. She looked extremely pretty, her hair swept back from the sides of her face and looped into soft swirls at the nape of her neck.

Jane shook her head, looking uncomfortable. 'I am perfectly well, Lady Edgeworthy,' she said. 'I do not wish to waste Dr Thompson's time.'

'I assure you that I should not consider it a waste of time,' he said. He glanced at his watch. 'I think I must be going, for I have a patient to see later. Accompany me to the door, Miss Trevor. If anything ails you, I may be able to help.'

'I shall certainly show you to the door,' Jane said and got up at once. 'But I am quite well, thank you.'

They left the room together. Lady Edgeworthy turned to Marianne and frowned. 'Did it seem to you that Jane was a little quiet? She is not usually so when the doctor is here.'

'Perhaps she does feel a little unwell. It has been very warm of late.'

'Yes, perhaps,' Lady Edgeworthy agreed. 'Tell me, what did you think of him, Marianne?'

'Doctor Thompson?' Marianne was silent for a moment. 'He

is an amiable, attractive man and seems to think just as he ought.'

'Yes, I have always believed him dedicated to his patients. He treats them all, whether they can pay him or not.'

'I thought that must be the case,' Marianne said. 'I think he must either have private means or several wealthy patients.'

'I believe he was a younger son. His private income is slight, but he does have several patients who can afford to pay him.'

'Perhaps he does not care much for money?'

'He is not married,' Lady Edgeworthy said. 'I asked him once why he had not taken a wife and he said that he could not afford it…' She wrinkled her brow. 'I have wondered if he has been blighted in love at some time…'

Marianne was about to reply when the companion walked into the room. Clearly Jane had not taken the doctor's offer to examine her, for she had not been absent long enough. However, she was looking a little happier, and the colour had come back to her cheeks.

'Are you feeling better?' Marianne asked.

'Oh…' Jane blushed. 'It was just a little headache and I am quite sure it will go very soon. Indeed, it has eased a little already.'

'If you have a headache, you must go and lie down until dinner,' Lady Edgeworthy told her. 'No, I insist, Jane. If you are no better at dinner, I shall have Miss Rudge make up a tisane for you.'

Jane got to her feet and left the room at once.

'She is such a foolish little thing,' Lady Edgeworthy said. 'Why would she not let Dr Thompson help her?'

'I cannot say,' Marianne said, but she was thoughtful. 'I

Marianne and the Marquis

think I shall go into the village in the morning, Aunt Bertha. I have written a letter for Mama and I wish to take it to the receiving office so that it may go on the mail coach.'

'One of the servants can take it for you, my dear.'

'I should like to go myself, if you do not need me for a few hours?'

'I did not ask you here to dance attendance on me every moment,' her great-aunt said. 'Of course you may go—but take one of the maids with you if you wish. I do not think you will come to harm, but there is a market on Saturdays, and you never know who may be there.'

'Thank you,' Marianne said and got up to kiss her cheek. 'I think I shall go up to change and write a short note to Jo to go with Mama's letter—and to Lucy, of course, for she must not be left out.' She smiled as she thought of her sisters and wondered what they were doing at home. She knew that Lucy would be missing her, for they had never before been apart, but Jo would keep her busy and not let her fall into too many daydreams.

She was thoughtful as she left her great-aunt and walked up the stairs. Jane had been very quiet, and she had gone quite pale for a while. Had she been upset because the doctor had paid some attention to Marianne?

No, surely that was wrong? Why should such a little thing upset Jane? Unless...she had a secret passion for the good doctor?

It seemed ridiculous at first, for Jane must be a few years older than Dr Thompson, who was no more than thirty or so—and yet she had seen something in Jane's eyes. She had been much happier when she returned from escorting him to the door...

Was it possible that they had an understanding? Jane might have thought she was about to lose him to a younger woman…which was quite foolish, of course. Marianne would not have encouraged him had he shown an interest, which he had not. She had merely been interested in what he had to say about the social conditions of the area. Jane could not have known that, of course, and she might have thought Marianne was concerned to attract his attention.

If Jane cared for the doctor, why had she not mentioned her feelings to her employer? Some employers did not encourage their staff to have followers, of course. Perhaps Jane thought she might be turned off if she allowed her partiality to show? And Lady Edgeworthy had just told Marianne that the doctor could not afford to marry…

Supposing that the legacies they had been left would enable them to marry? Marianne paused on the stairs as the awful thought struck her. Would they plot together to murder Lady Edgeworthy, knowing that the money she had left to them as individuals would be quite substantial when put together?

The possibility put a different complexion on the matter and was chilling. Marianne shivered, feeling suddenly cold all over. She had not believed that Jane was capable of such a thing…but a woman might do anything for the love of a man.

Without the means to marry, Jane was condemned to a life as companion to her employer. Lady Edgeworthy was kind to her, but others might not be in the future, and the legacy might not be enough to enable her to live comfortably without seeking further employment should Lady Edgeworthy die. Besides, if she was in love… Marianne did not wish to think ill of either Jane or the doctor, but it now seemed that she must consider them as possible culprits, and as yet she had not met Mr Joshua Hambleton.

Of course there was also the mysterious tenant at the house on the cliffs. She had seen him from a distance several times as she was walking about the estate, although as yet they had not come face to face. Quite often she would turn and see him staring in her direction, and she had wondered if he was following her—but why should he be? Besides, he had only recently taken up residence and had not been here when her great-aunt's medicine had been tampered with....

Chapter Three

'I missed my chance that morning, damn it,' Drew said. 'I was too slow to act, Robbie. I should have tackled him before he got into the boat.' He was feeling frustrated for there had been no further sightings of the French ship—and none at all of the man he sought.

'You can't be sure he was the one,' Robbie reasoned. 'He may just be one of the smugglers. You said the cave was empty, but you saw evidence that barrels had been stored there.'

'There were marks in the sand where they had stood,' Drew confirmed. 'The tide washes into the first cave, but the caverns go back a long way. I could not explore further at the time, for I had no means of lighting the path, but I think there is a man-made tunnel leading inland. I dare say there is a warren of tunnels all over this part of Cornwall, made by miners centuries ago when tin and copper were first discovered. The smugglers know of them and have turned their existence to their advantage.'

'That must be how they get the contraband through,'

Robbie said. 'It would be too dangerous to take packhorses through the village, because they run the risk of being betrayed, and on the open cliffs they would be bound to be seen. Even on a dark night, someone would be sure to notice and call out the militia.'

'Perhaps, though often the locals are remarkably close-mouthed on the subject. I think they take it to somewhere on Lady Edgeworthy's land,' Drew said. 'The tunnel must have its outlet there—and perhaps it is being transferred to an out-building somewhere on her estate until it is thought safe to move it inland. I dare say there may be several dropping zones before it reaches its final destination.'

'You do not suspect Lady Edgeworthy of being involved?'

'No, not at all,' Drew said. 'I am certain she does not know that her estate is being used as a cover. While the Revenue men watch the coast, the packhorses are already inland and heading for their next destination.'

'Will you approach her? Would she allow you to make a search?'

'For the moment there is probably nothing to find,' Drew said. 'I think the drop must have been made some time before we arrived—that is why I believe the man I saw being picked up is the one we are after. He was dropped when the cargo was brought ashore, and he had been…wherever he goes on his dirty business. The ship came in specially to take him off and they would not have done that unless he was important.'

'He might simply have been the one they trusted to sell the contraband,' Robbie suggested.

'Yes, you may be right, but I have a hunch that he was the French contact, though it is the English spy we need.' Drew frowned. 'I should have acted sooner, but I was looking at the ship and the boat. I did not realise that he was hiding in the cave, waiting to come out. I missed my chance to grab him, damn it!'

'He will come again,' Robbie said. 'If he has been successful this time, he will be back for more—whether it be gold for smuggled goods or information he can pass on to the French. Besides, it isn't the smugglers you want here—is it?'

'No, it is not. And you are right, he will come again,' Drew said. 'Next time I shall be waiting for him. I intend to follow the packhorses and see where they go—and then I shall have him!'

'If the smugglers don't see you first,' Robbie cautioned. 'It's madness to try this on your own, Captain. You should have asked some of your friends to help you.'

'I thought my ill health was a better cover,' Drew said. 'But I might send a letter to Hal Beverley, ask him if he is game for a lark—that should fetch him.'

'Aye, no doubt,' Robbie replied. 'He was as wild as you were in the old days, Captain, and that is saying something. Send for him if you wish, but ask Captain Harcourt—or Lord Harcourt, as I should say now—to come with him. Four of us will do better than three—and I'll wager that he is as bored with his life as you are. Besides, of the lot of you, he was the most sober…'

'Perhaps,' Drew agreed. Harcourt and Drew had been survivors on that day, when they were ambushed. 'Yes, I shall write to both Hal and Harcourt—but I doubt that Beverley will come. He has responsibilities enough these days. Hal's father demanded he sold out after his brother was killed. I have not seen anything of him since he came home some months back.'

'No doubt he has duties, as you do, my lord,' Robbie said

with a disapproving look. 'A man in your position has much to lose—and well you know it! A fine scandal there would be if it were known you were here under a false name. People would be bound to think the worst.'

'I know that you think me a fool to come here,' Drew said and grinned at him. 'But it amuses me, Robbie—and it was a favour to Jack…'

'And he saved your life at Salamanca,' Robbie said. 'You will go your own way as usual, Captain—but do not take too many risks. You should not forget that others depend on you…'

'I do not forget,' Drew replied and frowned, for he was neglecting his duty. 'But I have an agent who prefers a free hand with the estate, and for a while he shall have it. I promise you that I shall take no more risks than need be.'

Robbie's dour look spoke volumes, but he said no more.

Drew smiled as he left the house. He was remembering better times. They had indeed been a wild bunch in those days, carousing half the night, living life to the full…perhaps it was merely companionship that he missed.

Suddenly she was there in his head, a beautiful girl with sea-green eyes and spun-gold hair. He frowned as he recalled the girl who had called to him from the top of the cliffs as he climbed down to investigate what was going on in the cove. He had been annoyed that anyone was there, because she might have alerted the men in the boat that he was there, and it was only later that he had wondered if she was the beauty from the coach. Surely it was his imagination—it was unlikely that she would be here, so far from anywhere. A girl like that should be mixing in high society, chancing her luck in the marriage mart—unless she was already a wife? Yet something told him she was as innocent as she looked…and therefore far beyond him. A man like Drew Beck had nothing to do with innocent young ladies, however beautiful and spirited they might be.

Drew's eyes were shadowed with memories. War had sent him mad—the heat, the pain and the sheer horror of seeing those you loved as brothers fall into the dust and die slowly of fever or the gangrene that ate into neglected wounds. Yet the loss of comrades had driven him on, making him heedless of his own life, earning him several mentions in dispatches, besides a reputation for being fearless. He had been given medals and honours, all of which lay forgotten in a drawer, shut away with memories that had been too painful to remember.

Drew tasted the bitterness in his mouth and then thrust his thoughts away. It was over. He was no longer a soldier, but a man of consequence and wealth, his uncle's death making him responsible for more people than he could remember. Robbie was right when he said that he owed them a duty of care—but just this once he was going to court danger, to taste the spice of adventure again. And afterwards? Drew frowned. If he still lived, it would be time to settle down and take the wife his relatives and friends told him it was his duty to marry so that he could produce an heir…but he would choose a woman who understood what he needed, what kind of a man he was…a widow who would not demand the things he could not give.

Marianne was pleased as she left the receiving office that morning. It was situated in a building close to the inn, which was a busy place with coaches and carriages coming and going. She had left her letters for Mama, Jo and Lucy with the man who attended to such things, and been given three letters in return. Two were for Lady Edgeworthy and the other was for her from her sister Jo. She wondered what had caused Jo to spend some sixpences to write to her so soon and broke the seal in haste.

My dearest sister, Jo had scrawled, *I write to tell you that Aunt Wainwright has decided that I shall go with her to Bath next month. As you know, I had hoped that she would change her mind, but nothing else will do for her. I am to go to the Hall later today, where I am to be fitted for a new wardrobe. It appears that my aunt thinks I have nothing but rags and must be dressed properly so that I shall not shame her. How shall I bear it? I dare say we shall be at odds within a week, but I must try to remember what you and Mama have told me and behave as I ought. Enough of my troubles! Do write and tell me all your news, dearest. Your loving sister, Jo.*

Marianne was re-reading her letter as she walked along the path. She needed to fetch some trifles from the small village shop, which sold all manner of things a lady might need, including embroidery silks, ink and stationery, as well as acting as a small lending library. For the sake of a few pennies it was possible to borrow the works of various poets and popular authors. She was so engrossed in her thoughts that she did not see the gentleman walking towards her until they almost collided.

'Be careful, mistress,' he warned, reaching out to steady her as she tripped over him. 'I value my boots—they are my best and I may never find another pair to equal their comfort.'

Marianne looked down at his boots, which were black and long with pale buff cuffs at the top and which looked as if they had seen better days. She raised her inquiring gaze to his face, and felt a little jolt as she looked into his eyes. They were the colour of bluebells and his hair had the sheen of a raven's wing, cut short, as was the prevailing fashion. This was the man she had seen climbing down to the cove that day the French ship was in the bay. She had seen him several times since that morning as she walked about the estate, but always at a distance. She was sure now that he was also the man who had manoeuvred Lady Forester's damaged coach to the side of the road. Up close he was so large and powerful that he made her breath catch in her throat. His coat fitted superbly to broad shoulders and his breeches had been cut by a master tailor to cling like a second skin, though they, too, had seen better days. A gentleman, then, but perhaps down on his luck?

'Forgive me, sir,' Marianne said. 'I was reading my letter and I should not have been. I did not see you. I hope I did not tread too hard upon your toes?'

'I dare say I shall live,' Drew said and frowned. It *was* the beauty from the coach. His eyes had not deceived him that day on the cliffs, and he had glimpsed her as he walked about the estate, but had made no attempt to approach her, because it was best that he should not. The fewer people who knew he was here the better. 'I should have seen what was happening and stood aside. It was my fault.'

'Oh, no, you are too generous,' Marianne said. 'The letter is from my sister, you see…'

She laughed, softly, huskily, sending such a wave of hot desire rushing through him that he was shocked. He did not know her or anything about her, had seen her only once close to before, and yet somehow she had implanted herself into his mind, become a part of his dreams, for he had dreamed of her more than once, ridiculous as that was! Standing so close that he could smell a delightful perfume, which he imagined was uniquely hers, he was aware that she was an extremely desirable woman. He was conscious of a burning need in his loins, which made him draw back, because he was thinking the impossible.

She was speaking again. He crushed the rising need she aroused, bringing his thoughts back to what she was saying.

'I am entirely at fault. But I believe I have seen you…the other day at the top of the cliffs. I thought you might be my great-aunt's tenant? At Cliff House…'

'You are staying with Lady Edgeworthy? I thought she lived alone with a companion?' Drew frowned, his mind instantly alert, for the presence of a girl like this at the house might complicate matters, and not only because of the effect she had on his senses. 'For how long, may one inquire?'

'I have no idea,' Marianne said. 'For as long as my aunt needs me, I think.'

'I see…' He nodded his head. He must walk on! This would not do. He had no place in his life for dalliance with a girl like this! 'I am glad to have met you. Good morning, mistress.' He tipped his hat to her and moved on, frowning at his thoughts. If she perchance knew him, which was not impossible, for she obviously had good connections…she might reveal his true identity and that would be the end of all his hopes of remaining a shadow in the background. Besides, he needed all his wits about him, and he wanted no distractions in the shape of a girl like that! Drew knew his chances of trapping the French spy and the English traitor were slim, and would vanish into the mist if he became an object of interest to the community. Should his real name be known, he would be inundated with visitors and invitations, as he had been at Marlbeck before he made his escape—and that was the last thing he needed!

Marianne turned her head to watch him as he crossed the road to the inn and went inside. He had been friendly at first, but then his manner had changed suddenly, becoming almost rude. Why? What had she done or said to offend him?

She puzzled over it for a moment, then put it from her mind as she went into the tiny haberdashery shop. Its shelves and counters were crammed full of things that ladies needed, and she thought it was like a chest of treasure trove, knowing that she would always be happy to spend an hour or so here, spending her shillings on things for her sewing.

When the invitation to stay with her great-aunt had arrived, Marianne had imagined it would be for a few weeks, but Lady Edgeworthy was clearly hoping for something more. It was certainly a pleasant place to live. The village of Sawlebridge was large enough to support several small shops and it was but a pleasant carriage ride from Truro. She would find it no hardship to live here for some months, though she might begin to miss her mother and sisters after a while, but for the moment she was very content to be her great-aunt's guest.

She left the shop an hour or so later, carrying her silks and some lace to trim a nightgown. Her gaze strayed to the front of the posting inn a little further along the street, which consisted of several nice houses at one end, and finished in a huddle of fishermen's cottages at the other. There was also a forge, small baker's shop, an ironmonger's and a rather seedy-looking inn right at the far end. The man she had bumped into earlier was talking to a groom outside the posting inn, but he seemed to sense that she was looking at him and turned his gaze on her. For a moment their eyes met and held.

Marianne felt her cheeks growing warm. She turned away, walking in the opposite direction. It was a walk of some twenty minutes or more to her aunt's house, and much of it up a steep incline, but she strode out with a will. The very hot weather had gone and she enjoyed walking. After a while, she caught glimpses of the sea, which was white-crested with foam and looked dark grey. She had enjoyed herself. A visit to the village would always be a way of passing the hours in the mornings, because Aunt Bertha did not rise until noon.

To reach Sawlebridge House, Marianne had to branch away inland from the cliffs, although she had been on her great-aunt's land for some minutes. At the top of the cliffs, she looked back and noticed that the man she had just seen outside the inn appeared to be following her, because he had no need to come this way to reach his house. She decided that she would wait for him to come up with her.

'Did you wish to speak with me, sir?'

'My name is Beck—Drew Beck. I was not following you. I find it easier to come this way. Lady Edgeworthy gave me permission to take the shortcut across her land. I have been ill, you see.' Drew managed to cough twice behind his hand.

'I dare say it must be quicker and perhaps safer than the cliff road,' Marianne said with a cool nod. 'Perhaps I should introduce myself. I am Miss Marianne Horne—and Lady Edgeworthy is my great-aunt.'

'I believe you said as much earlier, though not your name.' Drew felt relieved. She did not appear to know his true identity, for if she had he believed she would immediately have said so.

'Are you planning a long stay, Mr Beck?'

'Perhaps a few months. The sea air is good for me. I need peace and quiet…time to rest and recuperate.'

Marianne's eyes went over him. She thought he looked extremely fit and healthy, though one's looks did not always reflect a true picture, of course. Yet he could hardly have put his shoulder to that coach the way he had if he were recovering from an illness. Her first instincts were to trust him, and yet she suspected him of lying about his health. However, she would give him the benefit of the doubt for the moment. She inclined her head politely, though she did not smile, because she sensed a reserve in him.

'Then no doubt we shall meet occasionally. My aunt welcomes visitors and she plans to give a dinner soon. She will probably invite you, but I am sure she will understand if you decline…for your health's sake.'

'If she invites me, I shall come.' Drew could have bitten his tongue off the moment he had spoken. He had intended to stay clear of all such affairs, but something about this girl had penetrated his armour. Besides, he would need an excuse to move freely over the Sawlebridge estate. 'Please tell Lady Edgeworthy that I shall call tomorrow.'

'Then you might as well come for tea,' Marianne said, slightly taken aback—she had thought he would decline. 'I am sure that Lady Edgeworthy will be delighted to receive you, Mr Beck.'

They had been walking together, falling naturally into step as they talked, but now a fork in the road meant that they must go in different directions.

'I think you must go that way, Miss Horne,' Drew said. 'My path is in this direction. We shall meet again soon.'

'Yes, of course. Goodday, sir—and be careful of the cove. I have been told that the tide comes in swiftly and it might be dangerous at certain times.'

Drew hesitated, then, 'Yes, I believe it might be very dangerous for the unwary, Miss Horne. Thank you for your advice—and be careful when walking on the cliffs. I know that more than one person has met with an accident there.'

Marianne was thoughtful as she walked on. There had been something odd in his manner as he spoke of the cove being dangerous for the unwary. Was he warning her to stay away from that part of the cliffs—and, if so, why?

He had told her his name, but a name meant nothing—and she had the strangest sensation, as if she ought to know him. As far as she could recall, they had never met before that morning—for one could not call a glance as they passed a meeting—but there was something about him that made her thoughtful. When their eyes met as she passed him in her uncle's coach, she had felt such an odd sensation—as if for one brief second they had communicated without words, as if they had always known each other. Oh, what a foolish girl she was! It must just be that chance meeting on the road that made her feel she had met him previously—or someone like him before.

She was aware of feeling a certain caution concerning him, though he seemed perfectly respectable—but who was he really and why had he taken the house at the top of the cliffs? And why was she always catching sight of him when she went out walking? He said he was here for his health, but in her opinion Mr Beck appeared to be perfectly well. It was not her business, of course, but it was curious.

The new tenant had told Aunt Bertha that he wished to be

alone for a while, but it seemed that he had changed his mind and was ready to dine with them. Marianne wondered about his true reasons for coming to Sawlebridge. She did not exactly mistrust him, but she sensed something hidden. Another mystery to solve.

However, a moment later she forgot Mr Beck, for a carriage had drawn up outside the front of her aunt's house and a man was getting out. Marianne knew that he had not seen her and she was able to observe him at her leisure. He was perhaps five and thirty and of medium height. His clothes proclaimed him a gentleman, but were of a sober cut and hue. Despite that, he was attractive with light brown hair, cut short and brushed forward in a fashionable style. As he turned towards her, she saw that he had a gentle, pleasant face. He had noticed her now and was staring at her with interest, waiting for her to reach him.

'We have not met,' he said, his eyes travelling over her with interest, 'but I think you must be Miss Marianne Horne. Lady Edgeworthy may have mentioned me? I am Joshua Hambleton.'

'Mr Hambleton, of course,' Marianne said and dipped slightly. She held out her hand to him, but instead of shaking it, he raised it to his lips to kiss it briefly.

'Charming, quite charming,' he murmured as Marianne removed her hand from his. 'I had heard that you were lovely, but I had not realised you would be so beautiful…'

Marianne felt slightly awkward, for his compliment was too much. 'Does Aunt Bertha expect you, sir? She did not mention it to me this morning.'

'She ought to have had my letter,' he said and frowned as though he did not care to be questioned. 'Though I have been used to visiting as I choose. Has she recovered her spirits?

When she wrote that you were coming down, I hoped for improvement. I do not like to see her so low.'

'Yes, she seems more comfortable now that I am here. She means to entertain more for my sake and I believe that may be what she needs. She has cut herself off from her friends here and I think she misses going into society as she did.'

'This place is rather isolated,' Joshua agreed, looking concerned. 'I have suggested that she should take a house in Bath and leave the management of the estate to me. I should be happy to take care of things here while she was away.'

'This is her home,' Marianne said. 'But a change of situation might benefit her. It is, of course, her own choice.'

'You must help me to persuade her,' Joshua said. 'I am sure you would enjoy a visit to Bath yourself.'

'No, I do not think that would be right. I am perfectly content here for the moment,' Marianne assured him. 'But perhaps in the winter, if my aunt should wish for it…but I would not presume to influence her one way or the other.'

She saw him frown. Her answer had not pleased him. She had a feeling that he was hiding his true sentiments—and she sensed that he was frustrated or angry about something.

'Oh, there you both are,' Jane said, coming out of the house. 'I wondered what was keeping you, Mr Hambleton— and I was beginning to fear that you had got lost, Marianne. It is not always easy to find your way about in a place that is new to you.'

'Oh, no, I was not lost. It is a fair walk from the village, and I stopped to speak to Aunt Bertha's tenant for a moment or two.'

'Tenant…' Joshua Hambleton looked at her through narrowed eyes. 'You mean at the cliff house, I suppose. It was unwise to let it to a fellow she knows nothing of. I cannot think why she did it.'

'Mr Beck seems a perfectly decent gentleman,' Jane said before Marianne could reply. 'Please come in and make yourself comfortable, Mr Hambleton. Lady Edgeworthy will be down shortly for nuncheon. Your room is ready for you as always.'

Marianne went into the house ahead of them. It was obvious that they were on good terms and knew each other well. They did not need her, and she wanted to change her gown and tidy herself before joining the others in the dining parlour.

It had been an interesting morning and she had a great deal to occupy her thoughts. There were two mysteries that needed to be solved here—but were they in any way connected? She had no idea for the moment. All she could do was to watch and listen.

Walking back to the house on the cliffs, Drew found thoughts of Miss Horne had invaded his head. He was thinking of her, of her eyes and her husky laughter—and her very kissable mouth. Such thoughts were a distraction. He was here for a purpose and had no time for dalliance. Besides, he must do nothing that might trigger her memory, for he believed that they might have met once years ago when they were both still children. He had been staying with his uncle at the time, and had encountered a pretty young girl in the woods. She could have been no more than ten or eleven, and he was fourteen. She had been picking blackberries and he had reached some that grew on a tall bush for her, eating some himself and teasing her with a ripe fruit until she took it from his fingers with her lips. It was an innocent encounter—he had been a boy then, untainted by all that was to come after. He had kissed her cheek and she had laughed, telling him that her papa would welcome him to the Vicarage, and that he should taste her mama's apple-and-blackberry pie, but he had never visited her at home, for the next day he had been sent away to school.

She had obviously forgotten him and the kiss he had given her. It piqued him a little, for he had remembered the incident shortly after she had told him her name. His pride was stung by the knowledge that she had not recognised him, though in truth there was no reason why she should. He could not quite remember—had he told her his name that day or merely that his uncle was the Marquis of Marlbeck? Perhaps he had told her that he was called Andrew, as he had been at his uncle's house in those days.

Was it only pride that had made him suggest a further meeting? Did he want to force her to remember? How foolish that would be! She was certainly beautiful, and he sensed that she had something more than that—a hidden fire that smouldered below the surface. She had been cool with him that morning, but in the woods he had known that the spark of mischief was there, and his new friend had enchanted him. Had he not been sent away, he would most certainly have sought her out again.

Damn it! It was an isolated incident from his childhood. He had not thought of it for years, and neither had she. It was unlikely that she would, which meant it was safe enough to visit Lady Edgeworthy. And yet he knew that the danger in meeting the beautiful Miss Horne again did not lie only in the possibility that she might one day remember a boy who had picked blackberries for her.

Drew smiled wryly. He was playing with fire and he knew it, but at the moment he didn't care. She moved him as few women ever had. He had felt the desire raging inside him, known that he wanted her urgently—though he had no idea why she had such a powerful effect on him. He was not a green youth to lust after any pretty girl.

He would be foolish to jeopardise a mission that meant so much to him for the sake of a woman, however lovely and desirable she might be. He was here to unmask Jack's spy— a man who might have betrayed Drew and his friends. If this man was still passing information to the enemy, he needed to be stopped. Only after the affair was settled would Drew be free to think of his own pleasure.

He pushed the thought of her from his mind. He had more important things to do than run after a pretty girl!

Marianne was dressing for dinner when she heard the voices in the garden below. She went to her open window and looked down, seeing that Jane was walking with Dr Thompson. They seemed to be talking earnestly, lost in each other, their expressions serious, almost anxious, and then the doctor said something and Jane laughed. Marianne could see her face, and in that moment she was transformed from the quiet mouse who knew her place as Lady Edgeworthy's companion into a girl who thrived on the attentions of her lover.

Now where had that thought come from? Marianne shook her head. It would be wrong to label them as lovers when she had no idea if it was true. She was certain that Jane felt something for the doctor, and it seemed to follow that he cared for her—but there was no sin in them enjoying each other's company.

Marianne would not have condemned the companion if she had sought solace in the arms of her lover, for her life must be dreary at times. At the beck and call of an elderly lady, she had no real freedom, or any life of her own. Yet she had accepted that when she took the position and it was no reason to try to harm her employer.

Could she have hoped that by adding laudanum to Lady Edgeworthy's medicine she would simply go to sleep and never wake again? If murder was planned, it was a kinder one than many. Lady Edgeworthy's death would set Jane free— and if she and the doctor had been left sufficient money to make a life together…it was certainly motive enough.

Marianne frowned—she did not like to think that Jane or the doctor could have plotted such a thing. It was unkind in her even to consider it! Having met Mr Hambleton, who seemed at first sight a pleasant gentleman, she found it difficult to believe that he would murder his cousin's wife. Lady Edgeworthy had been good to him, and it would be gross ingratitude to try to cut her life short simply for the money she might leave him in her will.

It seemed more and more likely that one of the maids had crept into Lady Edgeworthy's bedroom to borrow some laudanum and had fled when she cried out. Marianne decided to see if she could discover what the usual arrangement was for the distribution of powerful medicines to members of the household. Her great-aunt had told her that the butler held them under lock and key—but did the maids know that?

Leaving her bedchamber, Marianne went downstairs. She saw one of the maids carrying a tray of glass and silver into the dining room and followed her. Three girls were giggling together as they laid the table for dinner that evening, one of whom was Bessie, but they fell silent as they realised she was there.

'Is there something you need, Miss Horne?' one of the girls asked.

'Yes. I have a headache coming on. I need something to stop it or it may develop and I shall be prone on my bed. I wondered if there was anything that I might take for it?'

'Miss Rudge could make you one of her tisanes, miss,' the first girl suggested, looking concerned.

'I do not think that would serve. I need something stronger.'

'You need laudanum, miss,' Bessie said. 'Mr Jensen keeps it in his room under lock and key. He gave me some for the toothache some weeks ago and it took the pain away something wonderful. I did not use it all for I had the tooth drawn the next time I went to Truro—and I should be happy to fetch it for you.'

'Thank you, Bessie,' Marianne said. 'But I think perhaps a tisane will be sufficient after all.' Bessie had been so open and straightforward that she could not think her the kind of girl who would creep into her employer's room in the dead of night to steal laudanum. And if she had not, then someone else must have done so…unless her great-aunt had imagined the whole thing? She considered for a moment and then dismissed it. No, she did not think it was that. Lady Edgeworthy did not seem the kind of lady who would be given to foolish fears for nothing.

Marianne went out into the garden. It was a pleasant evening and she thought she would like a breath of air before dinner. She had not lied when she said that she had a bit of a headache, though it was rare that she needed to lie down on her bed.

There was not time enough to walk as far as the cliffs, so she decided to head for the stream. It was out of sight of the house and came up from the ground in a little spring, meandering down through a little valley where the rhododendron bushes grew in profusion. She had come too late to see their glory, but the leaves were dark and glossy and it was a pleasant place to walk.

She walked as far as the stream, wishing that she might go further, but knew that she must return or keep everyone waiting for their dinner. As she came through the wilderness of the rhododendrons, she saw a man walking towards her and she frowned. What was he doing here at this hour?

'Are you lost, Mr Beck?' she asked, for he was a long way from the path that led to the top of the cliffs.

'No, not at all, Miss Horne,' Drew said. 'I was bird-watching and I wandered further than I intended.'

'Indeed? What kind of birds were you watching?' Marianne frowned—surely there were more gulls to be seen from the cliffs and she had seen only sparrows bathing in the dust and a blackbird.

'I thought I saw an eagle,' Drew said. 'I am not certain now, for it is unlikely, don't you think?'

'Very unlikely,' Marianne said. 'There are not many tall trees here, Mr Beck. I do not imagine that golden eagles nest much in rhododendrons, do you?'

'No, of course not. I meant a fish eagle, of course. They are seabirds and sometimes nest on the cliffs—but this one seemed to fly inland. I dare say I was mistaken.'

'Yes, I imagine you were,' Marianne said. She had not heard of a fish eagle, and did not think it was a resident of Britain, but she could not argue the point for she did not know the habits of such a bird, or even if it existed. And yet she sensed that he was lying. He had improvised, saying the first thing that came into his head. Indeed, she wondered if he knew much about seabirds himself. If he had not been bird-watching as he claimed, what was he doing here? He surely could not be following her for how could he have known she would choose to come this way? 'Might it not have been just a large gull?'

'Yes, I dare say it might,' Drew said, cursing himself for the slip of the tongue. He had remembered now that the fish eagle was an African bird and fed on freshwater fish, and hoped that she would not notice his mistake. 'Do you walk this way often, Miss Horne?'

'Not often,' Marianne said. 'I imagine it will be pretty in early summer, but I like the views from the cliffs—as you do, Mr Beck. It is surprising what one may sometimes see from there, is it not?'

'Oh, indeed. I have seen the occasional seal and the gulls, of course.'

'I was thinking more of the ships one sees now and then. There was a ship anchored in the bay the other day—I thought it might have been French.'

'Did you? How strange! One would not expect it. We are still on difficult terms with the French, are we not?'

'I thought it might have belonged to smugglers.'

'Ah…' Drew looked at her through narrowed eyes. It was as he had feared when he knew there was to be a visitor to the estate. She had an inquiring mind and she liked to walk, which could prove dangerous if she saw too much. 'I suppose there is always that possibility. The strained relationship with France tempts men to bring in goods for which we are normally obliged to pay heavy taxes. If you did see such a ship, it might be best to forget it, Miss Horne. Desperate men sometimes do desperate things.'

'Are you warning me, sir?'

'For your own good,' Drew replied. 'Turn a blind eye for your own sake—and that of your great-aunt.'

'I wondered if you might know more about smugglers than you do about birds, sir,' Marianne said, for she had remembered something she had read in one of her father's natural history books. 'Good afternoon, sir. I think your eagle must have flown a long way from his home.'

Drew watched as she walked away. He could not help a wry grin, for she had caught him out. He must learn to think before he spoke another time. Fish eagle indeed! An osprey might have been more believable, though they tended to nest in Scotland rather than on the Cornish coast—but it was slightly more credible.

He sensed that Miss Horne was suspicious of him. She had not accepted his story of being ill—and she certainly didn't believe that he had been looking for an eagle, of any kind. He would have to be careful if he wanted to retain his false identity!

Marianne was lost in thought as she returned to the house. She was growing more and more certain that her great-aunt's tenant was not what he claimed to be—but who was he and why was he here?

As she approached the house, she saw that Joshua was standing in the garden. He appeared to be contemplating the view, but came to meet her as she walked through the shrubbery. He smiled at her in a way that she thought a little too ingratiating, and she decided that she did not quite like him—though that was unfair on such short acquaintance.

'Ah, there you are, Miss Horne. Miss Trevor told me that she thought that you had gone out for a stroll before dinner. Do you often walk in the evenings?'

'Not often,' Marianne said. 'I prefer the early morning, before most people are about. It is very peaceful then. I like to be up as soon as it is light enough.'

'There are some pretty walks on the estate, I believe. I do not often walk, for I prefer to ride—but I dare say it is good for one's health.'

'Oh, yes, though in the past I used to ride quite often,' Marianne said. 'My favourite walks are along the cliffs. There is a spectacular view from there on a clear day.'

'Yes, though in places they can be dangerous,' Joshua said. 'You must be careful, Miss Horne. It might be best to stay away from the cove. The walks are safer on the other side of the bay. It was at the cove that Lady Edgeworthy's cousin fell to his death, you know—such a tragic thing. He had lived here all his life, and should have known that the cliffs could be treacherous there.'

'Yes, that was strange, wasn't it?' Marianne said and frowned. 'Do you think he might have lost his way in a mist?'

'I have no idea. I was not here at the time,' Joshua Hambleton said. 'The accident happened while I was in Spain. I was with the army for a while. I took little part in the fighting, because I was employed as a communications officer at headquarters most of the time. My chest was never strong and I had to give up my commission some months ago. I came back here and Lady Edgeworthy was kind enough to let me live in her London house.'

'I am sorry that you were forced to give up your career, sir.'

'Yes, for it was quite promising. I might have gone into a diplomatic post afterwards, but someone else was preferred and I had to settle for a quieter life. I have a small income and I manage well enough.'

'That was disappointing for you,' Marianne said. 'But could you not have tried again later?'

'Perhaps.' He smiled and shrugged his shoulders. 'I confess I have become lazy and I am content to see my friends and entertain a little. I go on very well, you know. I have lately made some investments that bring me in a living. I am not an ambitious man, Miss Horne—but I live very comfortably.'

'I am glad you are content with your situation,' Marianne said. She sensed that he had controlled the frustration he had felt earlier and was now making an effort to be charming. Indeed, she felt that he had gone out of his way to explain his situation to her, and she was not sure why, for it was surely not her business to inquire. 'Changes in fortune are not always of one's own making—but it is rewarding to feel one has done something worthwhile, I think.'

'Yes, indeed,' he said and smiled at her, giving a nod of approval. 'What a sensible young lady you are, Miss Horne. You seem to think just as you ought on everything.'

'Perhaps not everything,' Marianne said and laughed. 'You do not know me yet, sir. You may not be so approving when you do.'

'I think you are teasing me,' he said. 'I doubt that I could ever disapprove of you, Miss Horne—or may I call you Marianne? Lady Edgeworthy is so very fond of you and I am glad you have come to be with her. She already seems much better. I am sure that is all to your credit.'

'I am glad you think so,' Marianne said. She did not give him the permission he sought to use her name, because something about him was not right. She could not say with any certainty what that might be, but she felt that his smile—indeed, everything about him!—was false. He did not feel as he spoke. He was trying to make a friend of her, though at first she had sensed he was annoyed that she had come.

If he had hoped to dispose of Lady Edgeworthy for the sake of her fortune, he would find Marianne's presence in the house a nuisance. But she must not jump to conclusions, because she had no real reason to suspect him of anything yet. It was just that she did not like him. It was most unfair of her to form an opinion when she knew nothing about him, but she could not help herself. She had liked and trusted Drew Beck from the first moment of speaking to him, even though she knew that he was hiding something from her—but she suspected that she knew his true reasons for being here. However, she felt no such confidence in Mr Hambleton and continued to be a little distant with him as they went into the house together.

Naturally, she must be polite to her aunt's guest, but she was not yet ready to trust him.

Marianne woke with a start. It was quite dark in her room and for a moment she lay wondering what had disturbed her sleep, then, hearing an odd sound, she threw back the covers and got out of bed. She reached for the tinder and lit the candle, which stood on a chest beside the bed, listening for the sound again.

All she could hear now was the wind in the trees and a spattering of rain against the window. Her instincts alert to danger, she unlocked her door and went along the passage to Lady Edgeworthy's room. She turned the handle very softly but it held and she felt a surge of relief. Her great-aunt was safe—but that noise might have been someone trying to enter the house.

She was not quite sure what it had been—perhaps a door that was stiff to open or something being dragged across a stone floor, but it had been strange…hollow and muffled.

Holding her chamber-stick tightly in her right hand, Marianne crept down the stairs on bare feet. She had heard nothing more since leaving her room, but she knew that she *had* heard something and she could not simply return to her room and pretend that it hadn't happened. She would never forgive herself if an intruder did some damage to the house, or, worse still, inflicted harm on Aunt Bertha.

Her room was situated at the back of the house, and so she instinctively turned that way. Suddenly, she saw a flickering light and knew that someone was coming from the wing of the house that contained the kitchens and servants' hall. Unsure what she ought to do, Marianne blew out her candle and drew back into the shelter of a tall clock, waiting and watching.

A man was coming along the hall, the light of his candle giving her a clear view of his face. It was Mr Hambleton! Marianne hesitated and then moved forward.

'You startled me, sir. I thought you were an intruder.'

Marianne had the advantage, for she could see him and he had clearly not known that she was there. He looked startled, his expression shocked.

'What are you doing, Miss Horne?' Joshua demanded. 'Why have you no candle?'

'It blew out,' Marianne told him. 'I heard an odd noise and came down to investigate.' She had noticed that he was fully dressed, which was quite odd in itself, and his coat sleeve had a film of cobwebs on it.

Joshua seemed to hesitate for a moment, then, 'You heard it, too? I came down to investigate some minutes ago. You may have heard me checking windows and doors.'

'Oh…' Marianne was not sure why, but she did not quite believe him. 'Do you think we should rouse the servants?'

'No, I have made sure that the house is safe,' he said and she caught the note of annoyance in his voice. 'I am sure it must have been the wind getting in some crack in the roof somewhere that we both heard, and then, as I said, you may have heard me checking. There is no need to cause an uproar, Miss Horne. It would only distress Lady Edgeworthy.'

'Yes, it would,' Marianne agreed. 'Goodnight, sir. I shall go back to my room.'

'Let me tend your candle for you,' he said. 'If you are a light sleeper, I suggest that you take more care when you come down another time, Miss Horne. Had I been an intruder, you might have been in some trouble.'

'Yes, I might,' Marianne said. 'It was fortunate that you were here to make sure we were safe, sir.'

Marianne turned away, guarding her candle flame. She frowned as she returned to her room and locked her door. Where had Joshua been and why was she certain that he had lied to her? He said that he, too, had been roused by a noise, but she thought that it was he who had made the noise. Whatever he had been doing, he clearly did not wish her to know about it.

Marianne was certain that his actions were suspicious.

She did not know what he hoped to gain by creeping about below stairs in the middle of the night, but she was sure that he was doing something he ought not. And it made her wonder if he had tried to give Lady Edgeworthy an overdose of laudanum in her peppermint cordial. He had everything to gain if she became very ill and died, for he was her main heir.

Oh, how horrid it was to have to consider such things! She did not even wish to think about it, but of course she must. Her great-aunt was relying on her to help her, and she must do all she could to prevent another attempt on her life.

She shivered as she got into bed and pulled up the covers. She could not rule out Dr Thompson and Miss Trevor, and of course Miss Rudge, though she was too elderly and too attached to her employer. However, Marianne's instincts told her that they were all innocent of any evil intent towards Lady Edgeworthy. Somehow her suspicions had become centred on Mr Joshua Hambleton. She ought to give herself more time to know him before she judged him, of course. She sighed as she turned over in bed. It was no use, she could not trust or like him…

Chapter Four

The next day was damp, a sudden rainstorm sweeping in from the sea in the early morning, forcing Marianne to stay indoors. She spent the morning finding small jobs that she might do for her great-aunt, though in a household that catered for so few there was little she could do other than arranging flowers and making an inventory of the jars on the shelves of the stillroom. She had tried to put the incident of the night before from her mind, because for the moment she had no intention of telling her great-aunt anything about it.

When Lady Edgeworthy came downstairs she looked a little pale and tired and said that she had been feeling sick during the night. However, she did not confide her thoughts until she and Marianne were alone in the best parlour later that afternoon.

'I dare say it was because I ate too much supper last night,' she said. 'I took a dose of my peppermint cordial before I went to bed, but it did not seem to suit me.'

'Perhaps it is time that you had a new preparation,' Marianne said. 'Could it have deteriorated over time?'

'It was the new bottle that Dr Thompson sent me,' her

great-aunt said. She frowned as she glanced round. They were alone in the parlour, but the door was not quite shut. 'I feel a little chilly, my dear. Will you be so good as to shut the door?'

Marianne got up to close the door. Returning to her chair, she asked the question uppermost in her mind. 'Was your medicine locked away last night?'

'Yes. I keep the key in my dressing box, but I cannot think that anyone…' Lady Edgeworthy shook her head. 'Why should anyone want to harm me? I have begun to think that I imagined it all that night. Perhaps I had used the laudanum myself—or it was Bessie, as you suggested.'

'No, I do not think so,' Marianne told her. 'I mentioned that I had a headache yesterday and Bessie told me that Mr Jensen had a supply of laudanum. She said nothing of you, and I think she might have, had she once borrowed some from you.'

'Then it must have been someone else—or my imagination.' Lady Edgeworthy looked upset. 'I do not know who it could be—perhaps it was all in my mind.'

'Perhaps,' Marianne said. 'But if I were you, I would find another hiding place for the key to your cabinet. It may be nothing, but I would throw the peppermint cordial away.'

'Yes, perhaps,' Lady Edgeworthy agreed. She gave a little shudder, for it was too awful to contemplate. 'We shall think of something else, Marianne. Are you certain that Mr Beck intends to take tea with us this afternoon?'

'Yes. At least he said that we might expect him. I met him last evening near the rhododendron valley. He was looking for birds.'

'Ah, yes, I believe I have mentioned that it is a hobby with him, though I imagine he would see more from the cliffs than that particular spot.'

'I suppose he may simply enjoy walking. The estate has many pretty walks and I believe he has permission to go where he will?' Marianne raised her fine brows.

'Well, yes, I suppose so,' Lady Edgeworthy agreed. 'When the cliff house belonged to my cousin, he treated this house as if it were his own. I was very fond of Cedric…' She sighed, because to speak of the young man she had loved was still so painful. 'I shall never understand why he fell that day. He knew the paths so well. I have never understood it…'

'You are perfectly certain it was an accident?'

'What else could it be?'

'I did tell you that I thought it possible that smugglers might be using the cove. Supposing he saw something he shouldn't and they killed him?'

'Good gracious!' Lady Edgeworthy put a hand to her chest in alarm. 'I have never considered the possibility that his death was not an accident for a moment. Nor do I wish to, Marianne. I am sure that Cedric fell…it could have been nothing else.∴.' She looked distressed at the idea that her cousin might have been murdered. Marianne tried to comfort her, wishing that she had not broached the subject.

'Please do not upset yourself, Aunt,' Marianne said. 'It was merely a thought that occurred to me.'

'No, no, it cannot be…'

As the door opened at that moment, admitting Mr Hambleton, Marianne made no further attempt to justify her suspicions. He came into the room, looking from one to the other as if sensing an atmosphere.

'I trust that you have not been arguing with Lady Edgeworthy, Miss Horne?' He spoke in a light teasing voice, but Marianne wondered if he hoped to cause dissent between them.

'No, of course not,' Lady Edgeworthy said at once. For some reason he had begun to irritate her. His letter had never arrived and she was a little annoyed that he had not let her know he was coming down. 'I was merely a little disturbed. Marianne was wondering if Cedric's fall was something other than an accident.'

'Indeed? How could that be?' Mr Hambleton frowned at her. 'I think there has been no suggestion of it before this.'

'Marianne thought there might be smugglers using the cove. If that were the case it might mean…for Cedric might have seen something he shouldn't…but, no, I do not think it.' Lady Edgeworthy fanned herself, obviously upset. 'Please, we shall say no more of this.'

'I am sure there is no foundation for such suspicions,' Joshua Hambleton said in a reassuring tone. He gave Marianne a warning look, as if blaming her for Lady Edgeworthy's agitation. 'We have never been troubled with activity of that kind here. I think your imagination has been playing tricks on you, Miss Horne. It was wrong of you to distress Lady Edgeworthy.'

At that moment Jane came into the room and announced that their visitor was on his way. 'I have just seen Mr Beck walking towards the house,' she said. 'He will be here at any moment…' Sensing an atmosphere, she glanced at their faces. 'Is something wrong?'

'Nothing at all,' Lady Edgeworthy said. She looked surprised as Mr Hambleton headed for the door. 'Will you not stay for tea, Joshua? I thought you might like to meet our tenant.'

'I have arranged to speak to someone in the village,' he said. 'I shall return in time for dinner, Lady Edgeworthy.' He smiled at her, threw Marianne a look that seemed to reprove her and went out of the room.

Marianne was standing by the window when Mr Beck was announced. She had not seen Mr Hambleton leave the house and thought that he must have used a side entrance. It occurred to her that he might not have wanted to meet their visitor, but she dismissed the thought, accepting that perhaps she was too suspicious. She had already distressed her great-aunt by suggesting that her cousin's death might not be an accident. To raise doubts about Mr Hambleton's sincerity would cause Lady Edgeworthy more anxiety. And for the moment she had no good reason to be suspicious of him. Just because she did not like him, it did not mean that he was a murderer or a fortune hunter.

'Good afternoon, ladies,' Drew said as he walked into the room. He bowed his head. 'Lady Edgeworthy, I trust you are well? Miss Horne—Miss Trevor. It is good to see you both in such beauty.'

'Oh, Mr Beck,' Jane trilled, her cheeks pink. 'Marianne is beautiful, but I am not pretty at all.'

'That isn't true,' Marianne said. 'Last evening I saw you laughing with Dr Thompson and I thought how attractive you looked when you were happy. You hide your light, Jane, and could make more of yourself if you wished.'

'Oh…' Jane's cheeks were hot and she looked uncomfortable. 'Yes, of course. I remember now that Dr Thompson called. He brought Lady Edgeworthy's medicine and we talked about something…I cannot recall what, but it was some amusing tale. He often makes us laugh, does he not, Lady Edgeworthy?'

'Yes, indeed, he does,' her employer said and frowned. 'When Thompson gave you the medicine, what did you do with it, Jane?'

'I took it to your room and left it on your dressing table. Did you not find it there?'

'Yes, of course. I recall it now,' Lady Edgeworthy said. 'You came from my room as I walked along the landing, and I put the medicine away myself.'

'Is something wrong?' Jane asked, looking anxious. She had a handkerchief in her hand, which she pleated nervously, a distinctly guilty look in her eyes.

'No, not at all,' her employer replied. 'We are forgetting our manners. Please sit down, Mr Beck. Jane, you may ring for tea if you will.'

Marianne came forward then, taking a seat on the small gilt-framed sofa. She had not missed the significance of the questions asked of Jane and wondered if the companion could have done something to contaminate the medicine. She was clearly nervous about something. It might be that she knew the peppermint cordial was contaminated and meant to make her employer ill—or it might be something entirely different.

'Have you seen any more of your eagle, Mr Beck?' she asked, deciding to put the peppermint cordial from her mind for the moment. Her gaze dwelled on his face, hoping that her question would at least give him an awkward moment or pause for thought.

'No, Miss Horne, I have not,' he said, seeming remarkably composed, though his eyes gleamed as he returned her look

'I think it must have been a hawk I saw or perhaps a large seabird, as you suggested.'

'I do not think I have ever seen an eagle on this part of the coast,' Lady Edgeworthy said. 'But then, I am not knowledgeable about these things.'

'I must confess that I have taken up the hobby only recently,' Drew said. 'I needed something to help me pass the time during my illness.'

'And exactly what was that?' Marianne asked. 'You seem much recovered, sir.'

'Yes, I am, thank you for your concern,' Drew said, a steely glint in his eyes, as if daring her to accuse him of something. 'I had a putrid fever of the lungs and was very ill for some weeks—but I believe the sea air is doing me the world of good.'

Lady Edgeworthy nodded her approval. 'Marianne tells me you like to walk, sir. You must feel free to go wherever you wish on the estate, Mr Beck. Just be careful of the cliffs in some places, for they are crumbling and may be dangerous.'

'Yes, your agent warned me of it,' Drew said. 'I was saddened to learn of the accident to your cousin. It was a severe loss for you.'

'Yes, it was,' Lady Edgeworthy agreed. 'However, it was some time ago now and I have my dear Marianne to keep me company—and Jane, of course. At the moment, my husband's cousin is staying with me. Mr Joshua Hambleton. I had hoped he would be here to meet you, but he had some pressing business. However, you may meet at my dinner party. I have decided to ask my friends for next Saturday evening. It is a long time since I entertained, for I could not raise the energy, but now that Marianne is here she will help me…will you not, my dear?'

'Yes, Aunt, of course. I shall write all the invitations and run any errands you care to ask. You must give me the names of your friends and it will be a pleasure to help you welcome them here.'

'Oh, there are no more than a dozen,' Lady Edgeworthy said, sitting forward in her chair and clearly animated. 'But they have been my neighbours since I first came here as a bride, and it is time I had them to dinner once more. I dare say you may have met Sir Edgar Bright and Mr John Pembroke, Mr Beck, for they are often in the village? Mr Pembroke is a man of business and Sir Edgar has a large estate just north of here.'

'I am not certain. I have not gone out in company much since I came here…' Drew saw Marianne's eyes on him. He knew that she was watching with interest and he smiled at the elderly lady. 'But I shall, of course, be delighted to meet them at your home—now that I feel so much better.'

'I knew that the air here would be good for you,' Lady Edgeworthy said, looking very pleased, as if she felt that she had contributed to his recovery. 'Ah, here is Bessie with our tea. Perhaps you would like to pour, Marianne? Jane will assist you.'

The conversation became general as they discussed the weather, the price of tea, which was so very expensive, and the continuing hostilities with the French. Austria had only recently declared war on France and there was hope that a solution would be found before too long.

'I believe my agent told me that you fought with Wellington at Salamanca?' Lady Edgeworthy said. 'It was my cousin's hope that he would become an officer in the light infantry one day…'

'Yes, I was at Salamanca, amongst other places,' Drew told her. 'I was called home some months ago on family business…and then my health…'

'Yes, how sad for you. You must miss your companions?'

'Yes, I do,' Drew admitted and there was the ring of truth in his voice. 'I have my batman with me. He looks after me at the house, just as he did in Spain.'

'Mr Hambleton was in Spain,' Lady Edgeworthy said. 'But I think he was not strong enough to fight. He was in charge of logistics…have I that right? I believe he means that he arranged for the transport of goods from one place to another?'

'Yes…' Drew frowned. 'I hope he was not one of the fools who were always losing what we most needed. It was often the case that vital supplies went astray. We lived on what we could buy or forage for ourselves—but supplies of ammunition were sometimes mislaid and that led to difficulties…'

'Well, I do not know how that may be, but Joshua had to sell out because he was prone to too many fevers.'

'What rank did he hold?' Drew asked politely.

'He was merely a lieutenant,' Lady Edgeworthy said. 'He could not afford to purchase his colours, you see. He worked his way up through the ranks, and then, just as he had risen to a position of some merit, he was forced to resign.'

'That was a shame,' Jane said. 'I know he suffers in the winter with his chest, because he asked Dr Thompson if he could recommend something—' She broke off and blushed. 'Perhaps I should not have said…'

'Mr Hambleton seems quite well at the moment,'

Marianne observed and then, to cover Jane's confusion, 'More tea, Mr Beck? Perhaps you would like another cake?'

'I have eaten three already,' Drew said and grinned at her. 'Do not tempt me, Miss Horne, for Robbie's cooking is not as enjoyable as these delicious trifles.'

'You should take advantage of my great-aunt's cook,' Marianne said. The sparkle in his eyes and his wicked look had made her heart race. At that moment something stirred within her, making her breathless—his eyes were so very blue, almost the colour of bluebells…and oddly familiar. She was sure she had looked into eyes like that once before, but it was a long time ago.

'I believe I must be going,' Drew said, getting to his feet. The puzzled expression in Marianne's eyes warned him that she had begun to wonder. It might be only a matter of time before she remembered him, as he had remembered her, and he would prefer that it did not happen here. 'I shall look forward to receiving your invitation, ma'am.'

'See Mr Beck out, Marianne,' Lady Edgeworthy said. 'Jane, you may pour me another cup of tea. I want to talk to you…'

Marianne left the room with some reluctance. She sensed there was something of a mystery about him, and though she thought she might know at least part of the answer, she was still not sure enough to be certain how she felt about him. She thought he might be trusted, but there were times when the look in his eyes made her feel a little strange.

At the door, Drew stopped and looked at her. 'You are frowning,' he said. 'You will cause lines to appear, Miss Horne. I assure you that there is nothing for you to concern yourself over.'

'Who are you?' she asked. 'I know that you call yourself

Mr Beck—and you say that you have been ill—but who are you really and why are you here?'

'It would be better if you did not ask such questions,' Drew said. 'Believe me, I mean no harm to your great-aunt or yourself.'

'I wish that I could be sure. It is all such a mystery…'

Drew frowned, for he sensed more here than her doubts concerning himself. 'You are worried about something?'

'Yes…' Marianne looked into his eyes. She hesitated, then, 'I do not know whether to trust you or not, sir—but I think that I need to trust someone.'

'If you decide that I am the one, come to the rhododendron valley tomorrow at midmorning,' Drew said. 'If you wish for my help, I shall do all that I can to serve you…'

'Thank you,' she said, her voice catching. She watched him walk away from her. She did know him from somewhere! The elusive memory was at the back of her mind, taunting her. She felt that she ought to remember him—but why?

Marianne spent a restless night dreaming. In the morning she knew that her dreams had frightened her, but she could not recall them. She seemed to remember that they concerned Mr Beck and the smugglers, but other than that the dreams had become a mist that vanished once she opened her eyes.

It was all nonsense! She laughed at herself and dismissed the dreams. Far more worrying was the thought that someone might have been tampering with her great-aunt's medicine once more.

She visited Lady Edgeworthy in her room before going out for her customary walk. Miss Rudge was tidying some clothes, but smiled and prepared to leave as Marianne entered. Her great-aunt was sitting up in bed with a tray of hot chocolate and biscuits beside her.

'Miss Rudge,' Marianne greeted her as she went out. 'Aunt, how are you this morning?'

'I feel very much better this morning,' she declared. 'I asked Miss Rudge to make me a peppermint tisane and that helped my digestion. I think it is better than Thompson's preparation and I shall not ask him for more just yet.'

'At least you know that your tisane is freshly prepared,' Marianne said. 'May I get you anything before I go out, Aunt?'

'Oh, no, my dear,' Lady Edgeworthy said. 'I approve of your habit of walking each morning. It brings colour to your cheeks and I am sure it is good for you. This afternoon you may help me write my invitations, but there is no reason for you to stay in the house on my behalf.'

'I am glad you are feeling better,' Marianne said. She kissed her great-aunt's cheek and left her, going downstairs. As she reached the hall, she saw that Mr Hambleton had just come in. He looked as if he had been riding, his boots splashed with something that might have been salt. Had he been down to the beach? 'Good morning, sir.'

'Good morning, Miss Horne,' he replied. 'Are you about to go walking? It is a lovely day, fresher than last week, but all the better for that, I think.'

'Yes, it will be pleasant near the cliffs,' Marianne said. 'Have you been riding?'

'Yes…yes, I went for a little ride about the estate. I always like to rise early when I am in the country. Had I known that you wished for exercise, I might have hired a horse for you from the local hostelry.'

'Thank you, but I am quite content to walk,' Marianne replied, feeling uncomfortable beneath his intent gaze. She felt a little guilty, because he was so obviously trying to be friendly towards her, and she could not help wishing that he would not.

Marianne nodded and went past him, out into the sunshine of a bright, late-summer morning. She supposed that the excessive heat of the summer must be almost over now, for it was nearly the end of August. She had told Mr Hambleton that it would be pleasant on the cliffs, but instead she turned inland, towards the rhododendron valley.

He was waiting for her in almost the same place as they had met previously. Marianne's heart quickened at the sight of him. She did not know why she should suddenly feel her spirits lift, but it was so and she smiled as she walked to greet him.

'Have you been waiting long, sir?'

'Oh, I wander about pretty much from first light,' Drew told her. 'It is amazing what one may see first thing…'

'You intrigue me,' Marianne said and gave him a wicked look. 'Don't tell me you spotted your eagle?'

'Ah, no, I fear I was mistaken there,' he said and grinned. 'What I saw was more interesting…a meeting in the cove between a local fisherman and one other.'

'One other? Do you mean a gentleman?'

'Of sorts,' Drew said and the look in his eyes sent a little shiver down her spine. She thought then that she would not like to be this man's enemy.

'Pray tell me what you mean?'

'If I am not mistaken, he is a disgraced army officer of junior rank—but I cannot be absolutely sure.'

Marianne frowned, for his words echoed thoughts she had

not realised were there until he spoke. 'Would you be speaking of Mr Joshua Hambleton?'

'That may be his name now,' Drew said. 'It was Lieutenant Joe Humble then—and he was dismissed from the service because he was caught cheating at cards. There may have been other things—misappropriation of army property—but I cannot be certain. The affair was brushed under the carpet for some reason.'

'Oh…' Marianne pursued her lips. 'Then it might not be the person I am thinking of. Mr Hambleton is Lady Edgeworthy's cousin by marriage.' She hesitated, wondering if she should tell him about the incident, when she had thought there might be an intruder in the house and discovered Mr Hambleton coming from the kitchen wing.

'Yes, I believe I have heard as much…' He shook his head. 'As in the case of the eagle, I may be mistaken. But you asked if you might trust me, Miss Horne. I shall now swear to you that I shall never do anything that would harm you or your family. Will you accept my word?'

Why should she accept his word? She hardly knew him, and yet something inside her was drawing her to him, telling her that he would never harm her, that she could tell him her thoughts…at least some of her thoughts!

His eyes were so blue, the colour of bluebells, and she felt herself drowning in their depths, forgetting what she had meant to say. For a moment she could not withdraw her gaze, and he seemed in like case for he made an odd sound and reached for her, drawing her close. At first his kiss was gentle and sweet, seeming to wrench her heart from her breast as her lips parted beneath his and she melted into him, the world fading as she gave herself up to the pleasure he evoked. In response to her surrender, Drew's kiss deepened, becoming fiercer, his desire leaping through his aroused body as he moulded her to him. His hands moved down her back, clasping her firm buttocks, pressing her against him as the hot desire raged inside him.

Marianne's body responded instinctively. For the moment she was not thinking, only feeling, reacting to his kiss with all the untapped passion that was in her. Passion she had not known existed until this moment, for he had awakened her dreaming spirit, forcing her to take the step between innocence and knowledge—the age-old knowledge that comes to a woman in love.

Marianne looked up at him in wonder, because she did not know what to expect from him now. She surprised an odd, slightly wistful expression in his eyes, and suddenly something clicked into place in her mind. She had been ten years old and picking blackberries and she had met a boy in the woods. He had reached up to pick those she could not reach and teased her…The memory was hazy, for she did not recall exactly what had happened, nor even what he had said to her, though she knew they had talked for a while.

'Did we meet in Marlbeck Woods years ago?'

'Yes…' Drew looked at her warily. 'You were picking blackberries. I thought it might have been you when you told me your name—you were the parson's daughter.'

'Yes…' Marianne wrinkled her brow. 'I can't recall anything, except that you picked blackberries for me, but I did remember your eyes because they were so blue.'

'We were children then. Why should you remember?'

'I don't know…' She shook her head. 'The memory is vague. I do not know why I remembered it just now.'

'Because I kissed you then and you laughed.'

'I dare say I did,' she said, her cheeks a little pink. 'It was a harmless incident, but…'

'I was a boy then,' Drew said. 'Impulsive and still naïve. I have no such excuse today. I kissed you because I find you irresistible, but I am sorry if I have offended you, Miss Horne. It was wrong of me to take advantage of you.'

Her eyes widened, their colour the hue of a mountain pool, clear and green, touched by sunshine. And then she smiled. 'You have robbed your action of any offence, sir. Nor can I pretend that I found it distasteful, for I did not—though I beg that you will not do it again without my permission.'

Drew laughed, for she was a breath of fresh air. It was her frankness, her open manner that fascinated him as much as her beauty. He had met women in society who might perhaps come near to her in looks, but none had made this direct appeal to his senses. At that moment he would have liked to take her down to the soft earth and lose himself in the sweetness of her flesh. Yet if he did that, she would hate him and he would be beyond redemption.

'I cannot promise that I shall wait for your answer,' he said, his eyes gleaming with laughter. 'But I shall ask if I feel the need to kiss you again, Miss Horne. Still, I asked you a question. Do you feel that you can trust me?'

'I am still not sure that I should,' Marianne said honestly. 'But I think that I shall. You see, I am afraid that someone may be attempting to murder Lady Edgeworthy.'

Drew's mind cleared instantly, all thought of seduction fled. 'Good grief! I sensed something was bothering you, but I did not realise it was so serious. What makes you think it?'

Marianne explained about the laudanum, and the medicine that had made her great-aunt feel worse instead of better.

'I know it isn't very much to go on,' she said. 'But someone tried to break into the house one night before I came. A maid had the toothache and came down to make herself a hot drink. She heard something and screamed, and then saw someone running away from the house. Aunt Bertha is being very brave and trying to convince herself that it was all a mistake, but underneath she is upset.'

'I should imagine she might be,' Drew said and frowned. 'I wonder…'

'Whether it might have something to do with what is going on here?' Marianne asked and saw his eyes narrow as he looked at her. 'You are not here to convalesce, Mr Beck—if that is your name. I think you are here to discover what the smugglers are up to, and the story of your ill health is merely to hide your real reasons for taking the house on the cliffs.'

'Not a particularly good cover if you have seen through it, Miss Horne,' Drew said and frowned. She had not yet recalled that his uncle had been the Marquis of Marlbeck, but she was an intelligent girl and it might only be a matter of time before she worked it out. He decided to trust her with at least a part of the truth. 'You are perfectly right, of course. I am here for reasons other than my health—and I believe that contraband is being stored on your great-aunt's land somewhere.'

'Yes, the thought had occurred to me,' Marianne agreed. 'I saw someone being rowed out to that ship in the bay. He appeared to be French, as did the ship, though I could be completely wrong.'

'You were not wrong,' Drew said, giving her a look of approval. 'Both the seaman and the ship were French, and it was dangerous for them to come in so close at that hour of the morning. I believe it was something to do with the tides— and of course they must have had good reason. I thought the man on the beach might be important, but now I am wondering if he was merely the go-between.'

'Because of the man you saw on the beach this morning?'

Drew inclined his head. 'You must forgive me if I do not tell you the whole story, Miss Horne—but it might be dangerous for both of us if you should let something slip. Indeed, I must advise you not to speak of the smugglers at all. If you were heard to voice your suspicions, it could put your life in jeopardy. Despite the myths that abound and the fact that they are called *gentlemen,* the smugglers are ruthless rogues.'

'I am sure you are right. If the attempts on my great-aunt's life were connected with this affair, I would imagine that mine might also be at risk. Someone must want to make sure that their activities carry on undetected—and for that reason they are prepared to do whatever is necessary.'

'Yes, that is a possibility,' Drew concurred. 'But we do not know if this is the case. Smuggling goes on in many parts of the Cornish coast, wherever there are accessible beaches and caves, though some of the northern cliffs are too dangerous for ships to approach. Many landowners turn a blind eye and are left gifts of brandy. You have not heard of anything like that happening?'

'No, for I mentioned the possibility of smuggling to my aunt and she did not think it could be so. Indeed, she was shocked at the idea.' Marianne frowned. 'It may be that the smugglers have nothing to do with this and that someone else wishes her dead.'

'Then you must ask who benefits from her will, I suppose.'

'My mama, who has not been here more than once in her

life, my sisters and I may have something, also Jane and Dr Thompson—but I believe the main heir is Mr Hambleton.'

'Our friend, Hambleton again,' Drew said. 'I should be very careful of that gentleman, Miss Horne. If he turns out to be the man I think him, he may indeed be dangerous—and I do not think he would hesitate to kill anyone who stood in his way.'

'Yes, I think it may be him, though he claims he was not here when Aunt Bertha's medicine was tampered with the first time.'

'Officially, perhaps,' Drew said. 'But do not forget the attempt to break into the house.'

'You think that he might have returned to finish his work?' Marianne felt sickened. 'Oh, how wicked! How could he?'

'If he and Lieutenant Humble are the same man, he could do it very easily, Miss Horne.'

'I see,' she said and nodded, her expression serious. 'In that case I must be especially watchful whilst he is in the house. I heard something the other night, something odd, but when I went downstairs I met Mr Hambleton coming from the servants' wing. He told me that he had also heard a noise and had checked the house for signs of an intruder.'

'But you do not believe him?'

'No. I think he was doing something that he did not wish me to know about. I should like to know exactly what it was.'

'Yes, it would be interesting to know—but be careful he does not realise that you are watching him. If he suspected that you knew what he was about…'

'I might end up falling to my death from the top of the cliffs,' Marianne said. 'Lady Edgeworthy told me that she had left much of her fortune to her cousin Cedric—but when he died she made a new will in Joshua's favour…'

'And where was Mr Hambleton at that time?'

'In Spain, he claims.' She grimaced. 'I do not like him and I am not sure that I would believe anything he told me. He may well have tampered with my aunt's medicine.'

'This is all speculation,' Drew said. 'We may have misjudged him—but please be careful, Miss Horne.'

'Perhaps you should call me Marianne. I think we have stepped over the bounds of formality this morning, sir.'

'Thank you, Miss Marianne,' Drew said and smiled at her. 'May I kiss you again?'

'No, Mr Beck, you may not,' Marianne said, but her eyes were bright with mischief. She had permitted the use of her name, but she was not yet ready to use his first name, for that was a different thing and would presume a friendship between them. It was of course perfectly acceptable for him to call her Miss Marianne, as this was often the case between acquaintances. 'We hardly know one another and I would not have you think that I am a woman of light morals. Perhaps one day…' Her cheeks grew warm. 'If we come to like each other…'

'Oh, I like you,' Drew said. 'But you are perfectly correct, Miss Marianne. I am engaged in a dangerous business, and so perchance are you. We need our wits about us and this is not the moment to indulge ourselves with a flirtation.'

Marianne was half-sorry that he had taken her refusal to be kissed so easily, for in truth she had been tempted to agree. 'I must go or I shall be late for nuncheon,' she said. 'I shall be busy for a few days, but perhaps…'

'We shall meet,' Drew said, an unholy light in his eyes. 'Be assured, Miss Marianne, we are destined to meet again soon…if only at your aunt's dinner.'

* * *

It had rained hard for three days. Marianne stood at the parlour window and looked out at the dripping trees. She would have braved a shower in the hope of meeting Mr Beck again, but it was pouring down and she could not go looking for him in such weather. He would probably be in his house waiting for the rain to stop, just as she was now.

'Miss Horne…' Marianne turned at the sound of Mr Hambleton's voice. 'I dare say you are feeling frustrated by the weather. I went out early this morning, but I fear I took a soaking, and I may suffer with my chest from it.' He coughed behind his hand. 'I really should not have gone, but I had to meet someone.'

'Was your business so important that it could not wait?'

'Yes, for it was to arrange a repair to my carriage wheel. I fear I must leave you tomorrow.'

'But you will miss Lady Edgeworthy's dinner party,' Marianne cried, for she was surprised at his leaving so soon. 'I think she will be disappointed, sir. Could you not arrange to stay another day?'

'It does you credit to think of her disappointment,' he replied and gave her what she could only think of as a simpering smile. 'Indeed, I have observed your manner towards her and I can only approve. You behave just as you ought, Miss Marianne—and I have formed a high opinion of you.' The look he gave her seemed to be indicating more than he was saying, but she pretended not to understand for she did not wish to know his feelings. Any attempt at flirtation or— heaven forbid!—courtship would be unwelcome to her. She hoped that she had read too much into his words, for it could only end in embarrassment.

'You are most kind, sir,' Marianne said, hiding her irritation as best she could. 'But my thought for my great-aunt is natural and born of affection. However, you have not answered my question.'

'I have business in town,' he replied apologetically. 'If I could defer it, I would, but I have no choice but to return. My visits are usually of a longer duration, and you may be sure that I shall return here again as soon as I am able.'

Marianne was silent. She did not know why she felt this prickling at the nape of the neck when they were alone, but she could not like him. She thought him false and sly, despite his attempts to charm her. Indeed, she had developed a dislike of him.

'You do not speak,' he said. 'I am encouraged to think that you are upset by my leaving so soon…and I may venture to say that I shall look forward to meeting you again.'

There was something in his look that made her want to recoil. If he imagined he was ingratiating himself with her, he was sadly mistaken. His false smiles only made her distrust him more, and she hoped that he would not press his friendship on her.

'You mistake my silence, sir,' she said. 'My disappointment is for my aunt's sake, not my own. Excuse me, I must fetch something from my room.'

Marianne walked past him and continued up the stairs. She did not glance back, but she was conscious that he was staring after her, and that she might have made him angry. He had no right to make up to her! She had done nothing to encourage him.

Marianne entered her great-aunt's bedroom. The medicine cupboard was locked, and it did not look as if anything had been disturbed. She was thoughtful as she walked along the hall to her own room. She had been watchful these last few days, checking on Jane as well as Mr Hambleton. So far she had seen no sign of interference of any kind with her great-aunt's medicines. Perhaps there was nothing to see. It might all have been in Lady Edgeworthy's mind—and yet the feeling that Mr Hambleton had something to hide had been growing steadily these past days.

She would feel safer once he had returned to London, though that still left Jane and the doctor—but she had always placed them low on her list of suspects. It was true that they had something to gain, but she could not believe that either of them would murder for money.

That left her with one real suspect. She would make sure that her great-aunt locked her door that night, and she would personally see that the medicine cupboard was locked when she said goodnight to Lady Edgeworthy.

It was odd that Mr Hambleton had decided to leave so soon. He must have known of his business in town before this visit, for Marianne had seen all the letters that were collected from the receiving office in the village. Mr Hambleton had not been sent an urgent message from town since he came down to Cornwall—so why had he decided to leave suddenly?

It did not matter, she decided. He would be far enough away to be sure that he could not harm Lady Edgeworthy. Her great-aunt had not reported any further meddling with her medicine these past few days, which might be because she had taken great care to see that nothing was left out at night, and the key was kept well hidden.

With Mr Hambleton gone, that would leave only Jane to

watch, and Marianne had almost concluded that the companion was blameless. She was fairly certain that Jane was in love with Dr Thompson, but that in itself was no sin. Her mind settled on that point, she was free to follow her own thoughts, and they turned towards Mr Beck and that kiss.

Marianne knew that she had behaved shockingly, for she had melted into his arms, offering no resistance, and he would be within his rights to believe himself encouraged. She would not be the first young woman to be seduced by a man's kisses, and she knew that something had responded deep inside her. There was a part of her that had wanted the kiss to go on and on for ever.

She would be foolish to so far forget herself that she allowed him such liberties in the future. He was handsome, bold and intriguing, and she had to acknowledge that she liked him—but she was still not sure that she could trust him. She held him blameless in the affair concerning her aunt, but she sensed that he was still hiding something from her.

He could not be so very wicked or her heart would not have responded to his kiss so willingly. No, she would not think ill of him, even though he was undoubtedly holding something back from her. Perhaps for her own safety? Yes, it could quite easily be that, she decided.

She was feeling very much better about things as she went down to the small parlour to join the others.

Chapter Five

After the heavy rain of the past few days the ground was soft underfoot as Marianne went for her walk the next morning. She knew that Joshua Hambleton had left soon after it was light, and could not help feeling pleased that he had gone, despite her great-aunt's disappointment that he would not be there for her dinner party.

As she walked in the direction of the rhododendron valley, Marianne was puzzled by hoof marks in the wet earth. She knew that Joshua had gone riding the previous morning, and the grooms sometimes exercised the carriage horses—but these seemed too many and too regular to have been one horse. Her suspicions were immediately aroused when quite suddenly the marks disappeared.

It was not possible for them to vanish at this point. She was puzzled as she looked around her, for there was nowhere that the horses—or ponies as the tracks seemed to indicate—could have disappeared into other than thin air. The valley of rhododendrons ended at the face of a rise that became rocky, but which looked impossible for even the sure-footed pack ponies that were often used for carting ore from the mines. Was there a hidden entrance here, somewhere that led into a cave…but surely it was too far inland?

Marianne moved towards a clump of tall bushes, a little hesitant, still puzzled by the disappearing tracks, and then she saw one of the bushes move and froze, fearing that she was about to be confronted by a smuggler. The next moment a man came out. He was wearing leather breeches and a miner's hat with a candle fastened to the front, his shirt open at the neck. He saw her at almost the same moment as she saw him and frowned.

'Marianne,' he said in a harsh tone. 'What the hell are you doing here? I thought you were going to leave this business to me?'

'Mr Beck,' she replied, raising her head proudly. His accusation was unfounded and put her on her mettle. 'There is no need for such language, sir. I came this way as I normally do and saw the tracks. I naturally wondered how they could simply evaporate like that.'

'Naturally,' he said, a reluctant smile tugging at his mouth. Most young women would not even have noticed the tracks, but he had realised from the start that she was not like most young women. 'If you look carefully, you will see that there are more shallow tracks leading to this clump of bushes. There is a carefully concealed entrance into a tunnel behind these bushes, and it leads into a set of caves. I imagine the caves have been in use for centuries and I believe that the ancient miners probably made the tunnel many years ago. There are some old iron workings at the far edge of your great-aunt's land, and they may perhaps have taken the ore out by sea.'

'Yes, that is possible, for the roads would have been impassable at certain times of the year,' Marianne said. 'When did you discover the tunnel?'

'Soon after I first came here,' Drew replied. 'I was not able to locate where they hid the contraband for a while, but I think we shall discover that these tracks lead to the old mine workings.'

'Does it not seem strange to you that they risked bringing goods in during such terrible rain?' Marianne asked. 'Surely they must have been aware that the tracks might be seen…and that they might be followed to their hiding place?'

'Perhaps they had no choice. Or perhaps a trap has been laid. In either case, I would ask you to stay away from this part of the estate for a few days. It may be simply that the smugglers have used the estate for a number of years without being discovered. Or they may have grown careless…either way, it could be dangerous to come here alone.'

'Yes, perhaps.' Marianne stared at him, her eyes dark with sudden apprehension. 'Do you think it may be a trap for you, Mr Beck? Are they trying to lure you to a place where they can arrange an accident for you? It might look too suspicious if you were to fall from the cliffs—but your body might never be discovered in a deserted mine shaft.'

'The thought had occurred to me, though I have been careful not to arouse suspicion.' Drew's eyes were thoughtful as he looked at her.

'I never believed your story of being ill,' Marianne reminded him. 'It is possible that others have become suspicious, too.'

'Then I shall take Robbie with me,' Drew said. 'I had hoped to be joined by a friend of mine, but he has not answered my letter. However, Robbie will watch my back, as he often did when we were in Spain.'

'He must be a good friend to you,' Marianne said. 'I shall take care not to come here again for a while. But I have news for you, too. Mr Hambleton left this morning. He says that he has business in London.'

'It was a long way to come for such a short visit. Something does not ring true here. You have done nothing to arouse his suspicions? It would need only a careless word or a look.'

'I have been confined to the house for three days because of the rain. He…seems to like me and I have tried not to let him see that I do not like him. I am sure he learned nothing from me, sir.'

'Then perhaps he truly had business in town.'

'Perhaps…'

'I shall rest easier knowing that he is not sleeping in the same house,' Drew said. 'I am sure that you locked your door at night—but even so…'

'I feel safer now that he has gone,' Marianne agreed. 'I am fairly sure that neither the doctor or Jane wish my great-aunt any harm, which means that he is the main suspect.'

'I believe he must always have been so,' Drew said. 'Whether or not he is the man I think him is another matter. I wonder…'

'What are you thinking?' Marianne saw his expression. 'Are you wondering if he left because he did not want to meet you at dinner? He also left the house rather hastily when you were expected to tea…and not by the front door. I was watching at the window and I did not see him leave. You have seen him, though from a distance. It may be that he has also seen you when you were not aware of it.'

'You are a clever girl,' Drew said and his eyes gleamed. 'It is possible that he did not want to meet a man who might be able to identify him as the disgraced Lieutenant Humble. Besides, his business here may have been done last night.'

'Yes, perhaps…'

'Now what are you thinking?'

'I am not sure. If he did tamper with my aunt's medicine, he must have been desperate for the legacy she intends to leave him. With me living in the house…' She shook her head. 'If he came down here secretly once before, he might do the same thing again.'

'You mean he may not have returned to London?'

'Yes, I suppose that is what I am thinking,' she said slowly. 'But I may be wronging him.'

'It is a pity I did not chance to see him out walking,' Drew said. 'When I caught sight of the man I thought I knew, he was too far away to be certain. I could be completely mistaken about all of this…'

'Then neither of us can be sure,' Marianne said. 'But I am delaying you. I dare say you are wishing me to blazes, for you have work to finish.'

'Would you care to know what I am wishing?'

Marianne saw the gleam in his eyes and her heart leapt— she knew without his saying that he wanted to kiss her. 'Perhaps it would not be wise to ask,' she said. 'I think that we must not let ourselves be distracted from the business in hand, sir.'

'May I kiss you, Miss Marianne?' he asked, his voice suddenly husky.

'No, Mr Beck, you may not,' she replied. She was on her mettle, deliberately keeping him at bay, for she knew that her heart was close to surrender. 'This is neither the time nor the occasion. I must return to the house—my aunt has several tasks for me. I shall see you tomorrow evening, if not before.'

'I must give you your way,' he said, but his bold look challenged her. 'But I warn you that it will not always be so—especially if you look at me like that, Marianne.'

'Goodday, sir,' she said. 'I shall look forward to tomorrow evening.'

'Be careful,' he cautioned. 'I cannot always be there to watch over you, though I shall come if you send for me.'

Marianne walked away without answering. The look in his eyes when he'd asked if he might kiss her had sent delicious shivers winging down her spine. She hoped he had not guessed how much she had wanted to say yes, but she knew that she must not give way to such urges. If anyone should see them kissing in such an isolated spot her reputation would be gone—and who was to say that it would stop at kissing? She knew that, once started, if he did not let her go, she might not want to break free of him.

He was attractive and she liked him. Indeed, she believed her feelings might be something much deeper, but she had no way of knowing his intentions. She did not even know if he was married. A part of her felt that she was ready to cast modesty aside and taste the delights of the pleasure they could find together, but she was a properly brought-up young lady and she knew that such behaviour would be the end of her hopes of a respectable marriage.

Men did not marry their mistresses—and though she knew that Drew Beck wanted to make love to her, loving her, wanting to marry her, were very different things.

Marianne was kept busy for the rest of the day and the following morning by requests from her aunt. Lady Edgeworthy was determined that her dinner party would be a splendid affair, and all the best linen had to be brought out and washed. Silver must be cleaned, and Marianne was sent to discover if the best china dinner service had been washed and prepared. Flowers were picked from the gardens and arranged in the various rooms the guests would use, and the maids were in a flurry of expectation. It was so long since their mistress had bothered to entertain in this way that they were anxious to make certain that everything was just right, and took it for granted that Marianne would know. For her part, she enjoyed all the flurry and the sense of expectation.

It was not until after tea that Marianne had a chance to slip away for a few moments. She decided that she would look to see if there were a few more roses that she might pick for a vase that was still empty, and made her way towards the rose arbour at the back of the house.

As she approached, she heard laughter coming from within its shelter and recognised the voices of Jane and Dr Thompson. She hesitated, not wanting to intrude on their privacy, but then they emerged, their arms about each other. From the way that Jane gazed up into his eyes, Marianne guessed that their relationship had reached another level. At that moment the doctor saw her and spoke to Jane. She looked at Marianne in her turn and blushed bright pink.

'Oh…what must you think of me?' she asked, looking distressed. 'I dare say you need me for something?'

'No. Everything is ready. I came only to see if there were more roses I could pick. I am sorry to intrude.' She turned away, but Jane came running after her, laying a hand on her arm.

'Please, you will not say anything to Lady Edgeworthy? I

shall tell her that we hope to marry soon…' She glanced back at the doctor, her cheeks pink. 'Doctor Thompson has just asked me to be his wife. We have been good friends for some years, but thought we could never marry—but now things have changed. He has heard that his uncle has left him some money. It is only a few thousand pounds, but it means that he can afford to take a wife at last.'

'I am pleased for you, Jane,' Marianne said. 'I know my great-aunt will miss you, but I am sure she will wish you every happiness.'

'She will not miss me so very much, for she has you now,' Jane said. 'However, I do not want to tell her today, because of the dinner party. In a day or two, Simon will call on her and we shall tell her together.'

'Yes, that must be for the best,' Marianne agreed. 'I am very happy for you, Jane. I suspected that perhaps you felt something.'

'I was a little jealous of you that day, when Simon came to tea,' Jane admitted. 'You are so beautiful and intelligent— and I am merely a companion. But he loves me and it was only because he had no money that he did not ask before.'

'I am sure that you will both be happy,' Marianne said. 'It is fortunate that Dr Thompson has been left some money— but Lady Edgeworthy may give you a present, Jane. You have been her companion for a long time.'

'Oh…' Jane shook her head. 'I do not expect it, Marianne. I am paid for what I do and I have been content here…but I could not help falling in love with him.'

'No. I think that one can never control these things,' Marianne said. She smiled at Jane. 'Do not let me disturb you. I dare say we have enough flowers.'

She turned and walked back to the house. Her great-aunt would miss her companion, and even though she might employ another one, it would be some time before she felt comfortable again. It was obvious that she would need Marianne to stay with her for some months to come.

Marianne went to her great-aunt's bedchamber once she had dressed ready for the evening. Lady Edgeworthy was sitting in an elbow chair, staring out of the window, a pensive expression on her face.

'Is something the matter, Aunt?' Marianne asked.

Her great-aunt turned to look at her. 'I was thinking of something,' she said. 'It is a decision I must make in the future—but it does not matter this evening, my dear.'

'I am very willing to listen, if you wish to tell me.'

'Perhaps tomorrow,' Lady Edgeworthy said and picked up her fan, which was made of stiffened buckram and painted with flowers. 'We must go down, Marianne. Our guests will be arriving quite soon.'

It was clear to Marianne that her great-aunt was anxious about something, but did not wish to spoil the evening they had all worked so hard to make perfect for her.

Jane was already in the large drawing room when they arrived. She was wearing a pale grey silk dress that Marianne had never seen before and her hair had been dressed in a much softer style. She had colour in her cheeks and her eyes glowed, evidence of the new confidence and happiness she had gained from the prospect of her marriage.

She smiled at Marianne and complimented her on her gown, which was the new pale blue silk that Mama had bought for her. Marianne told her that she looked lovely, too, and Jane blushed, shaking her head.

'It is quite true,' Lady Edgeworthy voiced her agreement. 'I have never seen you look quite so well, Jane.'

The guests had begun to arrive and were introduced to Marianne. Most of them were ladies and gentlemen of Lady Edgeworthy's age, apart from Dr Thompson and Mr Beck. However, they all seemed pleasant, friendly people who were delighted that their old friend had begun to entertain again, which they rightly put down to the visit of her great-niece.

'She seems in much better spirits,' Mr Pembroke said when he took Marianne into dinner. 'I was surprised when the invitation arrived, but Mrs Hammond told me you were staying, Miss Marianne, and the dinner was being given in your honour.'

'I think my great-aunt was missing her friends,' Marianne said. 'She was low in spirits when I arrived, but I believe she is feeling better now.' She was thoughtful as she sat down at the table. She had been placed between Mr Pembroke and Mr Beck. Drew had brought in Lady Edgeworthy, who was sitting on his left at the head of the table. Marianne glanced his way briefly, but resumed her conversation with Mr Pembroke until he turned away to talk to another lady.

'You look beautiful this evening,' Drew said, an unholy light in his eyes as he looked at her. 'That colour becomes you—but then, I believe you might look stunning in a flour sack.'

'You jest, sir,' Marianne said, because the wicked expression in his eyes was unsettling her. For a moment as she looked into his face, she was swept away to the day they had met in the rhododendron valley and he had kissed her. She knew a sharp sweet longing to have him kiss her again, but denied it. Now was not the time for such thoughts! She was not sure that the time would ever be right, for somehow she did not think that he had marriage in mind. 'I think Jane looks very well this evening. She is happy at last.'

'What do you know that you are keeping to yourself?' Drew asked, amused. 'Or perhaps this is the wrong time to ask?'

'Yes, it is,' she said softly.

'Then meet me tomorrow at our place.'

Marianne inclined her head. 'What do you think of the situation with France now that Austria has declared war on Napoleon Bonaparte?' she asked in a voice loud enough for others to hear.

'I believe that Wellington and the Allies will need to tame him,' Drew said, taking the subject seriously. 'He has rampaged all over Europe and must be contained one way or the other, though I do not know how it is to be achieved.'

'Surely the only way is to hang the fellow?' a gentleman said from the other side of the table. 'Damned upstart calls himself an emperor—madman, I call him!'

'Major Barr, you are unkind,' Lady Smythe reproved. 'I met Bonaparte in Egypt when my husband was in the diplomatic service. I found him charming—but of course that was some years ago now.'

'Napoleon Bonaparte is a dangerous man,' Drew said. 'If it were not for Wellington, we might have found ourselves under threat of invasion.'

'Oh, surely not?' the lady said and frowned. Her eyes narrowed as she looked at him, for she believed that she might have seen him when she was in London a few weeks previously, but could not be sure. For the moment the memory had eluded her.

'Military man yourself, are you?' Major Barr said. 'Sorry, didn't catch your rank?'

'I have none now,' Drew told him. 'But I was never more than a captain, sir.' He had preferred to remain a captain, for that way he stayed close to his men in the thick of battle, and had resisted all attempts to transfer him to headquarters, refusing promotion to a higher rank.

'Ah, Captain Beck.' Major Barr nodded his approval. 'Thought you had the cut of a military man—entitled to keep your rank if you wish, you know. Doesn't matter that you had to retire for your health's sake.'

Drew smiled, but made no reply and the conversation turned to general affairs. Marianne was conscious of him sitting beside her, but they did not have a chance for private conversation until much later that evening when he was leaving.

She went to the door with him. 'It was good of you to come, Captain Beck,' she said. 'I think you may as well use your title, for you are bound to be known by it now.'

'Yes,' Drew said ruefully. 'I liked Major Barr—just the kind of bulldog officer that we most admired in our junior days, but I wish that he had not made such a point of it.'

'Why?'

'I shall tell you tomorrow,' Drew said. 'If you will meet me?'

'Yes, I shall—a little earlier than last time. My aunt will need me later.'

'She seemed a little distracted at times this evening—do you think she has something on her mind?'

'Perhaps. Goodnight, sir. I must go back or I shall be missed.'

'Goodnight, sweet lady,' he said and kissed her hand.

Marianne was smiling as she went back to the drawing

room. There was still some mystery about Mr Beck, or Captain Beck as he was entitled to call himself—but was that his name at all? The smile left her face, for although she liked him very well, and her instincts told her that she could trust him, she was still sure that he was hiding something from her.

'What did you discover, Captain?' Robbie asked as they drank a glass of brandy together in the kitchen later that night. 'Do any of them know what is going on in the cove?'

'Lady Smythe may be a supporter of Bonaparte, but I doubt she is a traitor, just a woman won over by a young man's charm. I dare say Napoleon was charming enough when he was in Egypt. Major Barr would cheerfully hang any French spy that came his way. He could be a useful contact, Robbie. He invited me to dine with him, and I may do so…for he will know which Revenue officer I may rely on in an emergency.'

'You know where they took the stuff this time,' Robbie said, looking thoughtful. 'But if you want to catch them bringing it in, you must wait for another shipment, and that might not be for some weeks for they will need to move this lot on first.'

'Yes. One of us will need to keep watch, Robbie, because if they move it on we might discover where it goes from here, though it is likely that it will rest in many safe houses before it is sold. It is a pity that Hal did not answer my letter—three of us might have had more chance of catching them in the act.' He had deliberately asked only Robbie to accompany him down here, but now thought it might have been handy to have a burly groom to back them up.

'Well, they will not move it this night, because of the

company up at the house—too risky. Besides, they will probably wait for the ground to dry out. You might never have discovered their tracks if the ground had not been sodden when they took the ponies through. It was odd that they should choose to bring it in that night.'

'Yes, unless they had good reason. It had occurred to me that the mine workings might be one of their caches,' Drew said. 'But you are right, I could have searched for weeks before I found proof.' His thoughts were deep and complex, and he had too many theories to make sense of anything as yet. 'It is not the smuggling of contraband that bothers me, Robbie. It robs the government of much-needed taxes, but I would not have come here for that…I cannot give information against the smugglers yet. It is the spy I want—or perhaps I should say spies, for there must be more than one concerned in this affair. We know there is an Englishman, but there is also his French counterpart.'

'Do you think that Mr Hambleton is the man you seek?'

'I think that Lieutenant Humble may well be the traitor,' Drew said, his lips drawn into a thin line. 'If they are one and the same man…' his eyes were as cold as ice '…he deserves to hang for what he did!'

Robbie nodded. 'He will be dangerous, Captain. Not so much to you, because you know how to handle him, though a shot in the back would be his most likely way of getting rid of an enemy—but the old lady and the beautiful niece…'

'Lady Edgeworthy and Marianne Horne,' Drew said with a sharp glance at him. 'Give respect where it is due, if you please, Robbie.'

'Right you are, Captain. Taken a bit of a shine to the young one, have you?'

'That is not your business,' Drew said. 'I may allow you to be disrespectful to me on occasion—but not to Miss Horne.'

'Ah, so that's the way of it,' Robbie said and grinned. 'Congratulations, Captain. I wondered if you would ever settle for petticoat rule, being so wild as you were in the old days, but she is certainly a prize piece—and a lady to boot.'

'I should dismiss you instantly for insolence,' Drew said and laughed ruefully—his batman had never minced words, nor had he asked it of him. 'But I am not sure that anyone else would suit me quite as well.'

'I'll turn in now, sir, if you don't mind,' Robbie said, as unmoved as ever by his master's threats. 'On sentry duty tomorrow night.'

'Yes, goodnight, Robbie.'

Drew sat on in his chair, looking into space. Robbie's jest had made him consider his plans for the future. He certainly found Marianne irresistible—but marriage? He had expected to marry a suitable girl for the sake of an heir, but Marianne had got beneath his skin; she was like a fever in his blood. No other woman had ever made him feel this way.

He got up and began to pace about the room, much as a caged tiger might his prison. His thoughts were not comforting, for he was restless, plagued by memories.

Both Drew's parents had died when he was a small child. He could remember nothing of them. His uncle Marlbeck seemed a stern, remote man to the lonely boy he had been then, though later they had formed a kind of bond—but it was never love or even affection. Respect might have been a better word. Drew had been given into the care of a dry old tutor for years, and sent away to school at the age of fourteen. He was not sent for until he was eighteen, when he had been offered the choice of an academic life or the army. At that time his uncle had had a son he expected to inherit the title, but Barney had died of a fever a year or so later, and the estate had passed to Drew on his uncle's death.

Drew did not know if he was capable of loving someone. He had formed strong bonds with his friends, grieving for them deeply when they were lost in battle—but that was a different kind of love. No one had ever shown him softness or the kind of gentle love that came from a tender woman. He was not certain how he would respond to that kind of love…or if he could make a woman like Marianne happy. Would he chafe at the bonds of matrimony after a time? If he returned to his wild ways, it might destroy her. And that would be unforgivable!

Thus far he had thought only of the fierce desire she aroused in him. Robbie's jesting had made him consider more deeply. Perhaps now he should think of her instead of his own needs.

Marianne left the house early the next morning, for she wanted to keep her appointment with Drew and return before her great-aunt came downstairs. She had sensed that Lady Edgeworthy was anxious about something, and it would be best if they spoke privately in her room.

Her heart quickened as she saw Drew waiting for her and she smiled at him, anticipating that look in his eyes that set her heart racing. However, his expression was more serious than of late and she wondered if she had done something to offend him.

'You have news for me?' she asked as she reached him. 'Have you seen anything of Mr Hambleton?'

'No. I found the cache of brandy and what I imagine are

bales of silk in the old mine, as I expected—though not as much as I had expected. Robbie and I will take it in turns to keep watch at night and see where it is moved on to next—but you had something you wished to tell me?'

'It was merely that my aunt seemed anxious again. She would not tell me last night, but she may do later today. Oh…yes, I wanted to tell you that Jane and Dr Thompson are to be married. She told me yesterday evening and was so open and honest about her circumstances that I believe I can put aside any thought of her being the one to interfere with my aunt's medicine.'

'Then we must settle on Mr Hambleton,' Drew said. 'If he did not go to London, I wonder where he is? He must be staying somewhere nearby… Of course!'

'You have thought of something?'

'He will have gone to the next safe house to wait for the contraband to be brought there to him. He must be their agent in this country. It all fits so perfectly. I should have realised it before. You told me that he visits every few weeks—and that would be the perfect cover for his activities…'

'He did say that he had found a new source of income…' Marianne's eyes widened as she looked at him. 'Do you think…?'

'Everything seems to be pointing his way,' Drew said. 'So I must ask you again to be very careful.'

'Yes, I shall take care whenever he is staying with us,' Marianne said. 'And yet he may be more dangerous when he is not actually my aunt's guest.'

'Yes, perhaps,' Drew agreed. He hesitated—it was impossible to say the words that trembled on his lips, because he did not know what he wished to say to her. She was beautiful and the need to touch her and kiss her was strong—but was he fit to be the husband of a girl like this? 'The sooner this business is finished the better. I believe it would not be wise for you to walk this way again, Marianne. It may be better if you stay closer to the house for the time being.'

'But when shall I see you?' She spoke thoughtlessly from her heart and then wished she had not.

'I shall come to you when I have news,' Drew said, his voice harsher than he intended, because he was fighting against his own desires. 'If the smugglers suspect that I have discovered their hiding places, it may be dangerous for you to meet me. Send a note to the house if you need me and I shall come.'

Marianne stared at him, her cheeks flaming. Had she shown her feelings too plainly? Was this his way of telling her that he had meant only to flirt with her?

'I think I must return to the house,' she told him and turned away, her eyes pricking with the tears she was too proud to shed.

Drew stood watching her go. He knew that his brusque manner had hurt her and he cursed himself. She had begun to trust him and now she would think him a villain and harden her heart against him—but perhaps that was best. He did not know what might happen, for things were bound to become more dangerous in the next few days and weeks. And even if he survived, he would still be that same wild lonely spirit who had never known or given love. She deserved someone better. Someone who could love her and give her the tenderness she needed.

'Oh, there you are,' Jane said as Marianne entered the house. 'Lady… Is something wrong, Marianne? You look distressed.'

'No, it was just a bit of dust in my eyes,' Marianne lied and forced herself to smile. 'Did you mean to say that my aunt was asking for me?'

'Yes. I believe she is worried about something, but I do not know what it is,' Jane said. 'She asked if you would go up to her when you came in.'

'Thank you, I shall go now,' Marianne said. 'When do you expect Dr Thompson to call next?'

'On Friday as usual,' Jane said. 'I am a little nervous of telling her—though she has you, of course. Had you not been here, I should have delayed my wedding, but Simon wishes us to be married soon.'

'Do not concern yourself,' Marianne reassured her. 'My aunt will be happy for you and I shall stay with her until she is settled with a new companion.'

She went up the stairs and along the landing to her great-aunt's room, knocking and entering. Lady Edgeworthy was still in bed, a tray of hot chocolate and biscuits on the chest beside her bed. She had her writing slope on her lap and what looked like a pile of correspondence beside her.

'Are there any letters for me, Aunt?'

'Oh, no, these have not come today,' Lady Edgeworthy said. 'They are letters from friends and acquaintances who live too far from here to visit. I was just looking through them, Marianne.'

'If you wish to write some letters, I can return later.'

'No, my dear, it was just thoughts of the past...' Lady Edgeworthy sighed. 'I have been wondering if this estate is too much for a woman alone and whether it might be better to sell it and purchase a smaller house in Bath or somewhere of the sort.'

Marianne perched on the side of the bed, studying her aunt's face as she tried to judge what was on her mind. 'Is that is what you have been worrying about, Aunt Bertha?'

'Joshua has asked if he might purchase a lease on the estate,' Lady Edgeworthy said. 'He pointed out all the advantages, and even said that he might be able to borrow the funds if I wished to sell…'

'I think he ought not to press his claims,' Marianne said with a frown. She might have known he was at the back of this! 'This is your home, Aunt Bertha. You must do exactly as you please with it. Joshua Hambleton may be your rightful heir, but it is not yet his to command.'

'As to that, it was not my husband's estate and therefore Joshua does not have a natural right to it. My father left the property to me, but my husband rightly took it over, for it was his place to do so. Still, my father's will secured it to me and it was not entailed to my husband's relatives. After my cousin died, I believed that Joshua ought to inherit the estate, for my husband invested some of his own fortune here, though he was never a rich man. He had a title and I had money—it was a marriage of convenience, though we were happy together. We should have been happier had we had a child that lived…'

'Mama told me that part of it,' Marianne said. 'I am so sorry, Aunt. It must have been a great sorrow to you.'

'It was and yet I had Cedric. He was my aunt's child. She had him late in life and after she died he became like a son to me. His father was a military man and died of a fever in India. Cedric lived in the cliff house and visited me every day. I loved him and his death almost killed me, for he was young and it was such a shock…and then, a few months later, Joshua came to visit and for a while I thought perhaps…' She shook her head. 'I do not like to think ill of him, Marianne, but he was…a little threatening.'

'He threatened you?'

'Not exactly. It was more his manner than his words,' Lady Edgeworthy said. 'He seemed to imply that if I stayed here I should become morbid and might lose the balance of my mind…at least, that is how it seemed to me. He urged me to make the move to Bath for my health's sake—and he said it would be better for you to have more company.'

'Do not even consider selling your home for my sake,' Marianne said. 'I am happy here with you, and I think Mama and Lucy would be pleased to come and stay now that their period of mourning is over.'

'Well, that has put my mind to rest on your account,' her aunt said and smiled at her. 'But he may be right, you know. I have an agent to run the estate, but of late the income has not been what it once was, though of course the mine was finished ten years ago, and the farm does not truly pay for itself. I cannot imagine what Joshua wants with the place, unless he hopes to find another seam of copper or tin. It is possible, of course. I know that he visited the old mine workings when he first came down here.'

'He would need to discover a rich seam to open them up again, for it would be expensive,' Marianne said. She suspected that she knew the true reason for his desire to persuade Lady Edgeworthy to move to Bath and lease the estate to him. Under cover of looking for a new seam of copper or tin, he could carry on bringing in his smuggled goods without suspicion.

'I have told him that,' her aunt said, 'but he insists that he would find a way to make the estate pay.' She looked distressed. 'He made me feel as if I owed him the chance to restore his fortunes.'

'He has no right to put such pressure on you,' Marianne said. 'It is your home and only you can decide what you wish to do.'

'Yes, you are right,' Lady Edgeworthy said. She looked fondly at Marianne. 'It has given me such pleasure to have you here, my dear—and I should like to see your mama again. I must think about things, but I feel better for telling you what was on my mind.'

'That is why I am here,' Marianne said. 'I want to make your life more comfortable—and I shall not allow you to be bullied into making a decision that may not suit you.'

'You are such a comfort to me,' Lady Edgeworthy said. 'Jane is all very well in her way, but she is not like you, Marianne.'

'I want you to promise me that you will not worry about anything,' Marianne said. 'I am here and I shall not allow you to be browbeaten or made ill by worry.'

'I have begun to feel better since I stopped taking the peppermint cordial,' Lady Edgeworthy said. 'Perhaps it simply did not suit me.'

'Yes, perhaps,' Marianne agreed. Privately, she thought the answer lay in locking her cupboard and bedroom doors. If Mr Hambleton had hoped to avoid suspicion, perhaps laying the blame on Dr Thompson or Jane, he had discovered that his plans had come to nothing. Was that why he had now decided to try and force Lady Edgeworthy to leave her home?

What was he planning that needed extra security? There must surely be a reason for his wanting the estate to himself...

Chapter Six

Marianne woke early. Her thoughts had been muddled and uneasy, keeping her restless until past midnight and now she was awake again. Much of her concern was for her great-aunt, but she could not help wondering about the change in Captain Beck's manner. What had she done that had caused him to keep his distance? The difference in him had been marked and she could not think what had caused it—unless she had let something slip that made him believe she was setting her cap at him. She was not, of course, for even if he had been inclined to ask her, she could not think of marriage at this time. Her great-aunt was dependent on her for the immediate future at least. However, he might have realised that his attentions to her could result in her being compromised, and that in such an eventuality he would have no choice but to offer her marriage.

It was a humiliating thought and one that she found distressing. She would certainly not wish to be offered marriage in those circumstances!

Feeling restless, she decided that she would go down to the

village that morning. She had been hoping for a letter from Jo and was disappointed that nothing had come since her last short note. It was the first time that she had been apart from her sisters for more than a day or so and she missed them. She had written a letter to her mother, enclosing one each for Jo and Lucy.

To her delight, there were two addressed to her when she collected the letters and two for her great-aunt. She slipped them into her reticule and set off towards the drapery shop. As she did so, she saw a man cross the street and go into an inn. It was not the posting inn that most travellers used, but the shabby-looking place at the other end of the street, frequented by fishermen and the rougher elements of the village. He had not seen her, but Marianne recognised the coat he was wearing, though his back was towards her and a hat with a brim was pulled down low over his face.

She felt an icy tingle at the nape of her neck. Her instincts had not played her false. Mr Hambleton could not have gone to London when he said, for he would not have had time to complete his business and return. It must be that he had other business in the area…business that he kept separate from his visits to Sawlebridge House.

Marianne hesitated, for she knew that she could not enter such an inn. She would be noticed at once because no respectable young woman would set foot in such a place. Yet it would be wrong to let this opportunity slip away. On the verge of crossing the road, she saw another man approach and go inside. Once again, her instincts told her that she knew him, even though he was wearing the clothes of a fisherman.

What was Captain Beck doing dressed like that? Was he in disguise so that he could follow Mr Hambleton—or was there some other reason for his appearance? She knew so little of him. It was possible that he might be here for reasons other than he had told her. Could he be one of the smugglers himself?

No! She would not let herself think ill of him, even if his manner towards her the previous morning had been reserved and a little withdrawn. She would continue to trust him. It was all she could do, since she could not follow Joshua Hambleton into an inn of that nature.

Frowning, she crossed the street and went into the shop that had given her so much pleasure on her previous visit. She would buy some ribbons, buckram and velvet and fashion a pretty green bonnet to give Jane as a gift for her wedding.

Marianne was thoughtful as she walked home. The smuggling had clearly been going on around these parts for a while. What had changed? Why had Mr Hambleton decided that he needed to get her great-aunt out of the house now? It was unlikely that either she or Marianne would venture into the old mine workings. There must be some other reason...

Supposing the mine was not where they wished to store the contraband? Marianne suddenly recalled the night she had heard something and got up to investigate. She had seen Joshua coming from the kitchens and wondered what he had been doing there. She felt a tingling sensation at the nape of her neck as an explanation occurred to her. Could there be extensive cellars beneath the house—and a tunnel leading to them?

Marianne had always thought it odd that the pony tracks should be so easy to find the morning after it had rained so hard. Supposing Joshua Hambleton had realised that Drew was keeping watch for signs of smuggling activity and had decided to lead him to the old mine? He could have deliberately chosen a night when the ground was wet and planted a few barrels and packages to make Drew believe that he had found their hiding place. If a watch were being kept at the old mine, which she was sure it must be, that would leave the smugglers free to bring in their cargo at another place.

She was almost certain she was right. Surely it could be the only reason he wanted Lady Edgeworthy out of the house. If the smugglers planned to use the cellars for a special cargo, it might mean there was a secret way into them. And that meant that Joshua could come and go as he pleased. She felt cold all over.

She had reached the top of the hill. Marianne knew that she must tell Drew of her suspicions. Instead of going straight home, she would go to the house on the cliffs and leave a message for him.

She turned in the direction of Drew's house, walking swiftly now, because the detour would make her late for nuncheon.

As she approached the house, Marianne stopped to look down at the cove. The tide was right out that morning and there was a fairly wide beach. She was about to turn away when she saw two men suddenly appear, seemingly out of nowhere. They must have come from the cave Drew had spoken of and one of them was Joshua, the other a seaman who appeared to be local. She thought that they must have come from the village beach and rounded the cliff to reach the cave, which would have taken far less time than it had taken her to reach the top of the cliffs. From her position, they appeared to be having an argument, which ended with the seaman striding off towards the ridge of cliffs that cut the cove off from the village beach. At that very moment, Joshua looked up.

Marianne drew back immediately, but she was not sure whether or not he had caught sight of her. She walked quickly up to the front door of the cliff house and knocked. After a moment or two a man answered it. Everything about him shouted that this was an ex-soldier, and Marianne smiled inwardly as he looked at her with his one good eye. Given a parrot and a wooden leg, he would be a match for any pirate.

'You would be Miss Horne, I dare say,' he said, his one good eye fixing her with a gleam of interest. 'If you was wishful to see the captain, he ain't here. He should be back in an hour or two.'

'I must get home—I am expected,' Marianne replied and smiled at him. 'I have some news for Captain Beck.' She opened her reticule and took out a tiny notepad in a pretty enamelled case, using a little silver-cased pencil to write a few words about her suspicions concerning the cellars at Sawle-bridge House, and telling him that she had seen Joshua Hambleton on the beach. 'If you would be so kind as to give him this, sir.' She tore off a scrap of paper and gave it to the pirate.

'Name's Harris,' Robbie said. 'Robbie to the captain and my friends, miss. I'll give him your message right and tight. You'd best get home or you'll be in trouble.'

'Yes, I shall,' Marianne said. 'I am pleased to have met you, Mr Harris.'

'Likewise, I'm sure,' Robbie said and grinned at her. 'I ain't surprised the captain hardly knows where he's coming from.'

Marianne nodded and walked away. It was odd, but she felt as if she had been scrutinised and passed some sort of test. She would have to hurry now or she would be late.

* * *

After nuncheon, Marianne settled down to read the letters from her sisters. Lucy had written about some wild flowers she was pressing into a book, which was to be her journal, also a trip into Huntingdon with Mama and the new dress she was making.

I do miss you, dearest Marianne, she had written, *but Mama says that I must accept it because you will marry one day. Promise me that I can come and stay when you do, because I do not think I could bear it if I hardly ever saw you again! I am making you a present, but I must not tell you what, for I wish it to be a surprise for your birthday.*

Marianne smiled and folded the letter. She missed her sisters, too, but she knew that Lucy was just having one of her blue days, perhaps because it was raining. She turned to Jo's letter next.

Aunt Wainwright has put off our trip for a few weeks, because poor Uncle Wainwright had a fall from his horse and broke his arm. I think it shook him quite a bit and when I visited him he was in some pain. So we shall not go to Bath just yet, for which I am not sorry, especially as my uncle has given me permission to borrow as many books from his library as I please. He apologised for spoiling my pleasure and I told him that I would as soon visit him as go to Bath, which made him smile. He is rather a dear, you know, and it is a pity that she does not appreciate him, though I should not say it for Mama would be cross with me, but you know what I mean.

Enough of me! How are you, my dearest sister? And who is the mysterious Mr Beck of whom you last wrote? Do you really think there might be smugglers in the cove? How exciting! I do wish that I was there with you—so does Lucy.

We cut out a new dress in the back parlour the other day, but it wasn't as much fun as when you were with us. Besides, you are better at sewing than either of us, though I have been making hats and I think they have turned out very well. But I hope you are having fun and not thinking of us at all. Your loving sister, Jo.

Marianne read both letters again before placing them in her writing box, which was covered in red leather and edged with gold leaf. It was a particularly handsome thing and had been a present from her father. She ran her hand over the smooth leather and smiled, because her family was very precious to her. She supposed that she would always miss Papa, but she knew that she had been lucky to be brought up in such a happy home. She felt a little sorry for her Uncle Wainwright, who, as Jo said, was largely unappreciated by his wife.

How nice it would be if Aunt Bertha did ask her mama and Lucy to stay for a while. Jo, too, if she had not yet departed for Bath. She decided that she would write to her sisters and her mama again that evening.

Drew remained in his hiding place until the local fisherman had disappeared from view and Joshua Hambleton had gone into the cave once more. This time Drew had had a much better view of what was taking place, and he had caught enough of what they were saying to know that they were arguing about some goods that were due to be brought in in a few days' time.

Robbie had thought that it would be some weeks or months before they risked another cargo, but Drew had had his reservations. The barrels and bales he had discovered in the old mine workings were only a small part of a cargo; it wouldn't be worth the risk of being caught by the Revenue men to bring in so few barrels of brandy. That meant there had to be somewhere else—perhaps somewhere that had an underground tunnel leading to it.

The hoof marks he had followed were too obvious. He had felt it at the time, though he had wondered if it was just the smugglers being careless on a wet night. However, now that he was certain that the man who called himself Joshua Hambleton was the disgraced army officer Lieutenant Humble, he no longer thought the tracks were an accident. They were clearly meant to distract him, keep him busy watching the wrong place while a larger, more important cargo was brought in—and perhaps something, or someone, more important than contraband. He believed Jack had been right to suspect that the smuggling was a cover for something far more dangerous. Hambleton needed to be stopped! With his connections, it was possible that he was passing valuable information to the French.

But where was the new hiding place to be? Drew was thoughtful as he left his vigil. He had found only the one tunnel leading to the rhododendron valley, but there must be another. His quarry had not returned from the cave, so this was not a good time to explore, but he would certainly return there another time and try to discover if he had missed something the first time.

The drop had to be somewhere on the estate. Drew knew that there were several barns that were hardly used these days, but he had seen no sign of anything having been stored anywhere. He had probably been noticed walking about the estate. His presence at the cliff house had raised their suspicions, bringing Joshua Hambleton down here. It seemed obvious that he must be the mastermind behind what was going on—particularly if Jack was right and he was the one who had betrayed them to the French in Spain.

If Lieutenant Humble were the traitor, he was a ruthless man who cared more for money than loyalty to his friends, which meant that he would not stop at murder to get his own way. Marianne and her great-aunt might well be in danger.

Drew had intended to stay away from her, because he knew that if he met her often enough he would not be able to keep himself from making love to her. She deserved a better man than he was—or at least the man he had been—but he had found it hard to stay away from her, though at this moment marriage was far from his mind. Had she been less well connected, he would have asked her to be his mistress, but perhaps a flirtation would be all that either of them desired in the end. A few kisses could not harm anyone. If he knew that he was lying to himself, he refused to admit it.

Whatever the case, he would have to go to the house and warn her again, but first he must speak to Robbie.

Doctor Thompson had arrived early for tea and requested an interview with Lady Edgeworthy. Marianne went out into the garden, thinking that she would cut a few flowers until it was time for tea. She had spoken to her aunt's gardener earlier, and they had discussed where best the flowers for the house should be cut without spoiling the pretty garden. She had begun to place some sweet-scented roses with long stems into her basket when she saw Drew walking towards her. Her heart quickened at the sight of him, her eyes glowing though she fought down the urgent longing the sight of him aroused in her. She must remain cool and a little distant, for she did not wish him to believe that she was setting her cap at him.

'You got my note?'

'Yes, Robbie told me you had called. It seems that we both had the same idea, Marianne. I was not sure until I saw Lieutenant Humble again this morning. I do not know if he gave a false name when he joined the army—or whether he has since stolen the identity of your aunt's relative. Tell me, does she know him well?'

'I believe they had never met…until a few weeks after her cousin died.'

'So your great-aunt was grieving for a young man she loved and Joshua suddenly turns up, claiming to be her husband's cousin…' Drew's eyes narrowed. 'It sounds suspicious, do you not think so?'

'I have felt there was something false about him from the start,' Marianne declared. 'But Aunt Bertha seemed to like him…' She hesitated, then, 'I did not tell you in my note, but he has been trying to persuade her to lease him the estate and move to Bath for her health's sake. She is quite upset about it.'

'He needs a free hand on the estate,' Drew said. 'I think what I found was merely a decoy. They must be planning to bring in a much larger cargo—and perhaps more.'

'What do you mean?' Marianne's clear gaze made him hesitate. He knew that she was deliberately holding back from him, because he had hurt her at their last meeting.

He hesitated, then, 'I ought not to tell you, because it could mean more danger for you—and I fear that you may already be in more danger than you realise.'

Her eyes challenged him. 'But if you tell me, I shall be even more aware than I am now.'

'I do not know for certain, but I think that Humble or Hambleton, whatever he calls himself, may be working for the French in other ways.'

'You mean he is a spy?'

'Yes.' Drew frowned. 'He is a thoroughly unpleasant character—and would not hesitate to kill. If he tried to dispose of your great-aunt in a subtle way, it was only because he did not want to be suspected. Had you not come on the scene, her death might have been put down to natural causes and no one would ever have suspected him.'

'How could he be so callous when she has been nothing but generous towards him?' Marianne cried, her distress making her forget that she had meant to keep her distance with him. 'Oh, Drew, what shall I do?' She used his name without realising that it was revealing more than she wished or was wise.

'There isn't much you can do except remain watchful.' Drew moved towards her, wanting to comfort her, but resisting the impulse to pull her into his arms. 'He is quite possibly a ruthless impostor who came here with the intention of worming his way into her good books and stealing from her—to be left the estate would be beyond his dreams. Or he may have chosen her and the estate because it was ideal for his sly work. Either way, he had not bargained with you coming to stay.'

'Should I tell her of our suspicions?'

'Not yet,' Drew said. 'I need to catch him and his French counterpart in the act, Marianne. If he escapes, he may assume another identity and I shall lose him.'

She looked into his face, seeing his serious expression and sensing something deeper. 'This means a great deal to you, doesn't it?'

'I believe that he may have been responsible for an ambush that led to the deaths of twenty of my men and fellow officers. The mission we were on was secret, but the enemy was waiting for us. Someone betrayed us, and I now believe that it was the man we knew as Lieutenant Humble. He was in charge of the transport of ammunition, food, baggage. We hardly noticed him, except to complain when things were delayed—and perhaps he resented that. He certainly resented being dismissed from the army for cheating at the card table.'

'Oh, Drew,' Marianne said, her tone one of distress. 'You must have been so angry…so grieved by the loss of all those men.'

'It sent me mad for a while,' he said grimly. A nerve flicked in his cheek, his expression bleak. 'I had always been a little wild, but after that I cared nothing for my own life. I wanted to kill the enemy and to die…and I might have, had it not been for a good friend. He saved my life and brought me back from the brink.'

'Drew…' Marianne instinctively put out a hand to comfort him.

He groaned, his resolve breaking as he pulled her into his arms, holding her close and gazing down at her. Marianne smiled tentatively, her mouth opening slightly as he lowered his head to kiss her. She melted into him, her senses reeling as she gave herself up to the pleasure of being in his arms once more. Hurt pride vanished as she felt him shudder and knew that whatever was between them was something stronger than mere lust.

He gave her a rueful grin as he let her go at last. 'Forgive me, I forgot that I was meant to ask next time.'

'I do not think that I should have said no,' she said in a

husky voice. 'Though perhaps I ought, for this is not the behaviour of a modest young woman.'

'You need not fear me,' Drew said, touching her cheek
with his fingertips. 'I would never go beyond what you permitted. I have never taken an unwilling woman in my life,
and have too much respect for you to distress you in any way.
Moreover, until this business is settled, I dare not let myself
think of you, Marianne. I need my wits about me—and you
need yours. If Hambleton comes back here, you must be
very careful. If he suspected that we were more than
acquaintances, he might harm you in some way.'

'Yes, of course,' Marianne said, her mouth curving, for his
kiss had made her happy, despite her uncertainty about his
feelings towards her—and indeed her own for him. She
thought that she might have very strong feelings for this man,
who was still so much of a mystery to her—but without
marriage she could not allow herself to give way to them. Or
could she? No, no, it was impossible! She must concentrate
on the matter in mind. 'When I discovered Mr Hambleton
creeping about the house the last time I allowed him to think
that I believed him. I shall say nothing to antagonise him, for
my aunt's sake as much as my own.'

'She will not allow him to drive her from her home?'

'I think he might have succeeded had I not been here,'
Marianne said. 'But if they need to use the cellars he will no
doubt try to make sure that we hear nothing.'

'Yes.' Drew frowned. 'I wonder if it would not be better
if your aunt were to take a little holiday in Bath?'

'Perhaps…and yet, if he gains his own way, she might
never be able to return.'

'At least tell her to be careful how she refuses his request,'

Drew said. 'If you feel that either of you is in any danger, you must send word to me at once.'

'We both lock our doors at night,' Marianne told him. She heard the church clock strike the hour, its bell ringing out on the still air. 'I must go in. Will you stay and take tea with us?'

'Not this time,' Drew said. 'I mean to go down to the caves this evening when the tide begins to turn. I found one tunnel, but I think there must be another—one that leads to the cellars here.'

Marianne nodded. 'It has perhaps been blocked from this side, and that may have been what I heard that night. Do you not think that you might find it more easily from the cellars here?'

'Yes, I might,' Drew agreed. 'But I want to discover if I can find the entrance that leads from the caves first. I may come again soon. In the meantime, take care, my sweet lady.'

'Drew…' Marianne stood staring after him as he walked away. She smiled to herself as she turned and went into the house. She knew that he cared about her in his way, even if she did not know what his intentions might be for the future— at this moment, the fact that he felt something for her was enough to make her heart sing.

The next two days were damp and cool, though it did not rain hard. Marianne would have braved the walk to the cliffs, but her aunt had felt unwell for a couple of days and she had not wanted to leave her.

Jane was still with them, of course, though the banns were to be called in church the next Sunday.

'There is no reason for us to wait any longer,' Jane said to Marianne. 'Lady Edgeworthy will allow me to leave as soon as the banns are called, and we shall have time to do all the things we need by then. We do not intend to go away for our honeymoon, because neither of us particularly wants that and Dr Thompson is so busy. It will be wonderful to have a house of my own.' She blushed. 'Not that I have been unhappy here…'

'Nothing can compare with having your own home,' Marianne told her. 'It must be so exciting for you.'

'I am very happy,' Jane told her. 'I never expected to marry and I have all that I could want.'

Marianne could not doubt Jane's happiness, for she had a new spring in her step. Lady Edgeworthy was content that her companion should leave, and said that she would advertise for a new one soon.

'I shall give Jane five hundred pounds as a wedding gift,' she told Marianne. 'I had left her that amount in my will, but she may as well have it now—and I am intending to change my will anyway.'

'I am sure Jane will be delighted to have the money, Aunt.'

'Yes, I expect so. She deserves it—she has been a good friend to me for some years and may continue to be so, for she will not be living far away and I dare say she will call to see me now and then.' Lady Edgeworthy frowned. 'I have sent for my lawyer, Marianne. I have decided that Joshua should not be my main heir after all.'

'That is your decision, Aunt,' Marianne said. 'Did he know that you were intending to leave the estate to him?'

'I am not sure. I said nothing—but a copy of the will is in the bureau in the small parlour and I believe someone looked at it some weeks ago, before you came here.'

'Was it before the laudanum went missing?'

'Yes, before that…' Lady Edgeworthy shook her head. 'I think that perhaps I have been foolish, Marianne. I was very lonely after my cousin's death—and your mother was in mourning. I did not wish to intrude into her grief or yours. I believed that Joshua was genuinely my friend, but…now I am not so sure.'

'Had you ever met him before he came here after your cousin's tragic fall?'

'No…' Lady Edgeworthy looked at her. 'Why do you ask?'

'Are you sure that he is your husband's cousin?'

'I had no reason to question…' Lady Edgeworthy looked puzzled. 'Surely he must be Joshua? He knew things about the family…though there *were* some things he did not know. He said that he had been in Spain with the army and that he would have come years ago, but his father and my husband had quarrelled. I believed him.' She looked at Marianne. 'Have I been a fool?'

'No, I do not think so,' Marianne told her. 'You were lonely and perhaps you felt the need of someone after your cousin died. If he has taken advantage of your good nature, he is at fault, not you—but I cannot say for sure that he is not truly Joshua Hambleton.'

'My husband had a cousin, and Joshua is the right age, but we never spoke of him.' Lady Edgeworthy sighed. 'I think that perhaps we may take a trip to Bath after Jane's wedding, my dear—but I shall not lease the estate to Joshua. I might consider selling it one day, but not until I am sure that I would be happy living in Bath.'

'You must do just as you please,' Marianne said. 'I shall be happy to accompany you wherever you decide.'

'You are a good girl,' Lady Edgeworthy said. 'I am feeling a little tired. I think I shall lie down for a while before dinner.'

'You are not truly ill?'

'No, my dear, of course not.' Lady Edgeworthy smiled at her and patted her hand. 'I have had some restless nights thinking things through, but my mind is made up and I believe I shall sleep sounder now.'

Marianne was reassured. After her aunt had gone upstairs, she had a few words with Jane, who had been helping the housekeeper to sort through some linen for the seamstress to mend, and then went out into the garden. She walked as far as the small ornamental pond and then turned back. As she returned to the house, she saw that Joshua was getting down from his carriage. His arrival was bound to cause her aunt unease in the circumstances, and Marianne was angry that he should simply invite himself to stay without a by your leave. However, she knew that there was nothing much she could do about it for the moment. And then he turned and saw her, waiting for her to come up to him.

'You are back,' Marianne said, for it would not do to let him suspect that she knew he had not come from London. 'Did you finish your business in town?'

'Yes, it is done, and this visit I shall be able to stay longer with you and Lady Edgeworthy,' he said smiling at her. 'You have no idea how much I have looked forward to seeing you again, my dear Miss Marianne. How is Lady Edgeworthy feeling now?'

'Quite well, I think,' Marianne replied. How could he behave as if he were genuinely concerned for Aunt Bertha's health? It was difficult to keep her composure, for she would have liked to vent her opinion of his behaviour, but she knew that she must be careful and answered him calmly. 'She went up to rest and change for dinner. I have been taking the air.'

'I shall look forward to getting to know you much better this time,' he said, and the look in his eyes made her shudder inwardly. 'I did not forget you while I was away, Miss Marianne. I have brought you a gift.'

'I do not know you well enough to accept gifts, sir,' Marianne said. Her nerves were screaming and she wished that he would not look at her that way. Did he imagine that she cared for his regard? It took all her strength of character not to fly at him and box his ears. 'Excuse me, I must go in.'

She walked away from him, her back straight and her head high. Drew had told her to be careful of showing her dislike, and indeed she must, but it was hard—his manner set her teeth on edge. The more she saw of him, the more she believed that he had crept into her aunt's room intending to do her harm—to make her ill at least, if not to kill her.

If he had known that Lady Edgeworthy had left her estate to him, he might have seized any opportunity to gain it sooner, especially if he needed it for his nefarious activities.

She must be vigilant for her great-aunt's sake and her own. Once the will was changed, he might consider it was no longer in his interest to visit here.

Drew stood looking up at the windows of Sawlebridge House. He made it his habit to walk this way in the late evening, though he had so far refrained from making his presence known. As yet he had seen nothing suspicious, but if there was an underground tunnel leading here it was unlikely that he would, of course.

The last candle had been extinguished, and the house was

now in darkness. He waited for a few minutes longer, unsure of why he lingered, and then he saw a figure slip from the house and walk swiftly away into the shadows. His instincts told him who it was and he frowned. He had hoped that Hambleton would stay away from the house, but it seemed he had returned.

It was time that he brought in more help. If he was right, it could not be long before Hambleton made his move and he needed to be ready…

Marianne left the house early the next morning. She would walk to the rhododendron valley and see if perchance Drew happened to come that way. She wanted to tell him that Joshua had returned to the house and hear his opinion on the matter.

However, she was walking through the thick shrubbery when she heard someone speaking, and, recognising Joshua's voice, she froze, drawing back into the shelter of some very dense bushes as the voices came towards her.

'You said that you had the old woman eating out of your hand,' a harsh voice said as the men paused only a few feet away from where she was hidden. 'Yet she let the house to him—and I know he isn't what he claims to be. He has been everywhere on the estate, and he found the barrels you had us plant in the mine…'

'Well, that must have made him happy,' Joshua said in a sneering tone. 'As long as he and that man of his keep watching the old mine, we are in the clear.'

'Using the house as a store is dangerous. The tunnel hasn't been used for more than a hundred years and the roof looks as if it might collapse in places. I've done what I can to make

it safe, but I don't like it—and there will be noise. Supposing someone comes to investigate?'

'I shall be there to deal with it,' Joshua said. 'The mine was
the obvious place. He would have found it sooner or later. You
don't know Beck; he can be a devil! Better to lead him to the
mine and change our drop.'

'We've got a lot riding on this,' the other man said. 'Get
them out of the house or this may be the last run I do for you.'

'I've done my best, damn it! The old woman won't budge
and the girl is more stubborn than her aunt. I need this run to be
successful. Don't let me down, Bartlet, or you will be sorry…'

The two men had walked on and Marianne could no
longer hear what they were saying. She dare not move from
where she was standing until they had disappeared from
sight. She was feeling angry and sick inside. All their speculation had been right. Joshua Hambleton was planning to use
Lady Edgeworthy's cellars to store contraband—and he
would stop at nothing to protect his investment.

Marianne knew that she must visit the house on the cliffs.
She had to tell Drew about this as soon as possible!

Robbie answered the door to her. He frowned as he saw
her, recognising that she was upset about something.

'Come in, miss,' he said. 'The captain has gone out to meet
a friend of his in Truro, but I can take a message for you if
you've something to say.'

'Will you please tell him that I overheard something this
morning? It was early and I hid so that they did not see me—
but it was the man who calls himself Joshua Hambleton and
another, who looked as if he might be a fisherman. He was
angry because they had been forced to change their drop for

a cargo that is coming in soon—and Captain Beck was right. The mine was just a decoy and they are intending to use the cellars under Sawlebridge House.'

'He will not be best pleased to hear that, miss, for it places you in danger and the old lady.'

'Yes, I think it does, but there is nothing much I can do about it, except stay alert to the possibility.'

'Well, I'll tell him when he gets back, miss. You don't want to come in and wait for him?' Robbie narrowed his gaze. 'You didn't happen to hear when the drop is due to take place?'

'No, I am afraid I did not. Thank you for asking me in, but I must get back. I do not like to leave my aunt for long,' Marianne said. 'Captain Beck has gone to Truro to meet a friend?'

'Aye, he sent and asked him to come down. Their friendship goes back a long way, miss, and we may need an extra pair of hands.'

'Yes…' Marianne frowned. 'You should tell Captain Beck to be careful, for they suspect him of searching for something—they may think he is working for the Revenue.'

'Best they do, perhaps,' Robbie said with a dour look. 'Wouldn't do for the truth to be known. You get off then, miss. I'll tell him.'

Marianne nodded and left. It was only as she walked back to the house that she wondered what Drew's man had meant by saying that it would not do for the truth to be known.

Marianne met Jane as she entered the house. The companion was carrying a parcel wrapped in brown paper tied with string, and looked excited.

'Doctor Thompson ordered this for me in Truro,' she told Marianne. 'It is a gown he thought I might like to be married in. I came to ask if you would help me try it on. I think it may need some alteration, and I hoped you might pin it for me?'

'Yes, of course,' Marianne agreed at once. She thrust her worries concerning the smugglers and Joshua Hambleton to the back of her mind. She had done all she could for the moment and must leave it to Drew now. 'I should be very pleased to help you, Jane. Let us go into the small back parlour. My sewing box is there and so are my pins.'

'You are so neat with your work,' Jane said. 'I think you might have done well as a seamstress had you not been the daughter of gentry.'

'Yes, perhaps,' Marianne agreed with a smile. 'What colour is your dress, Jane?'

'I think it must be blue, because Dr Thompson says that I look well in blue. Shall we open it and see?'

They walked into the parlour together. Jane untied the strings and carefully unwrapped the gown. Her face was a picture to see as she lifted out the stylish, pale blue dress. Made of silk, it had short, puffed sleeves and a high waist with a slender skirt, which was embroidered at the hem with little crystals.

'Oh, how beautiful,' Jane cried, her eyes bright. She looked as though she might be on the verge of crying.

'Try it on, Jane,' Marianne urged. 'I will lock the door so that no one can walk in on you.'

'I have never had a gown like this before,' Jane said as Marianne turned the key in the door and then went over to the octagonal sewing table, which stood near the window. She took her pincushion from the silk-covered box at the bottom and brought it back to Jane. 'It is too stylish for me.'

'Nonsense!' Marianne laughed. 'It shows that Dr

Thompson thinks the world of you, as he ought. You will look beautiful on your wedding day.'

'I am so lucky,' Jane said, her eyes suspiciously moist. 'Both you and Lady Edgeworthy have been so kind. Some employers would have been angry or at least annoyed that they must find a new companion, but she was nothing but generous.'

'We are both very happy for you.'

Jane had slipped the gown on. Marianne fastened the little buttons at the back. 'I do not think it will need much alteration,' she said. She pinched in a small fold of material and pinned it. 'There, it is done. Now look at yourself in the mirror over the mantel.'

Jane did as she was bidden. She stared for a moment, as though she hardly knew herself.

'Is that really me?'

'Yes, of course it is,' Marianne said. 'I told you that you were lovely, but you would not believe me. Now you can see for yourself.'

'Simon has said—' Jane blushed and suddenly turned to hug Marianne. 'I am so happy!'

'You deserve your happiness. Now go upstairs and change into your own clothes again. If you bring the dress to me this afternoon, I will do the alterations—if you would like me to?'

'Would you really? I could do them myself, but you are so clever with your needle…'

'I shall enjoy working on such a lovely gown,' Marianne assured her. 'Now we must both hurry—my aunt will come downstairs in ten minutes.'

Jane nodded, gathering up the clothes she had discarded earlier. Marianne followed her up to the landing above and then turned in the direction of her own room. She was thoughtful as she washed her hands and tidied her hair. In another three weeks Jane would be married.

She was a little wistful as she went downstairs for nuncheon. She did not know when it would be possible for her to marry, even if Drew asked her. She did not even know when she would see him again.

'It was good of you to come this evening,' Major Barr said as he welcomed Drew to his house. 'We dine alone. I hope you will not be bored with the company of an old soldier?'

'Never, sir,' Drew said and smiled as he was offered a glass of Madeira. He tasted the wine and nodded approvingly. 'Very good. You must give me the name of your merchant.'

'Have it brought in—legally!' The major's beetle-bright eyes met Drew's. 'I was pleased to have your note, asking if you might dine this evening. Always glad of company and especially a man of your cut, sir. Are you going to tell me why you came down here? I ain't a fool and I never saw a man in ruder health.'

'I might have known I couldn't fool you,' Drew said with a rueful laugh. 'Unfortunately, I have probably not deceived those I wished to deceive either.'

'Is it to do with the smuggling? Captain Rogers was telling me the other day that they suspect the amount of drops has increased this last year or so. We've always had it, of course. One of the Revenue officers was killed just up the coast from here a few weeks back. He came across the *gentlemen* as they were transporting their goods. He was alone and they shot him. They left him for dead, but he lived long enough to tell the tale. He thought that at least one of them was a Sawlebridge man.'

'Rogers is one of the local Revenue officers?' Drew nodded. 'I thought you would know a good man I might call on. I may have discovered your ringleader—but it isn't because of the smuggling that I'm here. There's quite a bit more to it than that.'

'I imagined there might be,' Major Barr said. 'I am glad you came to me, Beck—if that is your name?'

'It's Marlbeck, actually,' Drew told him. 'But I should be grateful if you could keep that to yourself. I had asked a friend of mine to help me. He came to Truro to meet me, but he has other business he cannot neglect. I shall need Rogers and his men.'

'Do you know when they plan to make their next drop—and where?'

'I know where. I believe it may be within a few days, but I need the ringleader caught in the act.'

'Would you tell me why?'

'It is my belief that he is a go-between for a French spy. If I am right, he betrayed us to the enemy in Spain and twenty men died because of it.'

'Ah...' Major Barr nodded. 'Now I understand. I knew your uncle slightly, Marlbeck. Can't claim to have been his friend, but I should like to shake your hand.'

Drew smiled as he offered it. 'I knew I could count on you, sir. Robbie is a good man, served with me over there—but we shall need assistance at the right time.'

'Leave it with me. I'll see you have your men. And now we may eat. I hope you like your beef?'

'Thank you, sir. After living on Robbie's cooking for the past few weeks, it will be very welcome...'

And it would serve to take his mind from his other

problem, the very personal problem that concerned his feelings for Marianne. He knew that he had gained her trust, but he was very much afraid that he might do something in the future that would destroy it again.

Chapter Seven

'Ah, Marianne,' Joshua Hambleton said when he saw her the next morning. She had just come into the house with a basket of freshly-cut flowers. 'How nice it is to see a lady with flowers. It is pleasant to feel the sun once more, is it not?'

'Very pleasant, sir,' Marianne agreed. 'I hope to walk for a while when I have finished arranging the flowers.'

'Yes, of course, you *like* to walk,' he said. 'I should warn you not to go too near the cliff edge, for the heavy rain we had a few days ago may have damaged them. I should be very sorry if anything were to happen to you.'

If he had been in London, how would he have known of the rain? Marianne would have liked to ask, but she already knew the answer and she had to be careful. She had sensed something in his warning and wondered if he knew that she had seen him in the rhododendron walk. She had believed she was well hidden, but it was possible that he might have caught a glimpse of her gown as he walked past her hiding place.

'Do you think so?' she asked, giving no sign of her inner turmoil. 'I must abide by your warning, sir, for I know so little of the coast about here. I have been told that the tide turns very quickly in Sawlebridge Cove?'

'Yes, that is my understanding,' Joshua said. 'Though I do not know it well myself. I scarcely ever visit the beaches. I prefer to ride rather than walk, as I believe I may have mentioned before.'

'Perhaps,' Marianne said. Was he testing her—trying to discover what she knew? 'There are so many beautiful walks on this estate, are there not?'

'Yes, certainly…' Joshua hesitated and then moved towards her, an odd expression on his face. 'I do so admire you, Marianne. You have settled here so well. It must be hard for you to leave your family and come here, when perhaps you might have expected a Season in town.'

'Oh, no, that was out of the question,' Marianne told him. 'Mama could not possibly have afforded it. I might have gone to Bath with an aunt, but I was very pleased to come here instead.'

He gave her a look of speculation. 'I have suggested that Lady Edgeworthy might think of leasing the estate and house to me and retiring to Bath. I am sure it would suit her so much better. If you were to leave her, I think she might go into a decline, especially now that Miss Trevor is to marry.'

'I am not likely to leave her, at least until she is settled with a new companion, and even then I dare say she will have company. I have sisters who would be glad to come and stay—and Mama might even care to make her home with Lady Edgeworthy.'

Marianne could not help a note of defiance creeping into her voice, because it was so wrong of him to speak to her this way.

'I see…' He frowned, clearly frustrated. 'Well, I dare say you know best—though I am sure you will wish to marry one day.'

'Perhaps—though at the moment I have not met anyone whom I would wish to marry,' she said. 'Nor have I been asked.'

Joshua looked at her oddly for a moment, and then inclined his head.

Marianne did not turn her head as he walked away. She had a feeling that she had annoyed him, but she had no intention of siding with him against her great-aunt. Lady Edgeworthy would make up her own mind what she wanted to do.

She frowned as she went into the house, making her way to the flower room where she proceeded to fill the vases for the downstairs parlour, keeping a few roses for her aunt's bedroom. She would take them up to her before she went out for her walk and inquire if there was anything she wanted before she left.

She wondered briefly what Mr Hambleton was up to and where he had gone, but she could only be glad that he was out of the house. She would feel much safer if he took himself off for good!

'Are you sure about this?' Joshua Hambleton looked at the lawyer's clerk in annoyance. They had met in the Seafarer Inn to avoid being seen together by anyone who might know them. The man had been in Joshua's pay for some months now, and it was through him that he had learned of certain changes to Lady Edgeworthy's will. 'She has decided to change it yet again?'

'We had her letter this week,' the clerk said. 'You are to receive only a thousand pounds. The estate is to be divided between Marianne Horne, her mother and her sisters, Miss Marianne being the main heir. On her death, the house at Sawlebridge, the land and some money will be Miss Marianne's; the London house will go to Mrs Horne and the various other properties will be divided between the other two sisters—some one hundred and twenty thousand pounds in all, I believe.'

'Damn it!' Joshua Hambleton, alias Lieutenant Joe Humble and various other assumed names, seethed with frustration. 'I had the old woman eating out of my hand before *she* came. She is an interfering—' He swore beneath his breath, his mind working fast. He had a lot riding on the next drop of smuggled goods, because his French contact was coming in on the ship and would need somewhere safe to stay for a few weeks. They had important work to do and the house they had used for Raoul's hideaway was no longer available to them. 'It is a question of priorities…'

Joshua was thoughtful as he considered his options. He could dispose of Marianne in the same way as he had of Cedric Sawlebridge—an accident at the cliffs would be the easiest, for he had no doubt that she would ignore his warnings and walk there if she pleased. But another accident on the cliff tops might be one too many.

If he had succeeded in causing Lady Edgeworthy's death in easy stages, he might have inherited most of the money and been in the clear by now—but he knew that he dared not risk an investigation. If Lady Edgeworthy's death had looked suspicious, someone might have wanted to know more about him, and his credentials would not stand up to investigation.

He had worked for Joshua Hambleton as a secretary for some months after he was dismissed from the army, and when a sudden fever took his employer, he had seized on the idea of impersonating him. Hambleton had told him about his wealthy aunt, who would probably leave him nothing because of a quarrel between her husband and Hambleton's father.

Joshua had taken his employer's clothes, his possessions and what money he had, though it didn't amount to much. He had come down to Sawlebridge on the off chance to spy out the land. The first time he had visited under yet another false name and it was then that he had met Cedric Sawlebridge. They had drunk a few glasses of wine together—and, made unwary by the wine, Cedric had asked him to stay the night. On the way to the cliff house, Joshua had taken the opportunity to be rid of the man who stood between him and a fortune. At that time he had known nothing of the Horne family. Now it looked as if they might frustrate his ambitions.

Joshua had expensive tastes. He managed to pay for them at the moment, because of the money he made from the smuggling and information he was able to pass on to the French. He still had his contacts at Headquarters, despite his dismissal from the army, and obtained snippets of news for a few gold coins, though nothing of real importance had come his way for a while. It was for this reason that Raoul was coming over to stay for a few days or longer. He had some plan to break into a certain Government official's office and steal papers he said were of vital importance. Smuggling was a hanging offence in itself, as was passing information to the enemy. As for that other business in Spain… Joshua had nightmares about it sometimes, because he hadn't realised what he was doing when he accepted Raoul's gold that first time. A lot of men had died that day, and he knew that their blood was on his hands.

It was his shame and disgust at himself for causing so many deaths that led him to drink and cheat at cards, which in turn meant he was thrown out of the service without even the dignity of a court-martial. After that, he had become bitter, determined to get his revenge on the officers who looked at him as if he were a piece of excrement on the heel of their shiny boots. He had known that to live as one of them he needed a new name and money…lots of money.

The smuggling was never going to bring him that amount of gold, because there were too many palms to grease in order to be sure of a safe passage. He had hoped to give all that up once the old woman was dead, but since his plan had failed, he had decided on bringing in one last huge cargo, sufficient to make him wealthy enough so that he need not risk continuing this dangerous work. He had tried everything he could to get the old woman to move from the house for a few weeks, but she seemed determined to stay put—and now she was changing her will.

Wild thoughts of murdering her went through his mind. He could break her neck with his bare hands or put a ball through her head, but that would be too obvious and he might well end up by being hanged. It seemed as if there was one last chance to gain something from this business, though he knew it was a slim one. Marianne Horne had told him that there was no one she wished to marry—and she was to inherit most of the money. He believed that he had made a good impression with her, and she was, after all, a beautiful girl.

He decided that he would ask her to marry him. It need not be a marriage of long duration, for, once the money was his, he could arrange an accident and disappear somewhere—become someone else…

* * *

Drew sat on in the Seafarer's Inn after Joshua Hambleton had left. The man Hambleton had come to meet still sat staring sullenly into the fire. He looked so dissatisfied that Drew thought his business with Hambleton had not gone well. He had not been able to get close enough to hear what they were saying, but the expression on the face of the man who remained was enough to tell him that he felt disgruntled with his lot.

Drew summoned the barmaid, telling her to bring a jug of ale and a flask of rum to the table. He got up as the man finished his ale and looked as if he might leave, reaching him as he rose to his feet.

'Stay a moment, friend,' he said just as the barmaid brought the drinks he had ordered. 'I would ask for a few minutes of your time?'

'What do you want?' Bill Symonds said, his crafty eyes narrowed. The stranger might be dressed as a seaman, but he was used to serving quality and he knew it when he saw it, which that stingy devil Hambleton wasn't if he were any judge. He looked at the ale and rum. 'I don't tell what I know that easy.'

'And what makes you think I want information?' Drew's eyebrows rose.

'Because you wouldn't be bothering to buy me a drink if you didn't want something,' Symonds replied. 'Well, I'll tell you what I know—but I'll want something for my trouble.'

Drew nodded, taking two gold sovereigns from his pocket and laying them on the table. 'Tell me something interesting about the man who just left—his real name if you know it and what you told him that made him so angry. If what you say is what I need to know, there is more gold in my pocket for you.'

'That's easy,' Symonds said and took the coins, biting them before thrusting them into his coat pocket. 'He calls himself Joshua Hambleton, but I take leave to doubt it was the name he was born with—the Hambleton family was gentry and he ain't, though he acts like he were born to it. He wanted to know the details of a client's will.'

'And you work for the lawyer who made her will, is that so?'

'Aye, I'm the clerk, and little I get paid for my trouble.'

'So Hambleton, or whoever he is, paid you for information?'

'Yeah. He were pleased the first time, see, because the old lady left most of it to him, but she's gone and changed it again—probably found him out. Left it to her great-niece or most of it…' Symonds drank some of his ale. 'I can't tell you the name of the client, breach of confidentiality.'

Drew snorted in derision. 'Slightly late for an attack of conscience, I think. However, you need not supply the fine details. I imagine I know the lady in question.' He took another two coins and tossed them onto the table. 'If I were you, I should be more careful in future, sir. Otherwise your employer might find it prudent to dismiss you.'

He walked from the tavern, leaving Symonds to glower at his back as he picked up the coins.

Drew was thoughtful as he began the walk back to the house on the cliff tops. He did not think Joshua had noticed him at the inn, but he could not be certain. At this moment, however, he was more concerned for Marianne's safety than his own business. If Hambleton had been thwarted by Lady Edgeworthy's decision to change her will once more, he might become desperate.

* * *

Marianne had taken her sketchpad out into the garden. Her great-aunt was in the front parlour with her lawyer, who had come to the house at her request that morning, and Marianne had been asked if she would like to go out for a while. She had taken the chance to sit out in the garden, for it was a pleasant autumn day and she had a project in mind that would be best completed while the weather stayed fine.

It was her mama's birthday in a few weeks and she had decided that she would try to capture an image of Sawle-bridge House. She could colour it in with pastels after she had drawn it and perhaps have it framed. It might be expensive to send by carrier, but she could not let her mother's birthday go by without some token of her love. Mama would much prefer something like this to anything she could buy in the shops, even if she went into Truro.

She was happily preparing her outline drawing when a shadow fell across her shoulder and she looked round to see that Joshua Hambleton had come up to her unnoticed. She hid her feeling of annoyance as best she could, nodding her head in acknowledgement.

'I believe I offended you this morning, Marianne?'

'I do not think it proper that you should speak to me of something that is surely for my aunt to decide,' Marianne said, choosing her words with care. Something about him at that moment sent a shiver down her spine, and she sensed that he was angry, though he was doing his best to hide it.

'You are perfectly right,' Joshua said and sat down on the wooden bench beside her. 'I have come to apologise. My concern for Lady Edgeworthy may have led me to say too much.'

He was the perfect gentleman, contrite, anxious, all that he should be. Had Marianne not known him for the rogue he was, she might have been convinced of his sincerity. It was easy to understand why a lonely, elderly lady would have been taken in by his charm, for he was not ill looking and his manner was pleasant enough when he set out to please.

'Perhaps it would be best not to speak of this again, sir. You need not apologise to me, but I believe my great-aunt was a little upset.'

'Then I shall say no more to either her or you,' Joshua said. 'Will you think it impertinent of me if I say how much I admire you? You have so many talents… Miss Trevor told me that you had helped her with her wedding dress and I know you play the pianoforte—and now I see that you have an eye for detail. This is an excellent drawing.'

'It is a gift for my mother's birthday,' Marianne said, for she could speak of this without the need for caution. 'I shall colour it and frame it and send it to her by carrier.'

'Perhaps I could take it for you? My business takes me to many parts.'

'I think I shall not trouble you,' Marianne replied. 'Though it was kind of you to offer, sir.'

'You know I would do anything to please you.' He suddenly reached out and seized her hand, dropping to one knee on the grass before her. 'I have spoken of my deep regard before, Miss Marianne. I must speak now, though I realise that we do not know each other well. My feelings for you are such that I must ask respectfully if you would do me the honour of becoming my wife?'

For a moment Marianne was so shocked that she could not speak. When she could gather her thoughts sufficiently, she rose to her feet. Her instinctive reaction was one of disgust and horror, but she knew that she must hide her feelings.

'You do me honour, sir,' she replied as easily as she could manage, 'but you are quite right. I do not know you well enough to entertain your proposal of marriage.'

'But is there hope for me?' he persisted, rising to his feet. The way he looked at her sent slivers of ice down her spine and he must have sensed something, for his expression changed, a flash of anger in his eyes. 'Pray do not tell me that I may not even hope.'

'I fear that I must do so, sir,' Marianne said. 'Please do not press me more.'

'Am I to infer that you consider me unworthy of your consideration?' Joshua said, his gaze becoming cold and hostile.

'I do not mean to insult you,' Marianne said, 'but I…do not like you well enough to think of marriage, Mr Hambleton.'

Now the anger flashed in his eyes and she wished her last words unsaid. They had been unwise and she had made him her enemy, but his behaviour had been intolerable. She had thought he might try to kiss her, and she really could not bear such an intimacy.

'I see…then I shall not trouble you with my presence any longer,' he said and walked away.

Marianne stared after him for a few moments, then gathered her sketching things and took them into the house. The meeting with Joshua had unsettled her and she no longer felt peaceful enough to continue her work. She decided that she would go for a walk instead.

Hardly knowing why she did so, Marianne found her steps turning towards the cliffs. It was a while since she had walked this way, and three days since she had seen Drew. She had discovered that she was missing him far more than was good for her peace of mind, and her heart gave a great leap as she saw him walking towards her. She smiled a little tentatively as he came up to her.

'Marianne, were you coming to see me?'

'No…I am not sure,' she said and then burst out with it. 'Mr Hambleton asked me to marry him half an hour ago. I refused him as politely as I could manage, but I think he guessed that I dislike him—indeed, I fear I almost said it. It was very bad of me to be so rude, and not at all wise.'

She looked so contrite that Drew laughed. 'Well, he should not have had the effrontery to ask you. He is not worthy to kiss your feet! I should like to teach him his manners.'

'Oh…' Marianne blushed. 'I dare say it was a well-meant offer and I do not think myself above such a marriage—but I cannot like him and besides, I think he tried to kill my aunt. And he is involved with smugglers!' Her pent-up emotions tumbled out in hasty words. 'And if he were not, I could never marry him. He is a slimy toad!'

'I hope you did not say as much to him?'

'No, I was careful in my choice of words, except at the last—I told him I could not like him enough to think of marriage. Was that very rude of me? It made him angry.'

'I dare say it would,' Drew said. His eyes were warm with amusement as they dwelled on her flushed face. Her passion and her distress had tumbled out of her with charming innocence, making him aware of a need to protect her from Mr Hambleton and any other gentleman with similar intentions. Himself included, for he knew that he could bring her nothing but pain in the end. 'Feel no pity for him, Marianne. He has his own agenda for making you a proposal.'

'What do you mean?'

'Forgive me, it is not my place to say—but I was on my way to your aunt's house to warn you once more. I discovered something today that makes me think that you may be in some immediate danger from him...especially now that you have refused him.'

'You mean because of my aunt's will, I suppose. Aunt Bertha told me that she has decided to change it in favour of Mama, my sisters and me—though he is still to receive something.' Marianne frowned. 'Will you come back to the house with me now? I am sure that my aunt and Jane would be pleased with your company.'

'I shall walk part of the way with you,' Drew said as they turned in the direction of Sawlebridge House. 'There is one good thing in all this...' Marianne arched her fine brows. 'If Mr Hambleton knows that he will not benefit from her will, he may not bother to make any more attempts on her life.'

'I had not thought of that,' Marianne replied. 'Do you think he does know?'

'I am certain of it,' Drew said. 'He has been paying a clerk for information concerning her affairs, but he made a mistake today, for he gave only a half sovereign for the news that he was disinherited—and I paid more.'

Marianne looked at him. 'Have you considered that your own life may be in danger, sir? I do not think your activities in the district will have gone unnoticed.'

'I am safe enough as long as I go armed and keep my wits about me. I have no fear for my own safety. There was a time when I might have welcomed death, though that is behind me.

I promise you that I shall not be careless.' His eyes were a very dark blue as they dwelled on her face, sending little quivers coursing through her. 'It is your safety that concerns me, Marianne. I should not forgive myself if anything untoward were to happen to you. I know that you would not leave your aunt or I would urge you to go home to your family.'

'I should be a poor friend if I deserted her when she needed me,' Marianne said. 'Besides, Jane is to be married in just over two weeks from now. I have been helping her with her bride clothes and I am looking forward to seeing her wed.'

'Yes, I expect so,' Drew said and smiled oddly. 'Well, do not be surprised if you have a shadow haunting you wherever you walk—it will be either Robbie, me or someone I have asked to help us.'

She stopped walking, gazing up into his eyes, her face an open book for him to read. 'I thank you for your concern,' she said softly, 'but you must not worry for my sake. I think Mr Hambleton has other plans for the moment, plans that must take precedence over my death. I have been thinking that this next run must be something special…that he has good reason for wanting us to leave the house.'

'He may have decided that it is becoming too dangerous to continue his dangerous game,' Drew agreed. 'In his shoes I think I might risk one last cargo—a large one that would bring me in enough funds to set myself up in…whatever it is he has in mind.'

Marianne nodded and looked thoughtful. 'Yes, I believe he is hoping for something on those lines—but he has given up trying to persuade my great-aunt to leave the house. I do not know whether he still intends to use the cellars or whether he will change his mind.'

'There must be a wall blocking off the tunnel and perhaps part of the cellar itself,' Drew said. 'The house is old and it was probably installed many years ago. There may be some mechanism that releases it, as there often is in old houses. Many of the secret rooms that exist were built to hide Catholic priests in the days of the Tudors. I have looked for the entrance at the cliff side, but can find no sign of it. It might be easier to discover it from your side—' He broke off and looked at her. 'That does not mean that you should search for it. Perhaps I might be allowed to try one day—when Joshua is out?'

'I do not see why not,' Marianne replied. 'I should imagine that my great-aunt would prefer that it is sealed so that no one may enter that way.'

'Yes, I imagine she would,' Drew agreed. 'Will you ask her if I may come tomorrow?'

'Yes, when we are alone,' Marianne said. 'It may be awkward for Joshua now that I have refused him. I do not think he will be anxious to spend time in the house. He may even leave us again.'

'Send me word when he leaves and I shall come as soon as I am able,' Drew told her. 'I think the drop may be imminent, for he would not otherwise have returned so soon, and I have taken certain precautions. We may be able to catch them as they land and then none of this will matter.'

Marianne felt cold all over. 'I think you will be in some danger when that happens. Please take care, sir.'

'Yes, I shall,' Drew said. He reached out and touched her cheek, trailing his fingers down its softness. 'Do not worry for my sake, sweet nymph.'

'You should not call me that,' Marianne reproved, her heart racing. His look seemed to burn into her, making her aware of fierce longings she had not known she could feel. She hoped that he might take her into his arms and kiss her as he had before, but he merely smiled.

'I must go. You are in sight of the house and I think you safe enough now,' he told her. 'I have business elsewhere. I shall see you tomorrow unless I have your note to say it is not convenient. I shall know what you mean.'

'Yes, of course,' Marianne said. 'Farewell…until tomorrow…'

Drew nodded, but said no more as he turned away. She stood for a moment watching him walk back the way they had come, and then sighed. As she moved towards the house, a man came out, strolling towards her. She went forward with a smile as she recognised him, because she had liked the gentleman when they met and knew that he was one of her great-aunt's oldest friends.

'How nice to see you, Major Barr,' Marianne said. 'Have you seen Lady Edgeworthy?'

'Yes, we had a little chat. She told me that she had been changing her will and that Mr Hambleton was no longer her heir. I told her that I thought she was very wise. Seems a charming fellow on the face of it—but not sure he is everything he claims. Told her she would be sensible not to have him here again.'

'Oh…' Marianne did not know how to answer him, for he seemed to know what was happening here and she was not sure how he had gained his knowledge. 'Well, it is my aunt's affair. She must do just as she likes.'

'Yes, she said you had been a great support to her. The impertinent fellow wanted her to sell and move. Told her I could get her a decent price if she wanted to sell, but I hope she won't just yet. Hard to find good friends.' He smiled at her in a genial way. 'Did I see Beck walking off just now? Now there's a true friend to have in an emergency.'

'Yes, I believe so,' she said.

'Well, I must get off, I have things to do. I just wanted to make sure Lady Edgeworthy was going along nicely. She tells me that Mr Hambleton has decided to leave you again. Indeed, he took his leave before I arrived. Apparently, he had urgent business elsewhere.'

'Oh, I see,' Marianne said. 'Thank you for your neighbourly concern for my great-aunt, sir. I shall go in to her now, because she will be wondering where I have got to—it is well past teatime.'

'I should warn you that Lady Smythe is with your aunt,' Major Barr said. 'I left them to have a good gossip.'

Marianne nodded and went into the house. She decided to go up and tidy herself before going into her aunt's drawing room when she had company.

She came down some minutes later, pausing outside the door. Lady Smythe was talking rather loudly, and Marianne was struck as she heard Drew's name.

'Oh, yes, I am quite sure of it,' Lady Smythe said. 'I thought I had seen him in London—and I remembered this morning. We were not introduced, but someone pointed him out to me—he is the Marquis of Marlbeck. His uncle died a few months back and he came into the title, because the marquis's son had died…'

Marianne stood absolutely still, listening as her aunt

asked for more details. Surely it was not possible, and yet she had met him that day in Marlbeck Woods when they were children…and he had told her that he was staying with his uncle. Of course! She ought to have known it. There was a slight family resemblance, though she would never have put it all together unless she had overheard Lady Smythe.

Her heart was thudding, and her thoughts were whirling in confusion. Drew had deliberately concealed his identity from her—why? He had told her so much, why had he not trusted her enough to tell her who he really was? He must have known that she would not betray him.

She had thought him a gentleman of moderate means, an ex-army officer, but he was the Marquis of Marlbeck. And that meant marriage between them was out of the question. He was an important member of the aristocracy and could not be expected to think of marrying a parson's daughter. Her cheeks flamed as she recalled that he had told her he had no time for flirting with her for the moment. He must have thought she was setting her cap at him!

She knew the house he had inherited because she had been to the garden parties that were held there each summer. And she had been invited to a large gathering in the great hall that the last marquis had given for his neighbours a year or two before his death, but never to dinner or the balls that were sometimes held there. Marlbeck Manor was a very large house, furnished with countless treasures and resembled a museum more than a home, for the marquis had liked to show off his great wealth. However, he was a generous man, and had once, years ago, halted in his coach outside the Vicarage and given silver coins to the children, and he had also given permission for the Horne family to use his woods as they pleased. But the acquaintance stopped there.

Drew wore boots that had seen better days, but declared they were his favourites. It was a pretence, a sham, because he was one of the richest men in England, having inherited the estate and all the consequence that went with it.

Marianne's throat felt tight with tears, because Drew had not treated her well. He should have told her the truth. He should not have let her think there was hope! She would never be considered suitable as the wife of the Marquis of Marlbeck! All this time she had been nurturing a tiny seed of hope that perhaps one day…and he must have known it was impossible. His family and friends would be against it, of course they would, even if he cared enough…but he did not care. He had merely been flirting with her. How foolish she had been to think it could be more. Yes, she was at fault, for she had deceived herself. He had never actually said anything that entitled her to think he meant to make her an offer—and it was more than likely that he believed she would accept *carte blanche* to become his mistress. Many girls in her situation might have jumped at the chance.

Her cheeks felt hot as she recalled the last time they had kissed. She had surrendered to him completely, might even have considered the world well lost for love had he demanded it of her—but now she was angry. She turned away from the drawing room, feeling unable to face Lady Smythe or her aunt for the moment.

Drew had asked her to send word when Joshua Hambleton left, but that could wait for the morning. He had told her not to go down to the cellars, saying that he would come and search for the entrance to the tunnel himself—but she was in no mood for meekly obeying him.

Joshua had left the house, which meant it was perfectly safe for her to search herself. She decided that she would say nothing to her aunt until she had found something. If she found the entrance, it could easily be blocked from the inside, which would prevent the cellars ever being used for such a purpose again.

'You are very quiet this evening, my dear,' Lady Edgeworthy said when they were taking tea in the parlour after dinner. Her eyes dwelled on Marianne's face. 'Has something upset you?'

'No, nothing at all,' Marianne told her. 'Forgive me if I have not been good company. I had a slight headache earlier, but it has eased now.'

It was not quite the truth, because the pain she was experiencing was centred about her heart. She realised that she had become much too fond of Captain Beck, and it was difficult to know quite how to cope with the revelation that had dashed her secret hopes.

When she thought about it, she knew that Drew had said nothing to suggest that he wished to marry her. His kisses, his compliments—the smiles that made her heart beat very fast were mere flirtation. He belonged to the aristocracy and she was merely the daughter of a younger son of country gentry. He must imagine her ripe for seduction…or perhaps he was content with a few kisses?

Tears stung behind her eyes, but there was no way that she could let them fall in her present company. Besides, she was determined not to weep like a silly goose. She would find the tunnel when everyone had gone to bed that night, and then she would inform her aunt of the need to make it safe. She did not need Drew's help! She was perfectly capable of protecting her aunt and herself!

Somehow she managed to get through the evening without betraying herself. She played the pianoforte, putting all the pent-up passion inside her into a rousing performance that was greeted with applause from Jane and Lady Edgeworthy.

'If only I could play half as well,' Jane said. 'I shall miss you when I marry, Marianne. You must promise to visit me sometimes.'

'Yes, of course I shall,' Marianne replied. 'But you will always be welcome here—will she not, Aunt?'

'Yes, naturally,' Lady Edgeworthy said. 'Now I think I shall seek my bed, for it has been a long day. Will you come up with me, Marianne? I have something I wish to say to you.'

Marianne accompanied her great-aunt to her bedchamber. Lady Edgeworthy smiled at her and asked her to sit down. She did so on one of the stools and her aunt took the mahogany elbow chair, which was a fine example of Mr Chippendale's work, with pad feet and a solid square seat, covered with exquisite embroidery.

'Now we may talk privately for a moment,' she said. 'I have changed my will and your family will benefit, Marianne. We shall not go into details—but I wanted you to have this now.'

She handed Marianne a flat box. The girl took it, opening it slowly, feeling surprised and a little reluctant, because her great-aunt had already been more than generous. When she saw the beautiful creamy pearls inside, she was both shocked and overcome, for they were large and obviously expensive.

'These are very valuable, Aunt Bertha. I do not think you should give them to me—they must be precious to you.'

'My husband gave them to me when we were married,' Lady Edgeworthy said. 'But I have no use for them now—that style is for a young lady, not one of my age. And who else should I give them to if not you? You know my situation, Marianne.'

'Yes, I know,' Marianne said, her cheeks pink. 'I am delighted to have them, of course, and I do thank you—but I did not wish for such a gift. You have already made me a generous allowance. Besides, I came to visit only because I have always been fond of you, Aunt. I did not expect to be given things like this…'

'Do you think I do not know that?' Lady Edgeworthy's eyes were moist, warm with affection. 'The difference between you and that rogue…for that is what Major Barr tells me he is…' She shook her head. 'I do not know why I was ever fooled by him, but it is over. When he took his leave this morning, I told him that he must ask before he comes to stay again. I do not think he was best pleased, but I have decided that I shall break the habit. I do not wish him to come here again.'

'No, I should imagine that he was not pleased by the news,' Marianne said. 'I think you are well rid of him, Aunt—and I shall sleep more easily knowing that he has gone.'

'Yes, well, the thing is done and finished,' Lady Edgeworthy told her. 'I had no wish to lease my home or the estate to him, though I believe I shall need to seek some advice in how to bring things round here. However, I have good friends who may help me there—but I have decided that I shall write to your mama, Marianne. It is my wish that we shall all meet in Bath for a little visit together, and then…well, we shall see how we go on.' She looked at Marianne expectantly. 'I cannot be until after Jane's wedding, of course—but afterwards, would that please you?'

'Yes, of course it must,' Marianne told her. 'Lucy would love it of all things, and Mama, I am sure. Jo is promised to Aunt Wainwright, as I have told you, but we should see her there for it will be at just the same time, I believe. They were to have gone before this but for Uncle Wainwright's accident.'

'Yes, well, that was what decided me on it,' Lady Edgeworthy said. 'We shall all be together, and as I said, we must see what happens. I have it in mind to ask if your mama would like to make her home with me—but she may be settled where she is.'

'Oh…' Marianne looked at her in surprise. Before that afternoon, it would have opened so many possibilities, but now it could make little difference to her own happiness. 'I cannot speak for Mama, but I think she might like to live with you here, Aunt. She would enjoy a visit to Bath, I am sure—but she is used to a large country house, and I think she must find the Lodge cramped. Besides…' She shook her head. It was not for her to speak of her mother's discomfort at living on her sister's charity.

'As I said, it depends on many things,' Lady Edgeworthy said. 'But do you agree that I should write concerning the visit to Bath?'

'With all my heart,' Marianne said, 'for I shall have her birthday present ready by then and I may give it to her when we meet.'

She kissed her aunt's cheek and left her, walking along the hall to her own room. She was thoughtful, because she knew that once the smuggling was over Drew would leave the area; there was nothing to keep him here and he would naturally return to his home. She would go to Bath with her family and…

She shook her head. She must not dwell on the future. Tonight, she had more important work—she was determined to find the secret entrance in the cellars and have it blocked in before she told Drew of her discovery. However, she could not still the ache in her heart or her tortured thoughts, for she had allowed herself to dream of a future that included Drew. Lifting her head, she refused to let the tears fall. She had brought this disappointment on herself by allowing him to kiss her the way he had, and she had only herself to blame if he had taken unfair advantage of her feelings.

Chapter Eight

The house had been quiet for some time now. Marianne had not undressed, for it might be cold in the cellars. She picked up her chamber-stick, slipping the tinder-box into the pocket of her skirt in case she needed it. She opened her bedroom door very quietly and glanced out, listening for a moment before closing it softly behind her.

She was sure that the servants had retired to bed, for they went soon after their mistress. Their days were long, and, in some cases, arduous, for it was a big house and Lady Edgeworthy ought perhaps to have employed more servants than she presently had, though many of the rooms were not in use.

Going carefully down the stairs, Marianne turned towards the wing of the house where the kitchens were situated. She had visited them several times since she'd come to live here, because she had been used to an easygoing relationship with the servants at her own home, and had continued it here. Her smile and her polite manner, her warmth and her kindness towards her aunt had been noticed and won her many friends below stairs. Marianne would have been surprised had she been able to hear Mr and Mrs Jensen speak of her in the privacy of their own sitting room. It was the opinion of Mr Jensen that Miss Marianne Horne was fitted for higher things, and, he had told his wife, he wouldn't be surprised if she made a good match one day.

The kitchen had been left clean and tidy, and ready for the morning. Marianne made her way through it to the scullery and what she knew was the door to the wine cellar. The key was always kept on a hook close by the door. She knew, for she had seen Mr Jensen take it when he fetched up some wine Lady Edgeworthy had asked for. He had brought it to Marianne to be certain it was the right one, and he had told her that the cellar was always kept locked.

'I leave the key by the door just in case it is needed when I am out,' he told her. 'But I can tell you that anyone who used it without permission would be severely taken to task, miss.'

Marianne told him that she believed all the servants were to be trusted and he had smiled, well pleased with her answer.

She found the key where she had expected it to be and opened the door, locking it after her, and slipping the key into her pocket with her tinder-box. Taking a deep breath to ready herself, she held her candle in one hand, lighting the steep steps leading down to the cellar and placed her hand on the wooden rail, which hugged the wall on one side.

She walked carefully down them, lifting her gown so as not to fall over it and take a tumble, which might result in serious injury. It was chilly as she reached the bottom of the deep steps and she was pleased that she had not changed into a nightgown. Holding her candle aloft, she looked around her; seeing a tall candlestick on a table nearby, she lit it from her own, taking the larger stick with her and, after blowing out the flame, left her chamberstick in its place. She might need that later if there was much to explore and did not wish to waste it.

The tall stick gave her more light and she was able to see that there were three rows of wine racks. Most of them were stocked from top to bottom with bottles that had gathered dust, but there was a fourth right at the back of the cellar facing inwards, which was half-empty and looked as if it was the one in use. The cellar appeared to be smaller than she would have imagined and at first glance there seemed to be no possibility of a secret entrance—unless, of course, it was concealed behind the rack at the far end of the cellar? That seemed the most likely place to start. She was about to move towards it when she heard something—a sharp dragging sound similar to something she had heard once before.

Acting instinctively, she blew out her candle and drew back into the shadow of one of the tall wine racks. At first she could see nothing because it was very dark, but again she heard the dragging noise, followed by a heavy creaking, and her ears told her that it came from the far end of the cellar. She had been right to suspect that it must be the only possible way in.

The heavy wooden rack must have swung back somehow and, in doing so, one of the bottles fell out and smashed on the stone floor. Marianne heard a smothered oath, and recognised the voice instantly.

'Damn it! I hope that proud bitch didn't hear it and wake. If she comes down, it could ruin everything.' Mr Hambleton was carrying a candle and its light shed a yellow halo around where the two men stood, giving her a clear view of them.

'You said you would deal with her,' another voice accused. 'You should have lured her to the cliffs and thrown her over.

The goods will be safe enough hidden in the cavity behind the wine rack—but *he* needs a place to stay. He won't think much of being hidden in this hole!'

'Things have changed since last time. It will have to do until I can get him away. Besides, the alternative is a day spent in the caves. It would be too dangerous for him to travel immediately, in case they are keeping watch. He must come here and wait until it is dark. I can make sure that he has food and at least there is plenty of wine here.'

The other man laughed. 'That will please him, I dare say—but supposing they come in and find him?'

'Raoul has more sense,' Joshua said. 'Besides, I have a key in my pocket. If I leave it in the lock they would not be able to open the door from the other side without some trouble—enough time for him to hide himself anyway. He must take it or find himself somewhere else, I can do no more.' He scowled, clearly put out at the other's grumbling.

'He will not take kindly to such talk,' the other man said. 'You have taken his gold, as we all have, and he expects our loyalty. Do what you have to do and let us be gone. The less noise we make this night the better. If anyone were to raise the alarm now, it would ruin all our work.'

'Thank God it will soon be over,' Joshua said. 'It's our damned luck that the tides are against us tomorrow. They must come in on the high tide, for they cannot risk foundering on the rocks—and the tide will be right at six in the morning.'

'Light enough to be seen if there are any slip-ups,' the second man said. 'It's a damned risk, that's what I say, but it was his orders. Come on, let's get out of here.'

'I must place the key in the lock,' Joshua said and walked towards the steps. Marianne shrank further into the shadows, holding her breath as he passed her. If he discovered that she was there and had heard them talking… But he was returning and she could hear the two conspirators muttering together as they pulled the heavy wine rack closed behind them. 'Damn this thing—it wants greasing…'

The light had gone now and Marianne sighed with relief as she heard a clicking sound. The rack was back in place and no one would know that anyone had been here—apart from the smashed bottle, which could have been the work of careless servants.

She waited for a few minutes to be sure they had gone, and then reached into her pocket, lighting her candle from the tinder-box. Her heart was beating very fast and she felt a little sick as she walked back to the small table, lit the candle in her chamberstick and set the tall stick down, blowing out the flame.

She walked up the steep stone steps and unlocked the door, taking the key with her as she went into the scullery. Once there, she re-locked the door and pocketed the key. She now had both the keys to the cellar, which, she hoped, meant that no one could enter the house that way—and no one could walk in on their uninvited visitor by mistake and perhaps be killed.

Now what ought she to do? Marianne was thoughtful as she went upstairs, her mind going over what her next move should be. It was dark outside and she did not feel safe in walking to the cliff house, nor did she wish to wake the servants at this hour. Her anger with Drew had abated, and she knew it was her duty to inform him of what was happening. Her own hurt pride meant nothing when there was a French spy at liberty to come and go as he pleased.

The only solution she could think of was to go out at first light. She could call at the house on the cliffs and tell Robbie or Drew of what she had learned and then...after that it would be Drew's affair, not hers. She would hide the keys to the cellar in her room. Tomorrow, on her return, she would tell her aunt of her discovery and they could make sure that the workmen came in to close off the secret entrance in such a way that it could never again be opened from outside the house.

Going into her room, Marianne lay down fully clothed. She would rest, but she must not let herself fall asleep, because otherwise she would be too late to warn Drew.

She wished now that she had sent him a message earlier that day, but even though she might have told him that Joshua had left the house, she could not have told him all that she knew now.

It was damned cold crouching down amongst the rocks, waiting for the signal from the ship out in the bay. Drew was grateful for the warm coat that had seen him through his military days, blowing on his hands to warm them. He thought longingly of his bed at Marlbeck, and of a soft body lying beside him, a little smile curving his mouth as for a moment he indulged his dreams. He had them more often of late, and they were becoming more erotic, for she aroused his senses as no other woman ever had.

Damn them! If the ship that had been seen a few hours earlier further along the coast was the one he had been waiting for, they were taking their time getting a boat out. He was just wondering if he had been mistaken in her lines and it was a British vessel after all when the light flashed. He trained his spyglass in the direction it had come from, and found the ship as it sailed in closer, flashing the light twice more. It was answered almost instantly, and then he saw a boat set out from the ship. Something or someone was being brought in and he hoped it might be the man he was after. He did not care if the smugglers made a run for it or if their cargo was not taken, it was the Frenchie he was after—and Hambleton!

Something made him turn his head back towards the cliff tops and the house where he had been staying. It was just beginning to get light, and he could make out the figure of someone approaching the house…a woman wearing a dress of some pale colour with a dark cloak thrown over. The wind had blown her cloak back away from her body, pulling the soft material of her gown tight across her slender form, and it was the flash of a pale colour that had caught his eye.

He knew instinctively that it must be Marianne. What was she doing here at this hour? Surely she was not foolish enough to venture this way at such a time? She must know that it could be dangerous.

Drew cursed softly. He dared not move, because everything hung on surprise. If the smugglers took fright too soon, neither the contraband nor the French spy would be landed and all their work would be for nothing. Marianne's arrival at this moment was a deuced nuisance! It could ruin everything, but perhaps she would simply give up and go home when she realised that the house was empty…

He turned his gaze back towards the ship. He could do nothing to warn Marianne for the moment, because he needed to wait for the boat to land on the narrow strip of sand that was all that was visible at high tide.

Marianne had put her cloak on that morning, because it was cold, but the wind whipped it back from her body as she

paused at the top of the cliffs, pinning her dress against her
She was on her way to the house, but she had seen a ship in
the bay and a boat putting out from it. She hesitated for a
moment, but there was nothing she could do. She must warn
Drew at once!

She ran the rest of the way to the house and banged on the
door. There were no lights inside, and no one came to answer
her summons. She knew it was early and renewed her knocking,
banging as loud as she could, but still nothing stirred within the
house. Where had Drew gone? She felt a surge of frustration
and turned away. Her eyes strayed out to the bay once more and
she saw that a rowing boat was nearing the shore.

What could she do? She was a woman alone and she had no
weapon. Even if she could climb down to the cove there was no
way that she could prevent what was happening. A man had got
out of the boat and was wading ashore, others were unloading
some barrels and another boat was already on its way inshore.

'What are you doing here, *mademoiselle?*'

Marianne started and looked round. The man had come
upon her as she watched the activity on the shore below.
Where had he come from—and how had he seen her?

'Who are you?' she demanded, the words springing from
her lips without thought. 'Did you come in on the ship?' He
eyes narrowed, for suddenly she realised that this had all
been cleverly staged. He had spoken in English, but from his
accent he was French. The smugglers were landing their
cargo below, but this man—the man that Drew had been
waiting for—had been landed at some other place along the
coast and made his way here overland. 'Who have you come
to meet—is it Lieutenant Humble?'

'What do you know of him?' The Frenchman's gaze

narrowed suddenly in suspicion. When he first saw her, Raoul had thought her merely an innocent passer-by who had stumbled on what was happening in the bay by accident, but now he realised that she knew more than she should—and as such she was a danger to him. 'Did he send you here? Have you come in his place?'

Marianne shook her head—she realised too late that her careless words had led her into danger. She started to back away from him, but even as she did so, she heard a shout below her and saw men beginning to pour over the rocks that separated the village beach from the cove. Instantly, she knew that they were Revenue officers and she shouted, trying to attract their attention.

'Up here! The man you want is up here…'

The Frenchman swore and made a lunge at her. Marianne screamed and started to run back, away from the cliffs and the frantic scene below. She could hear gunfire and knew that a fight was going on, but she had no weapon or anyone to help her. She had seen this man's face and she understood that she was a danger to him. He would kill her if he could. Her only hope was to run as fast as she could…but he was gaining on her. Fright spurred her on, making her run faster. And then she caught her foot on an uneven patch of ground, stubbing her toe against a hidden piece of rock and twisting her ankle as she fell. She felt the sting of grazed flesh, but ignored it. She was up on her feet almost at once, but she could not run. Her ankle was too painful and she turned to face her attacker, her face proud.

'If you murder me, they will hang you,' she said. 'Go quickly before they come.'

'This is all his fault!' The man swore, in French this time, and moved purposefully towards her. 'Understand that I bear you no ill will, *mademoiselle*. If he had been waiting where he promised, none of this need have happened. He said that the old house was unsafe, for someone was living there, but he did not meet me as we had arranged and so I came here.'

'You came to the house you had used before…' Marianne understood what had happened. They must have used the cliff house to hide him sometimes, but Lady Edgeworthy's agent had let it, and Joshua had arranged to meet him somewhere else, to guide him through the tunnel—but something had gone wrong. Either they had missed each other in the dark, or Joshua had changed his mind.

'What do you know of him? Was this a trap he had set for me? Tell me and I may spare you.'

Marianne caught her breath. She had seen something behind him, something that gave her hope. 'You speak of the traitor—the man who calls himself Joshua Hambleton. You should not have placed your trust in such a man, *monsieur*. Go now, I beg you for your own sake…'

At that moment Drew sprang. He had heard her shout to warn the soldiers, and knew why she had called out. Scrambling up the cliffs as swiftly as he could manage it, he had been in time to see her fall, and he heard her speak out, saw how bravely she had faced her adversary. Now he rushed on the Frenchman, taking him down to the ground with him.

Raoul cursed—he had not been aware of the danger from behind. He fought back almost at once and for what seemed an eternity to Marianne, the struggle went on as the two men rolled over and over on the hard ground. She could not move even had she wanted, for she was frozen to the spot, her heart racing with fear. She gasped as she saw the Frenchman bring out a knife, trying to plunge it into Drew's chest, but Drew had a hand about his wrist and they tussled for possession, and then the knife went flying.

Marianne moved then, despite the pain; she seized on it, throwing it as far as she could. Yet still the fight went on and she was not sure which way it would go until Drew was suddenly sitting astride the Frenchman, banging his head on the ground until he stopped fighting and went limp.

Suddenly, another man was there, followed by yet another. Marianne caught a breath of sobbing relief as she recognised Robbie, but not the third man, whom she took to be one of the Revenue officers, for he was in uniform.

The Frenchman had stopped struggling. He was probably close to losing his senses for Drew had pounded him unmercifully, but she could see that he was still alive when they pulled him to his feet. He was swaying, his senses obviously disordered as more men came up to them, and his hands were bundled behind his back and tied with ropes. The soldiers took him away, one of their officers coming to inquire if Drew was all right. Marianne stood alone for a moment, and then Robbie came up to her.

'Are you all right, miss?' he asked, looking at her white face with concern. 'We spotted you just before he turned up, but we dared not move for fear they should put back to the ship.'

'But he was landed earlier and made his way over the cliffs,' Marianne told him. 'He was supposed to have met with Lieutenant Humble, but something went wrong. I think he must have stayed at the house sometimes in the past. When his contact was not there, he decided to find his own way here.' She took a step forward and stumbled, crying out with pain. Robbie caught her, supporting her, and then Drew was by her side. He took one look at her white face and swept her into his arms.

'I'll take her home, Rogers,' he said, glancing at the Revenue officer over her head. 'When you've cleared up here, go back to the house. I'll join you there, for we have some talking to do. We've got one of them, but it seems the other has slipped through our fingers.'

'Put me down,' Marianne said as he strode away from the others. 'If Robbie helped me, I am sure I could manage to get home.'

'Please do not be ridiculous,' Drew said sharply. 'What on earth brought you to the cliffs at this hour I have no idea, but I am certainly not letting you go home alone while that wretch Hambleton is still around! After what happened this night, he would as soon shoot you as look at you.'

'I came to warn you that the drop was early this morning,' Marianne said. 'I found the entrance to the cellars last night…they came to check on it and I heard them talking.'

Drew stopped and set her on her feet, looking at her in a stern manner. 'Then why did you not send me word? Why come here when you knew it would be dangerous?'

'I did not wish to rouse the servants last night. Besides, I thought it would be safe…that they would be on the beach…' She faltered and then her eyes flashed with sudden temper. 'You were waiting for them! You knew it was to be this morning. Why did you not tell me?'

'Because it was too dangerous,' Drew said. 'I have an insider working for me and have known what was going on since yesterday, but Hambleton was there at the house, and if I had told you, you might have let something slip…'

'How dare you?' Marianne said. Her fingers itched to slap him, but she kept her hands at her sides. 'I am not a fool though you may think it. Besides, had I not been there, you might have lost the spy. I was watching the ship and he came up to me in the dark. At first he may have thought I was Hambleton's go-between, because I was near the house. I think you ruined all their plans when you leased it from my aunt. If Hambleton wishes to kill anyone, it must be you…'

'All that is besides the point,' Drew snapped, because he had suddenly realised how close she had come to death, and the risks she had been taking. 'How do you think I would have felt if he had killed you? What of your aunt's feelings—your mother and sisters? Have you no thought for them? You are a headstrong, wilful girl and I have no patience with you.'

'Then go away and leave me alone,' Marianne said, close to tears. 'If you had not lied to me, I dare say I should never have—' She broke off, then said, 'You say that I am headstrong and wilful—but you are reckless and irresponsible. A man in your position should not be hiding on a windswept cliff waiting for French spies to land. You have people who rely on you for their living…' She choked back a sob. 'Leave me to make my own way home, my lord. I do not need your help.'

'Whether you need it or not, I intend to carry you home,' Drew said, and caught her up into his arms again. His expression was grim as he strode through the night and Marianne was too distressed to renew the argument.

She closed her eyes and tried not to think of the throbbing pain in her ankle, refusing to let the tears fall. It would shame her to cry, but she felt wretched and she wished that she wa anywhere but in his arms.

Drew did not speak again until he set her down outside her aunt's house. His expression had not lightened, his mouth wa set in a hard line.

'I need not tell you to continue to be careful. I believe tha Lieutenant Humble will be far away by now, for he mus know that his plans have gone wrong. However, you must sti be wary—he may want revenge.'

'Thank you for bringing me back,' Marianne said in a lov voice. Her ankle was hurting so much that she knew she could never have managed it alone. 'And for your warning

'You can manage on your own now? I have work I mu do,' he said harshly. 'Unfortunately, this business is no finished as I had hoped it would be by now.'

'Yes, of course I can manage.' Marianne turned from hir and limped towards the house, keeping her back straight. Fo pride's sake she would not let him see what even those few ster cost her. She knocked at the door and a moment later, Bess opened it to her. 'I have hurt my ankle…could you help me'

'Yes, of course, miss,' Bessie said. 'Wherever have yc been at this hour, Miss Marianne?'

Marianne glanced back. She saw that Drew had waited see her in, but now he was striding away. She had brought hir out of his way and he clearly still had much to do. They ha caught the smugglers in the act as he had hoped, and they ha the French spy—but the man who had betrayed them to th French had got away. He must be angry about that, for it wa the capture of the traitor that had brought him here in the fir place.

Marianne caught back her tears as she hobbled inside th

ouse. She thought that Drew blamed her for what had appened, and he was as angry with her as she had been with im when she discovered his true identity.

He would probably stay well clear of her now. The thought nade her want to weep, but she told herself she was being oolish. It could not matter that Drew was angry with her, ecause he had only wanted to seduce her in the first place. le was the Marquis of Marlbeck, and a man of his importance would never marry a girl of no fortune, even if she were f gentle birth.

'Shall we send for the doctor, miss?'

Marianne became aware of Bessie's anxious look as she elped her to a sofa. Her ankle was very painful, and, despite ating to make a fuss, Marianne realised that it needed attenon.

'Yes, I think perhaps I must trouble him,' she said. 'I tumbled on the cliffs and I am afraid I have twisted my nkle. I do not think it is broken, but I cannot be certain.'

'Best to be on the safe side,' Bessie said. 'I'll send a groom or him straight away. You just bide here, miss, and I'll bring ou a cup of tea in a moment. Unless you would like some-ning stronger?'

'No, I do not think so, thank you,' Marianne said. 'Tea will e very nice.'

She watched as the maid hurried away to send word to er aunt's groom. Her ankle was truly painful, but it was not at which caused the tears to trickle silently down her heeks.

Her display of temper would have given Drew a disgust f her...and she must cease to think of him by that name. If ey met in future, she must remember to call him by his

proper name. He was Marlbeck and now that the smuggling
ring had been broken he would leave here…and she would
never see him again.

'You must stay in bed for a few days, as the doctor bid you,'
Lady Edgeworthy told Marianne when she visited her in her
bedchamber later that day. 'You were lucky it was not much
worse, which it might have been. The cliffs are dangerous,
especially at that time of the morning. If you had seen where
you were going, you would not have tripped and fallen.'

Marianne had not told her that she was running from a
French spy who wished to kill her, because she did not wish
to distress her great-aunt further. Aunt Bertha was already
upset enough as it was.

'It was very foolish of me,' she said meekly. 'I shall not
do it again, Aunt. I promise.'

'I think I ought to write and ask your mama and sisters to
come here at once,' Lady Edgeworthy said. 'You have had a
nasty shock and if anything should happen…'

'I assure you that I am quite well,' Marianne told her. 'It
is just that my ankle hurts a little.'

'I think it hurts more than a little,' Lady Edgeworthy said.
'Jane told me that Dr Thompson said it was a nasty sprain. I
cannot imagine what made you go out so early, my dear!'

'I was awake early and I thought I should like to walk.'
Marianne gave her an apologetic smile. 'Please do not be
cross with me. I promise I shall never do anything so foolish
again.'

'Well, your mama may as well come here, you know. We
can all go on to Bath after Jane's wedding, and it will be nice
to have young people here again. Now, stay there and rest

and Jane will run any errands you need. I shall send her up to you in a little while.'

'Thank you, but I am quite content with my book for the moment.'

Marianne sighed as her aunt left her. She knew that Lady Edgeworthy was frightened because the accident had happened on the cliffs. Having lost Cedric in an accident there, she would naturally fear the worst, even though Marianne had not been near the cliff edge when she fell.

A little shudder went through her as she realised that she might well have died. It was dangerous to go too near the cliffs before it was light, even if there had been no smugglers. She ought to have roused Jensen the previous night and told him what had happened. Indeed, she must speak to him and tell him about the cellars, because she had both the keys and he might be looking for the one that usually hung beside the door.

However, she could not get out of bed, because she knew she must rest her ankle. It had begun to swell by the time the doctor arrived to look at it, and though he had bathed it with cold water and applied a bandage, it was extremely painful. She could ring for a maid, of course, and ask Mr Jensen to come, but that might set everyone wondering what had happened. She decided that when Jane came in to see her, she would ask for her writing slope and pen a note for Mr Jensen. In the meantime, she was very tired. Perhaps it was the medicine that the doctor had left her.

Closing her eyes, she drifted into a restful sleep.

When Jane looked in on her later, she smiled and tiptoed away again, going down to the parlour where Lady Edgeworthy was entertaining her visitor.

'She is sleeping,' Jane said. 'I think Dr Thompson gave her a draught to help her relax and it has worked very well.'

'Then I shall not disturb her,' Drew said. 'You will tell her that I called, if you please. I have to travel to London almost immediately, and after that I must visit my home. I shall hope to be down again in a few days—a week at the most.'

'Thank you for explaining everything to us,' Lady Edgeworthy said. 'Marianne did tell me that she thought there might be some smuggling going on—but I could not think it was so. It seems that we have been harbouring a traitor in our midst, Lord Marlbeck. I wish that I had known, for I should have liked to tell him what I think of such wickedness.'

'It is perhaps as well that you did not—he is a dangerous man,' Drew said. 'My hope is that he is far away from here, Lady Edgeworthy—but if you should see him again, you must send word immediately to Major Barr. He will know what to do.'

'I am most disturbed to know that my dearest Marianne was in danger last night. She never said a word of it to me, you know—nor has she mentioned the cellars.'

'I dare say she means to do so, however,' Drew said. 'I shall speak to your butler before I leave. He will know what must be done—but you will need to ask Marianne where the entrance is, for she has not told me.'

'I shall certainly do so when she is better,' Lady Edgeworthy told him. 'I am sorry that you are leaving, sir. I do hope that you will come back and visit us again—as yourself next time.'

'Thank you, you are most kind,' Drew said. He got up a little reluctantly, for he had hoped to see Marianne before he left. 'You will not forget to tell her that I called?'

'Of course not,' Lady Edgeworthy said. 'I have sent word for her mama, you know. It is my hope that the whole family will come down. We shall all attend Jane's wedding, and then we may go to Bath for a little visit.'

'That will make a pleasant change for you—but I hope you do not mean to give up your estate?'

'I am not sure that the income is what it should be,' Lady Edgeworthy said on a sigh. 'When the mine ran out it meant that we relied on the land, but that is not as fertile as it might be—the land is too stony.'

'Did you not know that there is a rich seam of copper in your mine?' Drew asked. 'I saw it when I went down looking for contraband. I know that the tin ore ran out, but I believe it would be worth opening up again for the copper. You would need advice on how best to go about it, but I am sure that it might be arranged without too much trouble.'

'Copper? Are you sure?' Lady Edgeworthy was surprised. 'It might make all the difference and it would bring more work to the men of the area. I shall have to consider this carefully.'

'Yes, of course,' Drew told her. 'I must leave you now, but we may talk about this another time.'

'Please see the marquis to the door,' Lady Edgeworthy said and Jane got up to oblige her.

'I hope to be back in time for your wedding,' Drew said to Jane as they reached the front door. 'You will not forget to tell Marianne that I called?'

'We shall tell her,' Jane promised. 'I might have woken her, but she looked so peaceful.'

'Oh, no, what I have to say to her can wait for a while.

Excuse me, I must go. This business is not yet settled and
there are people I must talk to.'

'Goodbye,' Jane said, smiled and went back into the house.

'Are you feeling better?' Jane asked as she took a tray of
tea and sweet cakes up to Marianne's bedroom a little later.
'You were sound asleep when I looked in earlier.'

'I think I was very tired for I did not sleep much last night,'
Marianne said and yawned. 'My ankle is throbbing, but I
expect it will for a day or two.'

'Yes, I dare say,' Jane said and laughed softly. 'If you will
go chasing French spies in the dead of night, Marianne!'

'What do you know of that?'

'Lord Marlbeck called earlier today on his way to
London,' Jane said. 'He asked to see you, but you were asleep
and he did not wish to disturb you. He told us all about the
smugglers landing their contraband on the beach. And that
by crying out a warning from the top of the cliffs, you had
helped them to catch the French spy.'

'Oh…' Marianne wrinkled her brow. 'In that case, you
may take these keys down to Mr Jensen and tell him that I
kept them with me so that no one could walk in on the smugglers and perhaps be harmed by them. They will discover that
the wine rack at the far end of the cellar can be moved forward
by means of a lever somewhere. It can be opened from the
other side, but I am not sure about this side—however, it
needs to be made safe so that no one can use it again.'

Jane looked at the keys. 'You must be very brave to have
gone down there and discovered it—and to have gone out to
the cliffs to warn Lord Marlbeck when you knew what was
happening. I do not think I should have cared for it.'

'I did not think about the danger to myself,' Marianne said honestly. 'I knew that it was important to Drew…Lord Marlbeck…to catch the traitor, but I think he got away. He did not keep his appointment with the French spy. He was meant to bring him here to this house and hide him in the cellars—but something went wrong and he was not there to meet him. When the Frenchman approached me he thought I might have been sent to guide him to the safe house, but when I saw the Revenue men pouring into the cove I shouted to them and…he attacked me. I do not know if he meant to silence me or to kill me, but I was frightened and I ran away. I caught my foot and fell, and because my ankle hurt I could not go on—and then Drew came and they fought. The Frenchman was taken away, but there was no sign of Joshua.'

'I think that is the most shocking thing of all,' Jane said. 'To think that we harboured a man like that in this house! We might have all been murdered in our beds.' She shuddered. 'I shall not sleep soundly until they have caught him.'

'Surely he will not dare to come here again? He must know that everything has gone wrong. The smugglers have been caught, and most of them are either dead or in prison.' Marianne felt a little sick. 'How awful that is, for I dare say that some of them were local fishermen trying to supplement their living. It was Mr Hambleton who brought in the French spy.'

'Yes, it seems that way,' Jane agreed. 'I sympathise with the wives and children they have left behind, but smuggling is wrong, Marianne. Simon does not approve, though he understands why men who cannot feed their children will do desperate things.'

'I do not think Drew would have come here for the smuggling,' Marianne said. 'But he wanted to catch the man who caused the deaths of his comrades—and now he has got away.'

'That cannot be your fault,' Jane said. 'Whatever the reason, it cannot change what happened. The French spy was caught—and much of that was because of your bravery in shouting to warn them.'

'Oh, no,' Marianne said. 'He was so angry with me for being there.'

'I dare say he was just anxious because he was afraid for you,' Jane said. 'But he came to inquire after you and told us everything—so there is nothing to worry for. Everyone thinks you were very brave, if a little…'

'Foolish?' Marianne supplied as she hesitated.

'Impetuous,' Jane said and smiled. 'I would never have had the courage to do as you did, Marianne.'

'Oh, let us talk of something else,' Marianne said, feeling as if she would scream if she heard one more word about those wretched smugglers. 'Have you everything you need for your wedding? We still have time to sew some pretty trifles if you need them…a night-chemise or something of the sort?'

'Oh, I have several pretty ones put away,' Jane told her. 'My life has been…quiet for some years and I have used my free time to make things I might need one day.' Her cheeks turned pink and she looked shy. 'I always dreamed that I might marry one day, though I did not truly believe it would happen.'

Marianne sat forward to take her hand. 'I am so very pleased for you,' she said. 'But I still think that when my ankle is better we might ask my aunt for the carriage and go into

Truro for a day. I am sure we could find something pretty for you there.'

'You are so kind,' Jane said. 'I shall pray that you will be as happy as I am one day, for I am sure that you will marry someone very nice quite soon.'

'Oh, no, I do not think it,' Marianne said, smothering a sigh. 'Perhaps one day, but not just yet.'

Drew had gone away without speaking to her, and she knew that he must be very angry with her. She had been angry with him for a time, but now she was regretting her show of temper. She was going to miss seeing him on her walks.

Chapter Nine

Marianne was sitting downstairs in the parlour two days later when Bessie came to her carrying a letter. She smiled as she handed it to her and asked if there were any little tasks she might perform for her.

'Oh, no, thank you,' Marianne said. 'I have a drink, my book and my needlework here beside me. And my ankle is so much better. If I need anything I am sure I can manage for myself.'

'The doctor said you were to rest, miss, and we are all happy to serve you.' Bessie's eyes shone with admiration. 'Everyone is saying that the French spy would have got away if it were not for you, miss.'

'I assure you that is nonsense,' Marianne said. 'He attacked me and I ran from him. If Lord Marlbeck had not been there, he might have killed me.'

'But you shouted and warned them, miss. I think that was very brave of you—and so does everyone here.'

Marianne shook her head and Bessie went away, leaving her to her letter. What she read there distressed her. The letter had come from her mother. It said that they had moved into the Lodge, which was very small and uncomfortable, and that the roof had leaked on to Lucy's bed without anyone knowing it and she had lain in it all night and for a few days she had been ill.

I cannot ask you to come home, for I know that your aunt needs you, Mrs Horne had written. *But it is very difficult. Jo is increasingly resentful of her Aunt Wainwright and says she shall not leave me, and Lucy is tearful. She cried for you when she was in her fever. Thankfully, she is on the mend and I believe she may soon recover, for she is young and strong. However, I am wondering if Aunt Bertha would allow her to come for a visit with you to lift her spirits. Forgive me for worrying you, my dearest, but it has been such an upsetting time. Your loving mother.*

Marianne stared at the letter for a moment. Her mother must have written this before she received Lady Edgeworthy's invitation to come and stay. She frowned over it, not certain whether to reply immediately or wait and see what happened.

'Ah, there you are, dearest.' Lady Edgeworthy came into the room at that moment. 'Bessie told me that you had a letter—is it from your mama?'

'Yes…please read it for yourself,' Marianne said and handed it to her. 'Poor Mama is so upset. I think it must have been a great wrench for her leaving the home to which she was taken as a bride, and Lucy seems to have taken it hard.'

'Yes, indeed.' Lady Edgeworthy read the letter and frowned. 'Poor little Lucy. Surely someone should have realised that the bed was damp?'

'Mama has only the one maid and Lily cannot be every-where. What with the move and all the upheaval that must have caused, I dare say she did not realise.'

'I did not realise that Cynthia's circumstances were so difficult. Why did she not tell me? Why didn't you tell me, Marianne?'

'Mama would never ask for anything,' Marianne told her. 'She should have told Uncle Wainwright that the Lodge would not be suitable, but of course she was grateful for a home.'

'Then it is just as well that I have invited her to make her home with me in future, is it not?'

'You will not tell her that you know? Mama would hate to accept charity.' Marianne looked at her doubtfully.

'Charity? What nonsense!' Lady Edgeworthy said robustly. 'I have been lonely and miserable. Having you here has made me realise what is missing from my life, Marianne. Cynthia is my family, and her children are also my family. You will all be doing me the greatest favour by living here and keeping me company for my declining years.'

'Oh, Aunt,' Marianne said, the shine of tears in her eyes. 'I shall write to Mama and urge her to come to us as soon as she can manage it—and I shall send her the money for her fare, for I have more than sufficient for my own needs.'

'I have already sent sufficient money for her journey,' Lady Edgeworthy said, 'for I very much wish to have your mother and sisters here, Marianne. Had you not arrived when you did, I think that rogue would have finished me. He would have hounded me to my grave.'

'I wonder if they have found him?' Marianne said and frowned. 'I do not think he would dare to come here again, nor will he go to your house in London, for it is the first place they would look.'

'We are well rid of him,' her great-aunt said. 'I cannot imagine why I ever thought he was charming.'

'I believe rogues are often charming,' Marianne said. 'That is why they are so dangerous.'

'Yes, I dare say you are right.' Lady Edgeworthy looked round as the door of the parlour opened and Bessie came in. 'You have a letter for me?'

'No, ma'am, a visitor—Major Barr has called to see you.'

'Oh, that is kind,' Lady Edgeworthy said. 'Pray ask him to come in, Bessie.' She looked at Marianne. 'He has called to discuss the mine. Lord Marlbeck told me that there may be a seam of rich copper in the old mine and I asked Major Barr if he would look into it for me.'

Major Barr came in at that moment. He inquired after Marianne's health and then settled down to talk to Lady Edgeworthy about the mine. Lord Marlbeck had seen copper, but it would need an expert to decide whether or not it was rich enough to warrant reopening the mine.

Marianne's thoughts drifted away. She was trying to be sensible and not think of Drew, but it was proving difficult to shut him out of her thoughts. If only he had stayed to say goodbye to her it would not have seemed so bad, but his departure without a word had left her feeling low in spirits. Yet she ought not to be, for her mother and at least one of her sisters would soon join her and in another few days they would celebrate Jane's wedding.

Marianne woke suddenly. The moon was shining in at her window, because she had not quite closed her curtains, and that must be the reason for her dream, which had been very muddled. She had been thinking about Mama and Lucy before she went to bed, and in her dream, her sister had called to her in a fever, but she could not reach her because there was a thick mist and a river to cross. She had called out for Drew to help her, but he had not answered her cry, though she could see his face through the mist.

Such a foolish dream! Marianne felt better as it faded. She knew that her dream had troubled her because of Mama's letter, and of course she missed Drew. She had grown accustomed to seeing him, and it would take time to forget the wonderful feeling of joy that his smile had given her.

But perhaps he would come back… Her thoughts were distracted as she caught sight of something moving in the garden. Was it merely a trick of the moonlight or had she seen a man's shadow near the far end of the garden? She shivered, closing the curtains and running back to bed. Thank goodness they had blocked the entrance into the cellars, though she was almost sure that Joshua would not dare to come here, because they would surely still be searching for him.

Her feeling of alarm eased as she recalled something that Drew had once told her. He had warned her that she might turn and see a shadow following her—someone that he had sent for her protection.

Yes, now that she thought about it, she realised that it had probably been someone sent to watch the house just in case Joshua Hambleton returned to the area. And if Drew had cared enough to make sure that she and her aunt were safe, perhaps he would return himself one day. The thought comforted her and she snuggled down in the warmth of her feather mattress to sleep again.

A letter arrived the next morning to say that Mrs Horne and Lucy would be with them by the middle of the next week. Jo was to stay with Aunt Wainwright until they went down to Bath.

She is reconciled to the idea now that we are all to visit Bath for a few weeks. She had been missing your good sense, Marianne, but I believe she will do well enough now.

Marianne's ankle had returned to normal by this time and she was able to walk about the house and garden quite freely. She spent the days between the receipt of her letter and her mama's arrival by helping to prepare their rooms. Bessie cleaned and polished them, airing the beds thoroughly, because, as she said, she did not want poor Miss Lucy to be ill again, then Marianne helped Bessie with the linen and arranged the various cushions and trinkets that had been added to Lucy's room to make it more comfortable.

The morning that her family were expected, she brought in flowers for her sister and mother's rooms. She had expected them to arrive in the morning—their letter had said they would stay overnight in Truro and come on the next day. However, it was almost three o'clock when they finally arrived in Uncle Wainwright's carriage.

Marianne flew out of the house to hug her sister, who burst into tears and said that she never wished to be parted from her again, for it had all been too horrible and she had thought she would die and never see her again.

'Lucy, my dearest,' Marianne hushed her. She drew back to look at her and was a little shocked to see how very pale she was, all her lovely colour quite gone. 'Was it so very bad at the Lodge?'

'It was horrid,' Lucy said. 'My room is so small and there is nowhere to put all my things. They had to take most of our things up to the attics and…it isn't like home at all.'

'Well, you have a lovely big room here,' Marianne said.

'If Mama agrees, you may all make your home here, and you need not go back to the Lodge ever again.'

'Marianne, my dear child,' Mrs Horne said and embraced her eldest daughter. 'I am very glad to be here. I am not sure that we may trespass on my aunt's good nature for ever, but it will be pleasant to stay for a few weeks—and a visit to Bath is something I have often thought I should enjoy.'

'Come in and get warm by the fire,' Marianne urged, for she still had hold of her sister's hand, which felt cold. The breeze was bitter at that moment and she hurried Lucy inside, not wanting her to take another chill.

For the next few minutes there was a flurry of greetings, as Lucy and Mama kissed Lady Edgeworthy and made themselves comfortable. Jane was introduced and refreshments were brought in. When everyone was settled and warm again, Marianne took her sister upstairs, leaving Mama and Lady Edgeworthy to talk by themselves for a little. Jane had gone to the kitchens to talk to Cook about something, and the two sisters were alone.

Lucy stood in the room Marianne and Bessie had so carefully prepared for her, her eyes moving slowly round it. It was furnished in shades of pink and cream, the furniture the prettiest that could be found amongst all the pieces that were used for the guest-rooms, and moved there to please her. Marianne had discovered some books of fairy stories and fables in the library and placed them on a delicate table, which stood in the window. A chair with a comfortable padded seat and wide back had been placed beside it so that she might sit and read or look out at the garden.

'Do you think you can be happy here, dearest?'

'Oh, yes,' Lucy said. 'I packed most of my favourite things

in my trunk and when they are unpacked it will be almost like home—and we may send for the rest of our things if Mama decides that we may stay here. I do hope she does—I do not want to go back to the Lodge.'

'I am sure she will once she understands how important it is for Aunt Bertha. I have not yet told Mama what had been going on here, but our aunt has been the victim of a cruel rogue, and she needs her family about her.'

Lucy looked at her with wide eyes. 'Poor Aunt Bertha! Do tell me everything,' she begged.

'Sit in your chair and I shall sit on the dressing stool,' Marianne said. 'It is a long story, which I am sure Aunt Bertha is now relating to Mama.'

She made light of her own part in the story, particularly the moment when she had feared for her life, because she did not want to distress her sister. Lucy was fascinated by the tale of smugglers' caves, secret tunnels and French spies, though she looked upset when she heard that an attempt had been made on Lady Edgeworthy's life.

'The wicked rogue!' she cried. 'I am glad that you discovered what he was up to, Marianne, and that the tunnel has been blocked up so that no one can get into the house that way.'

'I can assure you that it will never be used again,' Marianne said with a smile. 'So everything is all right and we may be happy together.'

'But what of Lord Marlbeck?' Lucy asked. 'You said that he wanted to catch Mr Hambleton because he was a traitor—have you heard from him since then? Do you know if that horrid man has been caught and punished?'

'No, there has been no word,' Marianne said, trying for

lightness. 'Jane told me that Lord Marlbeck hoped to come down again for her wedding, but he has not sent word. I dare say he has been busy. As the owner of Marlbeck—and various other estates—he will have too many responsibilities to think of us.'

'Oh…' Lucy stared at her. Marianne had written of someone called Mr Beck in her letters, and both she and Jo had thought that their sister rather liked him. 'You did not know that Mr Beck was the marquis until recently?'

'No. I suppose he wished to keep his identity a secret,' Marianne said, avoiding her sister's curious gaze. 'Anyway, we need not speak of him, for I dare say we shall not see him again or at least only for a brief visit. I think we should both change for dinner, dearest. After all, we have plenty of time to talk now.'

'Yes, it is so lovely of Aunt Bertha to let us come and stay,' Lucy said, her thoughts diverted. 'And it will be exciting to visit Bath. I am too young to be out, I know, but Mama says there will be lots of things for me to do there.'

'Yes, I think there must be,' Marianne said and smiled lovingly at her sister. 'I shall leave you now, because I want to talk to Mama before we go down for dinner, and I dare say she will have come up by now.'

Leaving Lucy to explore her room and discover all the treasures that had been brought there for her use, Marianne walked to her own bedchamber. Lucy's pleasure in such simple things had warmed her. She knew that she was very fortunate to have her family, and told herself that she would now put all thought of Lord Marlbeck from her mind. It was clear to her that he had forgotten her, for if he had wanted he might have written to her before this—or come down to see her.

* * *

Drew frowned as he looked across the table at Captain Harcourt. They were sharing a bottle of wine in the library at Marlbeck, for he had been forced to return to his estate on a matter of urgent business and Jack had posted down to join him.

'He has been questioned, but he won't break,' Jack said and fingered the spiralled glass stem before lifting the goblet to drink the deep red burgundy. 'We know his name is Raoul Viera and that he is working for Bonaparte, but more than that…' He shrugged. 'He claims that he is here on legitimate business and had no part in what took place on the beach that night.'

'He has not named Humble as his accomplice?'

'He says that he knows no one of that name,' Jack replied. 'We know what his business is, for certain documents have gone missing from Headquarters. We believe that these would have been passed on to Humble for money, and he would have sold them to Raoul. The culprit is being watched, because we hope that he may still attempt to pass the documents on. Humble will know that the smugglers were taken, but he may not know that we have the Frenchie. And it is possible that we may strike a deal with Raoul Viera.'

'What kind of a deal?'

'We want Humble,' Jack told him. 'He was responsible for the deaths of several men—and he has been selling secrets for some months now. We lost sight of him for a while, but then we realised that he had changed his name to Hambleton. As regards the Frenchie, he has some powerful friends this side of the Channel, and unless we have more evidence we might be forced to release him.'

'Then I wish I had finished him when I had the chance!' Drew cried angrily. 'He might have killed Marianne if I had not realised she was there and heard her cry out.'

'Do I know the lady in question?'

'I doubt it,' Drew said. 'What was all this for if you have decided to let the spy go?'

'It is the way things work in the diplomatic channels,' Jack said and smiled wryly. 'I dare say the life would not suit you, my friend. Sometimes it is better to have half a cake than nothing at all…'

'How do you know you can trust this Frenchie?'

'We don't, of course,' Jack said. 'We shall be very reluctant to let him go, make it appear that his friends have won the day. The papers have been changed, though the courier has no knowledge of that and will pass them on in good faith. He will be watched and followed, and arrested once he has done his work. If he makes contact with Humble, we shall keep him under surveillance until he passes the papers on to the Frenchie—and then we shall arrest him. We shall allow Raoul to return to France with the false information.'

'Did you have this in mind from the beginning?'

'It was always a possibility,' Jack said. 'We've known that information was getting out for several months, but it wasn't until a few weeks ago that I realised that our traitor might be a part of the chain.'

'And that is when you came to me. I am sorry I made a mess of it for you. I don't think I am cut out for this kind of work.'

'Perhaps not,' Jack said and laughed. 'You would prefer to shoot the lot of them and be done with it—lead the charge and mow them down come hell or high water!'

Drew smiled ruefully. 'It was different in those days, Jack. We were wild and heedless of life.'

'And now you have something to live for?' Jack grinned wickedly. 'Would that be Marianne?'

'Perhaps,' Drew said and sipped his wine thoughtfully. 'I cannot get her out of my head, Jack, though God knows I have tried, because I should not make her happy. Even so, she haunts me waking or sleeping. But seriously—do you think there is a chance that this clerk of yours will lead you to Humble?'

'Yes, I think there is a good chance. He may not realise that we know as much as we do—and he is probably desperate. He knows the smugglers were caught and he has lost his investment—it was a big cargo, Drew. If he can earn some French gold to tide him over…'

'I suppose it is worth a try,' Drew agreed, 'though I don't like the idea of letting that Frenchie loose.'

'He will be watched until he sets sail for France,' Jack said. 'He is but one of many, Drew. We have to deal with them as best we can. In this business there is no black and white, but only a murky grey. If we hung him, another would take his place. This way we might gain something from it.'

'Like the heads of some mythical creature?' Drew nodded. 'Cut one off and another grows. So is there anything I can do to help you?'

'Were you thinking of returning to Cornwall?'

'Yes, in a matter of days. My business is nearly finished here and I have a wedding to attend.'

'Not your own?' Drew shook his head. 'I trust you will invite me when that happens?'

'Naturally. What is it that you wish me to do for you?'

'Just keep your eyes open,' Jack said. 'If Humble is desperate, he may return to his lair like a wounded beast. If he should turn up, let me know and I'll see to it.'

'You are warning me not to break his neck, I imagine,' Drew said, a trace of grim humour about his mouth, because his own inclination would have been to shoot first and ask questions afterwards. 'I can only promise that I will restrain myself if it is possible…but he could be dangerous to people I care about.' If it were a question of Marianne's life or the traitor's, Drew knew that there could be only one choice.

'I know how you feel,' Jack pressed hard, 'but I want him tried and punished according to the law. Besides, he may have information we need.'

Drew inclined his head. 'If he dares to return, I shall do what I can,' he said and got to his feet. 'I think we have kept my chef waiting long enough, Jack. Let us go into dinner before he breaks every dish in the house.'

'Temperamental, is he?' Jack laughed and rose, lifting his glass. 'To absent friends,' he said and threw the glass into the fireplace where it shattered into tiny fragments.

'Damnation to the enemy!' Drew said and threw his glass to shatter against stone, the shards of their glasses mingling in the fireplace.

Later that night, Drew retired to his bedchamber, sighing as he sat in an armchair and allowed Robbie to pull off his boots. Slightly shabby, they were old friends and he clung to them despite the dozen or so pairs of newer ones in his dressing room. Had he employed a valet instead of his faithful batman, they would not have been tolerated.

'We shall go down to Cornwall in the morning,' he said.

'I had planned to wait another day, but I am uneasy, Robbie. Our business there may be unfinished. I think this time I shall take the curricle, and my groom—also the rascal, for he may come in useful to run errands.' He spoke of the young lad who acted as his tiger when he drove himself.

'I should say there is more than one affair unfinished, Captain,' Robbie said. 'Or have you got cold feet?'

'Damn you!' Drew said and glared at him. 'What the hell do you mean by that?'

'You know right enough,' Robbie said and took the boots with him as he left, because he allowed no one else to clean them. 'You'll regret it if you lose her—and don't scowl like that, because you know I'm right.'

'Get out!' Drew barked and reached for the decanter of brandy beside the bed. He was frowning as the door closed behind his batman. The devil of it was that Robbie *was* right.

He had left Sawlebridge in a hurry, because he had needed to speak to Jack, who was then in London. He had been furious that all his efforts had ended in failure. Oh, it was true that they had taken the French spy, and that was due to Marianne's warning, for if she had not been on the cliffs he would have got away. But it looked as if the Frenchie would be allowed to leave the country carrying his false information, and no retribution taken for past sins. It might be the way that the diplomatic world worked, but it wasn't for Drew. He would have liked to see both Humble and the French spy hang together.

It wasn't going to happen. The knowledge brought a bitter taste to his mouth, because Marianne could so easily have died. He had been furious with her for being there, and she had given him as good back. No, better! A reluctant smile tugged at his mouth. Her demure looks were deceiving. There was fire in her, as he had known when he kissed her, and though normally the sweetest of girls, she had a temper when roused.

She had been angry because he hadn't told her the truth of his identity, and perhaps she had a right, though she must have understood his reasons. After their quarrel that night, she would be within her rights to hate him. Drew knew that he might be able to overcome that if he tried—but he had been having second thoughts. Marianne was beautiful, desirable, brave and spirited—and he wanted her with every fibre of his being, wanted to wake up beside her and know that she belonged to him. And yet he had hesitated, half-afraid to take that final step.

Was this feeling that kept him wakeful at night merely lust or did he truly love her? At times, he felt that he knew, but at others he was uncertain. Supposing he woke up one day and discovered that he was restless, that the urge to return to his wild ways had become too strong to resist. It would not be fair to marry her if he could not be the kind of husband she deserved.

He might have cut his business short and returned to her before now, but he had hesitated, because he was afraid of himself…afraid that he might hurt her.

What did he know of love? He had never been shown how to love, never experienced the warmth of family affection or the little things that came from having loving parents and siblings. His uncle had treated him with scrupulous fairness, but he had never been loved…except perhaps by the men he had led into battle, which was another thing.

A woman like Marianne deserved so much more. Would it be fair to take his own happiness and perhaps risk ruining her life?

* * *

'You look beautiful, Jane,' Marianne said. 'Doctor Thompson chose wisely when he bought this dress for you.'

'I do look quite nice,' Jane said modestly. She touched the strand of lapis lazuli beads at her neck, which had been given to her that morning by Lady Edgeworthy as a personal gift as well as the five hundred pounds. 'Everything is so pretty— especially the bonnet that you made for me, Marianne. You have spoiled me, because you have given me two hats.'

'I had finished the green one before I saw your dress,' Marianne told her with a smile. 'So I thought you should have two. One is from me—but the other was paid for by Lucy and Mama, so it is their gift to you, even though I fashioned it for you.'

'Well, you are all very kind,' Jane said and gathered up her posy of flowers, picked from the garden by Lucy that morning and tied with a blue ribbon. Mrs Horne had lent her a white leather prayer book to carry, and she had an old lace garter that had belonged to Lady Edgeworthy as a girl. 'I think I am ready to go down now, Marianne.'

Marianne nodded and kissed her, following Jane from the room. She stood back and allowed Jane to go down the stairs ahead of her so that everyone could admire her and shower her with good wishes and compliments. And then they were all trooping out to the carriages. Marianne was to go in the first with Jane and Major Barr, who had agreed to give Jane away in place of the father she had lost years before. Lady Edgeworthy, Mama and Lucy would follow in the second carriage.

It was just a short drive to the church, which stood at the edge of the estate. A small crowd of villagers had gathered outside the church to see her arrive, and when the wedding party entered, they followed behind and sat on the pews at the back. Amongst the general noise and chatter, one more guest slipped in unnoticed and took his seat in a pew near the back of the church.

Marianne was Jane's maid of honour, and Mr Pembroke stood up with Dr Thompson as his best man. The congregation rose for the first hymn and their voices filled the small church with song, for it was a popular wedding. Doctor Thompson was generally liked, even worshipped by some of the poor folk he attended, and the whole village had turned out to see him wed.

Marianne had moist eyes as she watched her friend take her vows, for Jane's happiness shone out of her like a beacon. She took the bride's posy when Jane and Dr Thompson went to sign the register, and then the bride and groom were back and the bells were ringing out as they all walked from the church.

Jane was showered by rose petals and ducked her head as she ran laughing towards the carriage waiting to take her back to the house. Lady Edgeworthy was giving a small reception for them, and it would be a merry party that gathered there that afternoon.

It was just as Marianne was about to get into her aunt's carriage that something made her turn her head. Her eyes were drawn to a man who was staring at her, and her heart began to race as he inclined his head to her.

Drew had come back for Jane's wedding just as he had promised! For a moment hope soared within her, but in another moment it vanished, for there had been time enough for him to speak to her as they waited for the happy pair to come out of church had he wished it. Besides, he had looked serious, the bold smile that always made her heart sing unaccountably missing.

Was he still angry with her? Her own anger had cooled. She understood that he might have had good reason for not telling her his real name, and yet it did not explain his behaviour since that night. If he cared for her at all, he would surely have written. Even if he were too busy to come down before, he could have sent her a note.

She ducked her head as she got into the carriage. She must hide her feelings of disappointment, because it was Jane's wedding day and she did not wish to spoil it for her friend.

All Jane's guests were known to her, other than two gentlemen who were friends of Dr Thompson. One was a man in his late years, who merely smiled at her and walked away to talk to Major Barr about something. However, the second gentleman was a man of perhaps thirty, tall and attractive, with soft dark eyes. He told her that he was also a doctor, but he worked in London and his patients were the poor of the slums of the city.

'Simon chose to come here,' he told Marianne. 'But I have found my vocation in London, for there is so much poverty and few to care for the weak and the helpless.'

'You must be dedicated to your work, Doctor Barton,' she said. 'I admire you for your compassion. I know that Dr Thompson is much troubled by the condition of many of those he treats here, and I dare say it may be worse in town.'

'At least here they have fresh air,' Doctor Barton said. 'Though I imagine the work in the mines is as hard as the factories and there is not much to choose between the two.'

'No, I suppose not,' Marianne said. 'It is good to know that someone like you does what he can.'

'I am fortunate enough to have inherited enough money to allow me to do my work as I please,' he told her with a smile. 'I have a good house and a comfortable living, and consider that it is my privilege to help others.'

Marianne nodded approvingly. 'You are a generous man, sir.'

'Oh, no, I should not want you to think me deserving of too much praise,' Dr Barton said. 'I enjoy my life and I have many friends, though as yet no wife. I envy Simon and his good fortune. Jane is a lovely girl and just the kind of wife a doctor needs.'

'Yes, she is,' Marianne said. 'She is looking my way. Excuse me, I must go. Perhaps we may speak again later?'

'I should like that very much,' he said, his eyes warm with admiration as they rested on her face.

Marianne went over to Jane, who wanted to show her something. She had a slender box in her hand, which she opened to show Marianne a gold chain set with sapphires and diamonds.

'Look what Lord Marlbeck sent for me,' she said. 'Is it not wonderful? I cannot imagine why he has given me such a gift. It must be very expensive and I could never have expected it.'

'I believe he is extremely wealthy,' Marianne said. 'I am sure he thought you deserved it, Jane. I think he likes Dr Thompson.' She glanced across the room and saw that Dr Thompson, Dr Barton and Lord Marlbeck were talking together and apparently enjoying each other's company, because they were laughing.

'Yes, but it was very kind,' Jane said, 'though I am not sure that I shall ever have the occasion to wear something like this.'

'Then you may keep it for the future,' Marianne told her. 'Perhaps for your daughter's wedding?'

'Oh yes, if we have one,' Jane said. 'Everyone has been generous to us, Marianne. We have so many lovely gifts, and the villagers sent us a cask of brandy…though I am not sure that it ever paid duty.'

'I dare say it may not have,' Marianne said and laughed. 'But I should not let it concern you. It is their way of thanking Dr Thompson for all he has done for them.'

Mr Pembroke came up to them then, engaging Jane in conversation. Marianne walked away to speak to her sister, who was talking to Major Barr and seemed to be getting on very well with him. Lucy turned as Marianne came up to her.

'Major Barr has a copy of Grimms' *Fairytales,* which he has promised to lend me—is that not kind of him?'

'Yes, indeed,' Marianne said. Her eyes strayed to where the three gentlemen had been standing, her heart jerking as she saw that Drew was no longer with them. Where had he gone? For a moment her throat was tight and the tears burned as she imagined that he had left without speaking to her.

'Marianne?'

His voice behind her made her heart race. She closed her eyes for a moment, turning to him in the instant it took to open them again.

'Lord Marlbeck,' she said. 'It was good of you to come down for Jane's wedding. She was very pleased with your gift. It was beautiful.'

'A mere bauble I picked up in town,' Dew said, his eyes on her face. 'I did not come down just for her wedding, Marianne.'

'Did you come to catch another French spy?' Lucy asked. She smiled at him engagingly, her innocent manner free of any restraint. 'It all sounds very exciting, Lord Marlbeck. Did you catch all the smugglers—or did some get away? Have you caught the traitor yet?'

'Lucy,' Marianne reproved gently. 'This is neither the time or the place to ask such questions.'

'Oh, I do not mind,' Drew said, giving Lucy an indulgent look. 'I need no telling that you are Marianne's youngest sister, Miss Lucy. Shall we take some food into the garden and then you may ask all the questions you like?'

'Oh, yes,' Lucy said. 'Aunt Bertha's cook makes wonderful cakes. Do you like cake, sir?'

'I do if it is good,' Drew said. 'Let us see what there is to choose from, shall we?' He offered her his arm, and Lucy took it, for all the world as if she had known him her whole life.

Marianne watched as they walked across the room together, envying her sister's easy manner with Drew. She felt constrained with him, uneasy, and she had sensed a reserve in him.

'May I fetch you anything?' Dr Barton asked from behind her. Marianne turned to face him, forcing herself to smile naturally. He was a pleasant gentleman and she liked him, but a part of her was conscious only of Drew and Lucy as they laughed together and then disappeared through the open French doors to the garden with their plate of cakes.

'Oh, no, nothing for the moment,' Marianne said. 'I am supposed to be looking after the guests. I must make sure that everyone has what they like—and tell Bessie when more food needs bringing through from the kitchen.'

'Yes, of course,' he said, but looked disappointed. 'I understand you are to visit Bath soon? I shall be there shortly myself, for I have a medical lecture to attend. We are at last beginning to make some progress in the art of medicine, though there is still so much we do not understand. I shall stay for a few days with my brother, who resides in the town. Perhaps I shall see you there?'

'Yes, perhaps,' Marianne agreed. 'I must go, for Bessie is waiting for a signal.'

She went to speak to Bessie, who wanted to know whether they should bring in the trifles and sweetmeats that had been left in the cold pantry until some of the food had been cleared. Marianne spent some minutes with her and then passed on to one of the other guests, who wanted to know where she could refresh herself.

After that, the wedding speeches began and it was a while before Marianne was free. She had seen Lucy return to the large parlour alone, but did not get a chance to speak to her until Jane had gone upstairs to change her gown.

'Did Lord Marlbeck leave?' she asked Lucy.

'Yes,' Lucy said and smiled at her. 'He is so nice, Marianne. He said that he had something he ought to do, but would call on us tomorrow morning at about eleven.'

'I see…' Marianne smiled, but her heart felt as if it would break. Had he wanted to see her alone, he would have found some way of speaking to her in private. No doubt he simply wanted to tell them the latest news concerning Lieutenant Jumble or whatever the rogue was calling himself now. Well, I dare say he had other reasons for coming down here. It would not have been just for the wedding.'

Her heart ached but she kept her smile in place. She was determined that no one should guess how much she was hurting inside.

Chapter Ten

'**W**here are you going, Marianne?' Mrs Horne asked th[e] next morning as Marianne came downstairs wearing a heav[y] silk shawl about her shoulders. 'I wanted to talk to you abo[ut] my decision concerning your great-aunt's request that w[e] make our home with her.'

'Aunt Bertha asked me if I would walk down to the villag[e] for her,' Marianne said. 'She needs a particular shade of gre[en] for her embroidery and she says that I have a good eye f[or] colour. I am happy to go, for it will be a pleasant wal[k], Mama.'

'Of course you must oblige your aunt,' Mrs Horne said a[nd] nodded her approval. 'As you know, we are to go to Bath [in] a day or so. I think Jo and your Aunt Wainwright may co[me] down the following week, and we shall stay there for perha[ps] three weeks in all—after that, we shall return here.'

'Yes, I knew that was Aunt Bertha's intention,' Marian[ne] said. 'I think she had considered living in Bath, but that w[as] before she thought of asking you and my sisters to live he[re]. This is a big house and much of it was not being used befo[re]

…ou came. I believe she feels very much happier now, and I
…are say she would prefer to live here most of the time.'

'I believe it might suit us all,' Mrs Horne said. 'If we stay,
shall send for Lily to join us, because she has been very loyal
…nd we shall need extra help in the house if it is to be opened
…p as it ought.'

'Yes, Aunt Bertha spoke of needing another girl to help
…essie.'

'She tells me that she would like to spend some time in
…ondon next spring. Neither of us have been to London for
…ears, and it would be a chance for you and Jo—unless you
…ave both found husbands before then.' Mrs Horne looked
…t her speculatively. 'Was there anything you wished to tell
…ne, dearest?'

'No, Mama—should there be?'

'Only you can say. Your great-aunt hinted that you might
…uite like Lord Marlbeck?'

'Yes, I do like him,' Marianne agreed. 'But I do not expect
…im to make me a proposal of marriage, Mama.'

'No? Then your aunt is mistaken. I thought it unlikely, for
…e gap is too wide, Marianne. You are very pretty, dearest,
…nd I am sure you will meet a great many gentlemen who are
…ware of that—but the marquis must look higher than a
…icar's daughter for his wife. It would be foolish to expect
…'

'I know that,' Marianne said, fighting the urge to break
…own and weep in her mother's soft arms. 'He…likes me, but
…e must have commitments to his family.'

'I do not think he has a great deal of family,' Mrs Horne
…id. 'But he does have the honour of his name to consider.
…think he mixes with a rare set in London, quite above our

touch—or even your Uncle Wainwright's circle, I imagine For my part, I should be happy to see you settled with a nice gentleman, someone more like your father…' She hesitated then, 'Dr Barton has asked if he may call on us when we are in Bath. I saw you talking to him at the wedding, Marianne.'

'He is a dedicated man and his conversation was interesting, Mama. I do not think I had realised how much poverty there is in the world. We were so fortunate while Papa lived.'

'Your papa was a good man,' Mrs Horne said. 'Agatha has told me several times that I should marry again, and I have thought of it because it would have been hard to continue as we were. Lord Wainwright is kind, but my sister…' She shook her head. 'However, that is behind me—I have made up my mind to accept your great-aunt's offer to live with her. We get on very well, and she was lonely before we came. If I live here, she will not need a companion so I shall save her that expense, and I believe we shall be content together after all my girls have gone.'

'I do not think that will be just yet, Mama. Lucy is too young to think of marriage, and Jo says she does not wish to—though she may change her mind if she meets someone she truly likes.'

'And what of you, my love?'

'I am happy enough for the moment, Mama.'

Mrs Horne smiled. 'Then we shall let things take their course. It will be pleasant to amuse ourselves in Bath and you never know who we may meet there.'

Marianne agreed and they parted. Her mother went to consult with Cook concerning the day's menus and what should be done with the leftovers from the wedding, for she had heard of some deserving cases in the village from M

Pembroke and it was better to pass on any unwanted food than to waste it. Marianne went out, leaving by the French windows at the back of the house. She did not know if she would be back by the time Lord Marlbeck came to visit, but it did not matter—they could have nothing to say to one another. After all, had he particularly wanted to speak to her, he would have told her of his intention to visit, and not her sister.

She had not walked down to the village for some time and she would enjoy the exercise.

Drew frowned as he left Sawlebridge House later that morning. He had spent twenty minutes visiting with Mrs Horne and Lucy, but there had been no sign of Marianne, and Lady Edgeworthy was of course still in her room, for it was not yet noon.

'I am afraid that Mr Hambleton, as Lady Edgeworthy knew him—though he has several aliases, I understand—is still at liberty,' Drew told them in answer to their anxious questions. 'He is being searched for and I am sure it will not be long before he is brought to book, but for the moment it is still best to take care.'

'That is worrying,' Mrs Horne said. 'I wonder if I should have prevented Marianne from leaving earlier? She went out for a walk and I saw no reason to stop her. I do hope she is safe! She has been gone for more than an hour, though that in itself is no cause for alarm. My daughter has always enjoyed long walks.'

'So I believe,' Drew said. 'I understand that we are neighbours. You live in the Vicarage, which is quite close to my estate, do you not?'

'We did, but no longer,' Mrs Horne told him. 'My husband died just over a year ago and we moved to the Lodge on my brother-in-law's estate, but it was not as comfortable as it might have been and we are all to live here in the future. We go to Bath in…three days from now. Yes, it is but three days. How time flies, to be sure. It is for a visit of some three weeks, and then we shall return here—though we may go to London in the spring.'

'I had not realised that you had come for more than a stay of some weeks' duration,' Drew said and frowned. 'I had hoped to call on you when you returned…but no matter. I believe the wedding went very well yesterday?'

'Oh, yes,' Mrs Horne said and looked thoughtful. 'Jane was overwhelmed with all the kindness she received, but it is always so at weddings, do you not think so, sir? Are you planning a long stay here yourself, my lord?'

'I am not sure,' Drew said. 'My plans are uncertain. I might be called away at any time. I have duties to the estate, which I may have neglected of late—and there is this business of that rogue Hambleton. I should like to see that finished.'

'I believe we should all feel better if he were behind bars.'

'Yes, indeed,' Drew agreed. 'We must hope that it will happen soon. I think I must take up no more of your time. Please tell Miss Marianne I was disappointed not to have seen her.'

'I am sorry you missed her. She went out on an errand, but that might have waited until later. I am sure she would have been here had she known you meant to call, sir.'

'Oh, but she did, Mama,' Lucy said, 'for I told her.'

'Lucy…' her mother reproved. 'I am sure she did not perfectly understand what you said, my dear. She would not have been rude for the world.'

'It does not matter,' Drew said. 'No doubt we shall see each other one of these days, for we both like to walk.'

He took his leave of them. It seemed clear to him that Marianne had gone out rather than stay and greet him, and perhaps he could not blame her. Perhaps it was for the best that his thing should end here. A part of him was tempted to linger in the gardens and accost her on her return; that part of him wanted to hold her and kiss her until she melted into his body as she had done on another occasion. He knew that no other woman had ever made him feel this urgent need, and yet it seemed that it was an ill-fated affair, doomed to failure. For he was not worthy of her and knew that in the end his restless spirit would bring her down. To hell with it! He knew that he could not simply walk away without at least seeing her once more.

He was about to set out for the cliff house, where he was staying once more, but then something made him change course without his consciously intending it and he found that he was heading in the direction of the rhododendron valley.

Marianne saw Drew coming towards her. She hugged her shawl tightly about her shoulders, for she had started to shiver, and she did not want him to think that it was on his account. She had delayed her return to the house, because she needed time alone to think, but she made no attempt to avoid him now. If they must say the things that needed to be said, let it be here, away from her family's loving eyes so that she need not pretend for their sakes. Yes, it would be good to have it out, and know finally what his intentions were.

'Your mother told me you had gone to the village, but I thought I might find you here.' He gave her an accusing look. 'Why did you go out when you knew I meant to call?'

'I had an errand for my aunt,' Marianne said, though she knew that she could have put it off had she wished. 'Mama and Lucy were there to receive you. I did not think you had anything in particular to say to me, sir—surely, if you had, you would have said as much at the wedding?' Her eyes threw a challenge at him, daring him to speak.

Drew felt a surge of frustration, wanting to take her by the shoulders and shake her. She must know what she meant to him! And yet how could she when he was not certain of his own intentions? Even now, despite his burning need to draw her down with him and know her intimately, he hesitated to speak.

'I should have liked to talk to you.'

'You have found me. I shall listen if you have anything you feel you need to say…such as an apology?' She was proud, determined not to let him see how close to tears she actually felt inside.

'Perhaps it should be you who apologises,' Drew said, a glint in his eye. 'You were to have sent word when Hambleton left Sawlebridge House—and you were not supposed to go looking for the entrance to that tunnel yourself! Supposing they had discovered you?'

'Well, it has been blocked up now and no real harm was done,' Marianne said, lifting her head proudly. 'I was on my way to warn you but you were not at the house.'

'I was crouching further down the cliff, keeping watch for the boat to land. I saw you, but there was nothing I could do—had I tried to attract your attention, it would have ruined everything.'

'Your French spy did not come that way. He must have put into shore further up the coast. As I tried to tell you before he was to have met Mr Hambleton and they missed each other. I think when he realised that something had gone wrong, he came to the house on the cliffs because he had stayed there before. Mr Hambleton was most annoyed when he learned it had been rented to you.'

'Yes, I dare say. I wonder…'

'What?' She raised her brows at him.

'Whether Mr Hambleton deliberately avoided the meeting. He might have discovered that we were waiting for the smugglers…'

'Yes, perhaps,' Marianne said. 'He has not been caught yet?'

'Unfortunately not, but I believe it may happen soon— though it is possible that he is holed up here somewhere, too frightened to move.'

'Is that why you are here?'

'It was a part of my reason for coming down, yes. I had other reasons…the wedding, for one.'

'Jane looked lovely, did she not?' Marianne avoided looking at him.

'Yes, as brides do, so they tell me.' His voice was ironic. 'I have not attended many weddings, and those I did were hasty affairs when we were campaigning. We did not have the benefit of a church or flowers then.'

'Perhaps the bride was just as lovely?'

'Yes,' he agreed. 'I did not notice. I have never been interested in such things. My parents died when I was young. I was sent away to school and I learned some hard lessons there. Love…softness…marriage—' He broke off for he could see that her eyes were bright with what might be tears. 'I have never known these things. I am not sure that I know how to love or even what it means.'

'I see…' Marianne swallowed hard. 'It is quite easy if one has experienced it,' she said, managing to hold her head high and keep her voice steady. She would not beg for his love! 'But I understand that it might be harder for…someone who has never known love.'

'I suppose I fear it.' Drew made the admission with difficulty. 'I fear to hurt and be hurt.'

'Yes, of course. I believe you have made yourself plain,' she said, her throat tight with emotion. 'For myself, I do not look for marriage in the near future. My great-aunt is no longer alone, but Lucy was very ill recently and she broke her heart for me. I shall not think of leaving her until she is more herself again. Now, if you will excuse me, Lord Marlbeck, I must go home before my family begins to worry—and it is getting chilly.'

She pulled her shawl tighter about her and walked past him, her head high. Tears were pricking behind her eyes, but she was too proud to let them fall. It was clear that his feelings for her had been merely that of a man tempted by a pretty girl. He had never intended more than a flirtation.

Drew turned his head and watched her go. He was a wretched fool! He wanted to catch her up, take her into his arms and kiss her until neither of them could stop what must happen then, for he would be committed and there would be no drawing back. Yet something held him. He was once again the lonely boy watching from inside school windows as other boys went running to their mothers' arms. He had built this wall around his heart brick by brick and it was damnably painful tearing it down!

How could he promise to love her for ever when he did not know how?

* * *

Marianne brushed her tears away impatiently with the back of her hand. She must not cry. It would be so foolish. Weeping and breaking her heart would do no good. Drew did not love her. He had told her that he was afraid to love, but she did not understand him. One either loved or one did not—it was as natural as breathing to her.

She had always loved her mother and sisters—and particularly Papa. The memory of being held in her father's arms one particular day when she was a small child, swept over her, bringing the tears she had fought so hard to hold back. She had tripped and fallen, cutting her knee. Her father had caught her up in his arms, comforting her, bathing her knee and kissing it better before giving her into her mother's care.

'Oh, Papa,' she whispered, 'what shall I do? I do love him so much—and he does not love me…'

Had her father been alive she knew that she could have asked him how to accept her pain, but she did not wish to distress her mother or sister. She must somehow find the strength to deal with it herself.

'This came for you while you were out, Captain,' Robbie said, handing him a sealed letter as he entered the house an hour or so later. 'The lad who delivered it said it was urgent and the gentleman wanted an answer, but I had no way of knowing when you would return.'

Drew took the paper and broke the seal. He read the cryptic message with a frown and gave it back to Robbie. 'What do you make of that?'

'If you wish to find the man who calls himself Joshua Hambleton, come to the old mine at nine this evening. Come alone and you will need fifty guineas for the information, but it will be worth your while,' Robbie read aloud. 'Sounds a bit smoky to me, Captain. I should be wary of this if I were you.'

'Yes, I agree,' Drew said. 'And yet I think I must go, Robbie. Jack is banking on the hope that Humble will walk into his trap—but he may disappear, never to be seen again.' He frowned. His anger against the traitor seemed to have cooled, for taking revenge on Lieutenant Humble would not bring his friends back. 'It would not matter so much if it were not for…'

'The old lady and the beauty?' Robbie said and Drew nodded. 'Well, you please yourself, Captain. Go if you think it right, but you'll not be alone—I'll be at your back.'

'Yes, thank you,' Drew said. 'But you must keep well hidden. If this note is genuine, I do not want him to be scared off…whoever he is…'

'Might it be the lawyer's clerk? Did he not give you information before?'

'Yes, he did,' Drew agreed and frowned. 'I would have expected him to want to meet in the safety of the inn, but it could be him.'

'Supposing it is a trap? Humble may have sent the note himself to lure you there.'

'Then I shall know how to deal with him,' Drew said. 'Jack wants him alive, but if it were necessary I should not hesitate to kill him.'

'We'll both of us be armed,' Robbie said. 'At the first sign that he means to murder you, I shall shoot him—in the back if I have to.'

'Fighting talk,' Drew said and smiled oddly.

Robbie's loyalty made him feel better. He had been feeling wretched since he had let Marianne walk away from him cursing himself for a fool and a coward. How could he have hurt her, as he knew he had? Excuses were worth nothing—he knew that the memory of her face would haunt his dreams. He must go to her, beg her forgiveness…try to explain the thoughts that were so tangled he hardly understood them himself.

He decided that he would leave it for a night. She might refuse to see him if he went too soon, and a little time for reflection might help him to sort out his own thoughts.

If all went well, this night might see an end to the business of the traitor and the French spy. In the morning he would seek Marianne out and try to explain the things he had made such a mess of earlier.

'Is something the matter?' Mrs Horne asked of her daughter later that afternoon when they were sitting together in the parlour. 'You look a little pale, dearest. I do hope you are not coming down with a chill?'

'No, I do not think so,' Marianne said. 'But I do have a little headache. I think I shall lie down for an hour or so before dinner—if you do not mind?'

'Of course not,' her mother and aunt said together.

'We do not want you to sicken with anything when we are about to leave for Bath,' Mrs Horne said, looking anxious.

'We have decided that we shall go tomorrow, if you are well enough,' Lady Edgeworthy informed her. 'Cynthia and I have decided that there is no point in delaying things, because we have already secured a house for the duration of our visit, and I know that some of my friends are in Bath at the moment. Besides, the weather is fine; if we wait, it may change.'

'I am sure I shall be much better in the morning,' Marianne said. 'I had better start packing my trunk, for we do not want to be late tomorrow.'

'Bessie will do it for you,' Mrs Horne said. 'Lucy has already packed her own, and she was going to make a start on mine. She is excited, though I have told her that she will not be able to attend the Assembly because she is too young.'

'I dare say there will be plenty of visiting to amuse her,' Lady Edgeworthy said. 'Lucy will be able to accompany us on drives and walks, and all manner of things. It will be quite exciting to go out in company again. I am looking forward to seeing old friends.'

Marianne nodded her head and left the parlour. The news that they were to leave for Bath immediately was unsettling. She had expected to be here another two days…but what difference did it make? A sob rose in her throat, but she held it back. She was determined not to give way to tears and spoil the promised visit for everyone else. She must put a smile on her face and accept that she had been foolish to imagine that Drew cared for her. His words had been clear enough. He had no idea of marriage, and had thought of her as someone to amuse himself with while he waited to trap the traitor.

Nothing would be changed because they were leaving for Bath two days early. She must learn to cope with her heartache and hope that in time it would become easier. She had her family around her, and in Bath they might see Jo when she came down with Aunt Wainwright. She lifted her head, a look of pride on her face. She would not lie down on her bed and cry, she would find Lucy and they would pack Mama's trunk and her own together.

* * *

It was very dark that night. Drew thought that he would not have chosen to be out in such weather for a sudden storm had blown up, whipping the sea into a frenzy about the rocks out in the bay. His lantern was all the light they carried, for Robbie was forced to keep in his shadow in case they were being watched as they left the house and made their way towards the old mine.

Drew's pistol was primed and loaded, ready for instant use should it be needed, as was the weapon Robbie carried. They had not spoken since they left the house, because they both knew that this was in all likelihood a trap. When they were almost at the mine, Drew blew out the candle in his lantern, plunging them into darkness. For a moment neither were able to see, but gradually their eyes became used to the darkness. Now they had separated, Drew going ahead, Robbie watching from a distance.

Drew could see no sign of anyone waiting at the appointed place. He knew that he was a few minutes early, and he squatted down on his haunches, resting, as he had learned to do in the army, knowing that he was less of a target for an assassin's pistol. He waited for some minutes, feeling the chill wind as it whipped about his head, blowing his hair and making him wish himself back at the house.

There was no sign of anyone, and after perhaps twenty minutes had passed, he began to think that Robbie had been right—it was either a wild-goose chase or a trap. He got to his feet and began to walk closer to the mine entrance, won-dering if the writer of the letter was waiting in the shadows for him to come closer. Looking about him, he did not see what was at his feet, and his boot kicked against something…soft and yet bulky. Dropping to his knees, his hands reached out and discovered a body.

'Damn it!' he muttered and felt for his tinder-box. As he lit the lantern once more, the yellow light fell on to the face of a man he recognised as the clerk who had once given him information. His eyes were open, staring straight up at him sightlessly. 'Robbie!' He got to his feet and waved the lantern, bringing his batman to him in seconds. 'You were right. It was my informant from the lawyer's office, but someone else got here first. The poor devil never saw it coming.'

'Lieutenant Humble?'

'Perhaps…' Drew looked at the man's pale face. 'Why on earth did he choose to meet here? There's nothing we can do for him, and I've no mind to hang around here any longer. I'll send word to Major Barr in the morning. He is the Justice of the Peace in these parts. He can sort out what happened.'

'Aye, that's the most sensible thing you've said for the past few hours,' Robbie said. 'Let's get back to the house. It will be a wonder if we don't both catch our death of cold.'

'I never catch colds,' Drew said and promptly sneezed. 'Damn it! We could both do with a rum toddy, Robbie. I should never have come on this fool's errand.'

'I'll second that,' Robbie said. 'Whoever did this will have seen you're not alone. I doubt if he will come after you, Captain. He will be in hiding for the moment.'

'At least we know he must be holed up somewhere in the district,' Drew said as they trudged back to the house. The wind was howling and a driving rain had set in, soaking them through to the skin by the time they were home.

'You've done all you can. Best you leave it to the militia now, Captain,' Robbie said as they got inside and he put a pan of rum on the kitchen fire to heat. 'You had best get out of those clothes. Why don't you go to bed? I'll bring you a hot toddy when it's ready.'

'Anyone would think I was a child or an invalid! I've endured worse than this on campaign.'

'Aye, so you have,' Robbie said. 'But there's always a first time to be ill, my lord, and I've seen you in a fever afore this.'

'Don't start that,' Drew said and promptly sneezed three times. 'Fool! Not you, me. I'll take your advice, but see you get your own things off, man. You wouldn't want me as your nurse.'

Drew left him in the kitchen and went into his own bed-chamber. There was no fire here, but he stripped off and rubbed himself down with a towel. He was gripped with icy shivers as he got into bed, cursing himself for being idiot enough to respond to the note. And yet it was probable that the dead man had had valuable information to pass on—if only Drew had got to him first! He pulled the covers up around his neck, because he was feeling shivery and took the hot drink Robbie brought him gratefully, holding it in his hands and appreciating the warmth.

'This will sort me out,' he told Robbie. 'I shall be fine once I've drunk this. I told you, I never get colds. I'll be back to normal in a couple of hours.'

But in the morning he was far from fine. He was right to say he didn't get colds, for it was a nasty fever he had taken and when Robbie went in to wake him, he was out of his head, tossing and turning, his skin burning up.

'Well, now, here's a fine to-do,' Robbie said. 'There's a dead man lying out there by the mine, and his murderer roaming the countryside at will—but how am I to do half a dozen things at once? Leave you while you're this ill, I can't, Captain. The rascal can go for the doctor, and I'll send Harry to inform about Master Lawyer's clerk, but as for that rogue…' He shook his head. 'There's no more we can do for the moment.'

'Marianne…' Drew cried, starting up from his pillows. His eyes were dark with fever and he did not know what he did. 'I didn't mean to hurt you…come back…'

'She'll have to wait for the moment, Captain,' Robbie said. 'A fine mess you've made of things by the sound of it. Anyone could see that she is a real lady. You'll end up a lonely old man if you lose her.'

Grumbling to himself, Robbie lit a fire in the grate and then went back to the kitchen. He would heat the warming pan and wrap it in a cloth, and then put it in the bed with the captain. He knew that Drew was a strong man, for he had nursed him through worse than this in Spain, but the fevers then had been brought about by his wounds. He wasn't sure why the captain had succumbed this time for it was true that he seldom took chills, but he would weather it. And while the captain lay here in a fever that murderer was out there somewhere—roaming free and at liberty to do more harm.

Marianne stopped to look in the window of a shop selling pretty hats. Lucy was hanging on her arm, pulling at her because she had seen a blue bonnet that would match the redingote that Jo had made for her from the blue velvet bought at Huntingdon market.

'Shall we ask how much it is?' Lucy asked, looking longingly at the bonnet. 'Do you think we can afford it?'

'I think we might if it is not too ruinous,' Marianne said

with a teasing smile. 'Yes, of course you may have it, dearest. Aunt Bertha gave me an allowance when I first went to live with her and I have not spent a penny of it as yet, for I had what Uncle Wainwright gave me. Let us go in and you shall try it on—and I might try that green one…'

Lucy sent her a look of delight for she had never had so much fun in her life and was thoroughly enjoying their visit to Bath. Once inside the shop she tried on at least ten hats, but in the end she bought the one she had admired in the window. Marianne did not buy anything. She had tried on one or two she liked, but she knew that she and Jo could make them as well as the milliner who had fashioned these, and she enjoyed doing it, especially as her friends were all so complimentary and often asked where she had bought her hats.

When they came out of the shop, they had to stop to allow two ladies to enter. Marianne was about to pass by with a nod in greeting, but the young lady suddenly took hold of her arm and exclaimed in delight.

'Oh, it is you, Miss Horne! I thought I saw you the other day, but Mama told me I must be mistaken—I am so glad to have bumped into you like this. We are giving a little dance this weekend. The invitations have already gone out, but you will not mind that, I hope. Please do say you will come!'

'Miss Forester,' Marianne said and smiled at her enthusiastic welcome. 'This is my sister Lucy. I am in Bath with my great-aunt and my mother.'

'Then you must all come, must they not, Mama?' Henriette looked at her mother pleadingly. 'Do say they shall!'

'Yes, certainly, if you wish it,' Lady Forester said with an indulgent look. 'You were so kind to take us up in your carriage, Miss Horne. I believe I was too upset to thank you

as I ought—please say that you will come to Henr
dance. We have only just arrived in Bath and she do
know many girls of her own age as yet.'

'Lucy is not out yet…'

'Oh, but it is a private affair and Henriette is not so
older,' Lady Forester said. 'Where are you living? I sha
on your mama and ask her if she will bring you both.'

'A real dance,' Lucy said, her eyes shining. 'Do sa
Marianne.'

'Well, if Mama permits,' Marianne agreed. 'Lady
worthy has taken a house in Queen Square and will be p
to welcome you, I know. It is very kind of you to inv
Lady Forester.'

'Not at all,' she replied. 'It is nothing compared t
you did for us that day, Miss Horne. And now we m
on, Henriette. We have a lot to do this morning.'

She nodded and guided her daughter into the shop. Ma
and Lucy walked on. Lucy looked at her sister curiousl

'You didn't tell me anything about them?'

'I had forgotten,' Marianne said truthfully. So muc
happened to her since she went to live with her great-au
the trivial incident had slipped from her mind. 'It was n
Their carriage had broken a wheel. It was being cleared
side of the road and I took them up as far as the neare
Anyone would have done the same.'

'Yes, perhaps,' Lucy said, 'but isn't it fortunate th
were the one? A private dance is so much nicer th
Assembly, Marianne—don't you think so?'

'Perhaps,' her sister agreed. 'Since we have not b
the Assembly yet, I cannot truly say—but it will be pl
if Mama agrees.'

* * *

Mrs Horne had been a little doubtful when Lucy told her that they had been invited to the dance of a lady she did not know. However, when Lady Forester called the next morning to invite them personally, she was pleased to accept.

'It is just the thing,' she told Marianne. 'We shall no doubt meet and make many new friends at the pump room and the Assembly, but it is always nice to be able to claim an acquaintance—and as it is a small private affair, Lucy may come with us, which is even better.'

'Yes, Mama,' Marianne said. 'I was thinking—' She broke off as Bessie came into the room. She and Miss Rudge had accompanied them to Bath, because Lady Edgeworthy felt that they would do better with some of their own maids to look after them, though the house had come with a full complement of servants.

'Yes, Bessie?' her mistress asked. 'Did you wish to speak to me?'

'There's a visitor, ma'am—only he asked for Miss Marianne and I wasn't sure if she was at home to a gentleman.'

Marianne's heart raced wildly. 'Who is it, Bessie?' For an instant she hoped that it might be Drew, but in the next moment her hope had faded.

'Doctor Barton, miss. He said that he had heard you were in Bath and thought that he would call.'

'Oh, how kind of him,' Lady Edgeworthy said. 'Ask him to come in, Bessie. We shall have some tea—and some Madeira for the gentleman, if you please.'

Marianne got to her feet and went over to the window, gazing out at the pretty back garden. She needed a minute to compose herself, because her disappointment was so sharp that she felt close to tears. They had been in Bath five days now, and it was stupid to imagine that Drew would follow her here. Why should he? He had made his feelings clear at their last meeting. She must control these foolish longings and accept that she might never see him again. Behind her she could hear the exchange of greetings, and knew that she must turn and smile at their visitor. No one must suspect that her heart was breaking little by little.

Drew was standing by the window looking out at the sea. He turned his head as Robbie brought in a can of hot water for him to shave. It was the first time that he had shaved himself in five days, and he was still feeling a little under the weather, though he had recovered sufficiently by the third day to send Robbie to ask Major Barr to call on him.

'Major Barr sent word that he will call at eleven this morning,' Robbie said. 'I dare say he has been waiting to see if there is any sign of that rogue, but I doubt if they will find him. Wherever he is, he knows how to keep out of sight.'

'He'll need food and water. He has to come out of hiding sooner or later. Unless someone is harbouring him, of course,' Drew said and frowned. 'He must have contacts in the area, but I'm damned if I know where to look. He seems to have the knack of disappearing…'

'Major Barr may have something to tell you,' Robbie suggested.

However, when he called later that morning, the Justice of the Peace was as frustrated as they were. 'Seems to have disappeared from the face of the earth,' he said. 'We've had men out searching all the empty barns and ruins in the district

Even sent some volunteer miners down that old shaft—but so far there's no sign of him. If it was Hambleton, he probably cut and ran for it after he killed Symonds.'

'Ah, yes, Symonds, the name had escaped me,' Drew said and looked thoughtful. 'Well, if Hambleton has gone, so much the better. I have been worried about Lady Edgeworthy and her visitors.' Frustrated would have been a better word, for in his weakened state he had been unable to rise from his bed.

'Well, they are in Bath for the moment,' Major Barr said. 'To tell you the truth, I had hoped we might have it all finished and done by the time they come back—but he can't be found and there's not much more we can do.'

'In Bath?' Drew nodded. 'I had forgotten they intended to go for a visit. Yes, it would be good to have it all sewn up before they return. I think perhaps I shall go to Bath myself. Lady Edgeworthy may know something of Hambleton's lifestyle that we do not.'

'Doubt it myself,' Major Barr said. 'But ask her by all means. I dare say you'll be glad to see the back of this place after your illness.'

'It wasn't the most comfortable of places to be ill,' Drew said with a wry smile, 'and Robbie has had hard work of it to look after me. At least in Bath we shall be sure of a comfortable inn and someone to cook for us.'

'Come and dine with me this evening,' the major said. 'At least I can offer you some decent beef.'

'Thank you, but another time,' Drew said. 'I think we may leave this afternoon. I have business that will not wait.'

Henriette came up to Marianne and Mrs Horne a few moments after they had entered the ballroom at the Assembly

Hall. She was looking very pretty in a dress of pale pink silk with a ruffled hem and a demure neckline.

'Is Lucy not here this evening?' she asked.

'She is not out,' Mrs Horne told her. 'She may come to your private dance, Henriette, and I am sure she will be happy to walk out with you to the library or the shops, but I do not want her to attend public affairs like this for another year or so.'

'Oh, yes, I shall enjoy having her at my dance,' Henriette said. 'There are so many people here and we do not know the half of them…' Her words died away as her gaze fell on a gentleman who had just entered the ballroom. 'Oh! Surely that is…*him*…'

Marianne turned to look at the gentleman who had brought a delicate blush to Henriette's cheeks, and her heart jerked as she saw that it was Drew. He seemed to be looking for someone and, catching her eye, began to walk towards where the three of them stood.

Marianne would have fled if there were anywhere to go, but she was in a ballroom and she could not simply leave without an explanation to her mama. She decided to be cool but polite, for she must not let him see that his sudden arrival had thrown her into confusion.

'Good evening, ladies,' Drew said as he reached them. 'Mrs Horne, Marianne…Miss Forester, I seem to remember?'

'Oh, yes,' Henriette breathed, her eyes glowing as she gazed up at him. 'Mama told you our names, of course, but I do not recall yours, sir.'

'This is Lord Marlbeck,' Mrs Horne said, looking from Henriette to Drew. 'You seem to have met briefly?'

'Lord Marlbeck…' Henriette said and her voice carried a tinge of surprise. 'Oh, it was when our coach came off the road and Marianne took us up in her carriage as far as the next inn. Lord Marlbeck helped us, for Mama was likely to have hysterics had he not come along when he did.' The look she gave him was unashamedly adoring, and it was clear that she was brimming with excitement at having discovered her rescuer was a marquis.

Lady Forester had been talking to another lady, but she came up to them at that moment. 'Ah, there you are, Henriette.' She looked at Drew, but gave no sign of recognition.

'Mama, this is Lord Marlbeck. You recall that he helped us when we had an accident to our coach…'

'Lord Marlbeck?' Lady Forester's tone seemed to question the validity of her daughter's words for a moment, her eyes going over him sharply. However, she could find no fault with his appearance because he was dressed in perfect taste that evening, his coat the work of a master tailor, and his cravat a pristine waterfall that many a dandy would envy. Suddenly she was smiling her approval. 'Yes, I remember perfectly. It was so kind of you to help us that day, sir.'

'It was nothing,' Drew said in a dismissive tone. The set of his jaw was hard and Marianne sensed that he was angry. She guessed that it was a struggle for him to control his impatience. She could hear the music playing in the background and knew that the dancing was about to begin as he said, 'Would you give me the honour of this dance, Miss—'

'Oh, yes, thank you,' Henriette said before he could finish and looked at him expectantly. 'I have been longing to dance, my lord.'

Drew's eyes flashed with some pent-up emotion that Marianne thought might possibly be frustration, but he gave his hand to Henriette and led her away to join the other dancers who were forming into groups.

'They make a pretty sight, do they not?' Lady Forester said, nodding indulgently. 'Are you much acquainted with Lord Marlbeck, Mrs Horne?'

'He is an acquaintance of Lady Edgeworthy, with whom we are staying,' Mrs Horne replied. 'Marianne knows him better than I do myself.'

Lady Forester nodded, but what she was about to say was lost to Marianne, for at that moment a gentleman of their acquaintance came up to her and asked if he might have the pleasure of that dance. She gave him her hand and they took their places at the end of a line of ladies and gentlemen. It was a progressive dance in which all the participants danced with each other as well as their particular partner. And being at one end of the line, while Drew was at the other, it was a while before she found herself curtsying to him, and giving him her hand.

He threw her an exasperated look. 'You knew it was you I intended to ask, Marianne.'

'Henriette thought otherwise.' She gave him a cool nod and they parted to walk down the line and then joined hands again to dance back up. 'She is a charming girl and I am sure you cannot regret your choice.'

'Jade!' Drew hissed at her and gave her an awful look, which made her smile inwardly.

As she naturally progressed to the next gentleman in the line she had no further chance to speak with him, until after the dance was finished. Drew escorted Henriette to her mother, thanked her for the dance and walked straight back to where Marianne stood with her mama and two other ladies

'Marianne, I believe you promised me the next dance,' he said and took her arm, leading her away to where dancers were collecting for what it became clear was to be a waltz.

'I am not sure that I should be dancing this,' Marianne said. 'Is it not true that most young ladies dare not accept unless they have been given special permission?'

'You are not most young ladies and I have no time for such nonsense,' Drew said grimly. 'If you do not dance with me, I shall drag you outside to the balcony and kiss you in full view of the room.'

'You are very forward, sir,' Marianne said coolly, though her heart had begun to race wildly. She lifted her head, gazing into his eyes in a challenging manner, determined to give him no quarter. 'Especially when the last time we spoke you gave me to understand that there could be nothing between us.'

The music had begun and she was in his arms, her head tipped to look up at him, his hand at the small of her back, their bodies too close for her comfort. She hoped that he was not aware it had become difficult for her to breathe. Already she was feeling herself relax, their feet, bodies and hearts as one as they danced. They were so in tune that it was like floating through air, a heavenly sensation that made her feel as if she wanted to melt into him and fly away.

'I am all kinds of a fool,' Drew said. 'You must know that there is something between us, Marianne…something that is stronger than both of us. It is perhaps the nearest thing to love that I can feel.'

Marianne looked at him uncertainly as their dance came to an end. In his arms she had felt as if she wanted to stay there for ever, but now she was not sure what he was saying. Her own love for him was overwhelming, and she knew that without him her life would have no real meaning—but just what did he feel for her?

'I do not believe this is the right moment to speak of these

things,' she said as they walked towards her mother. 'Perhap
if you called tomorrow?'

'I shall take you driving, if you will permit me?'

'Yes, thank you. In the morning at ten?'

'I shall be there,' Drew promised. 'If you will excuse me
I think I shall leave before I am obliged to dance with mor
innocent young girls who have match-making mamas.'

'Lord Marlbeck!' Marianne's eyes flashed at him indig
nantly. 'You are unkind.'

Drew grinned, made his bow to her and walked away withou
looking to the left or right. Marianne watched him go, he
thoughts in some confusion. Did he mean to offer her marriage
Surely he had not been thinking of offering her *carte blanche*
He must know that she would never accept such an offer.

'Has Lord Marlbeck gone?' Henriette said as she came t
join Marianne. 'Mama was going to ask him to my dance.'

'Yes, unfortunately he had another appointment,' Mari
anne said. 'But I dare say you will meet again soon.'

'You do not happen to know where he is staying?'

'No, I am afraid not,' Marianne replied. She turned as
gentleman came up to her and bowed.

'Good evening, Miss Horne. We were introduced earlie
I wonder if I may have the honour of this dance, please?'

'Oh…' Marianne saw that Henriette was also being aske
to dance and she need not fear to leave her standing alon
'Yes, thank you, sir. You are most kind.'

The dance was once again a progressive and Mariann
found that she was enjoying herself as she passed from on
partner to the next. None of them made her breathless, b
she was able to smile and laugh, and at the end of the evenin
told her mama that it had been a pleasant evening.

'It was a pity that Lucy and Aunt Bertha were not with us, but tomorrow we are invited to a private party, and the day after that is Miss Forester's dance.'

'Yes…' Mrs Horne looked thoughtful. 'I think Lady Forester would have been pleased if Lord Marlbeck had stayed longer. She quizzed me about him after he had left, and she was interested to know that we had once lived within walking distance of his estate. She asked me if it were true that he was one of the wealthiest men in England, but I told her I could not answer her question for I did not know.'

'What a thing to ask!' Marianne said and laughed. 'No wonder poor Drew made such a hasty retreat. If he has been the subject of such scrutiny by match-making mamas, as he calls them, it is not to be wondered at if he shies off dancing with their daughters.'

'Poor Drew?' Mrs Horne raised her brows. 'I was not aware that you were on such terms with Lord Marlbeck, Marianne?'

'Oh…' Marianne blushed—it had been a slip of the tongue. 'We did become…friends, I suppose, before you came down, Mama. I suppose I should not have spoken so freely, but he told me that his friends call him Drew.'

'I see…' Mrs Horne studied her face. 'Have you anything more to tell me, Marianne?'

'Lord Marlbeck has asked if he may take me driving in the morning, and I have said yes… I hope that was acceptable, Mama?'

'Yes, perfectly acceptable,' her mother said and smiled. 'I do not believe I have seen you smile as much for days as you did this evening.' She kissed her cheek. 'Sleep well, my darling. You will want to look your best in the morning.'

Marianne nodded and went into her own room. She closed her door and leaned against it, feeling a sudden wave of apprehension. Her mama was clearly imagining an understanding between her and Drew—but what were his intentions towards her really?

She moved towards her dressing table, sitting down to unpin her hair, looking at her reflection as she struggled to unfasten the hooks at the nape of her neck. Slipping her gown off, she stepped out of it and laid it carefully over a chair for Bessie to press and put away in the morning. It was her best evening gown and she would need it again for Henriette's dance, because although they had ordered a new one it would not be finished in time.

Getting into bed, Marianne blew out her candle and closed her eyes, but sleep did not come immediately. Drew was still a mystery to her. She could not help feeling a little apprehensive about what he would say to her in the morning.

Chapter Eleven

Marianne dressed in a carriage gown of green velvet, adding a matching pelisse and a bonnet tied with crimson ribbons and decorated with a bunch of cherries. She had made it herself, but it was as stylish as any she had seen in the fashionable milliners in Bath, and she was happy that it complemented her gown.

Drew arrived punctually. Marianne was with Lucy upstairs, and Mrs Horne invited him into the parlour where she and Lady Edgeworthy were sitting. Marianne heard his voice and, kissing her sister's cheek, picked up her reticule and went downstairs. He turned to look at her as she entered the room, and his eyes lit with what she imagined must be a mixture of pleasure and approval. He came towards her. She offered her hand. He took it, lifting it to his lips to kiss it hastely.

'You look beautiful, Marianne,' he said. 'Are you ready to leave?'

'Yes, thank you,' she said and glanced at her mama. 'I am not perfectly sure how long we shall be…'

'Your mama has invited me to take nuncheon with you,' Drew told her, and the look of satisfaction in his eyes made her tremble inwardly. 'I have promised we shall return by half-past twelve.'

Marianne nodded, turning to lead the way outside to where his horses were being held by a young tiger. Drew assisted Marianne into his curricle and climbed up beside her, taking the reins. He nodded to the lad.

'Climb up, you rascal,' he said. 'And mind you behave yourself.'

'Yes, milord,' the lad said. 'Don't I always?'

Drew ignored him. For a few minutes he concentrated on his horses. Apart from one smile, he did not look at Marianne until they had cleared the traffic of the busy streets.

'I thought we would drive into the countryside, for it is quite pretty around here,' he said. 'Did you enjoy your evening?'

'Yes, it was very pleasant. Miss Forester was disappointed that you left so early, and so, I believe, was her mama.'

'Marianne,' he warned, giving her a look that took her breath. 'Think yourself fortunate that I do not allow the rascal to drive my horses or you would receive instant punishment for that remark.'

'Why do you call him that?' Marianne said, determined not to let him fluster her. 'Has he no other name?'

'I have no idea,' Drew said and grinned at her. 'He came down the chimney into my bedroom at Marlbeck when I first came home from the army. The imp was so terrified of what his master would do to him if he was discovered and blamed for being in the wrong place that I gave his master twenty pounds for him and took him on as my tiger. He has his use despite a propensity for insolence.' He glanced over his shoulder. 'Tell Miss Marianne your name, rascal—if you have one.'

'Don't know,' the lad replied. 'Him what owned me called me 'ere you or blasted boy. Reckon I answer to anything, milord.'

'There you are,' Drew said. 'Rascal will do for now. It suits him.'

Marianne had to admit privately that it did, for the boy was hardly angelic. He had a snub nose, ginger hair and a big gap in his front teeth when he grinned, which he did most of the time, and especially when Drew spoke to him. Apparently, he was happy in his present work.

'You seem to have some odd servants, my lord,' she said and her lips quivered as she looked at Drew. 'Robbie is a pirate if ever I saw one.'

Drew gave a shout of laughter. 'He would love that,' he said. 'He calls you the Beauty…'

Marianne saw the look of unholy glee and cast her eyes downward. It made her heart race to know that she had been a matter of discussion between master and servant, though in truth they were more like friends.

'You are an unusual man,' she said at last. 'I have not met many men of your rank, my lord, but I had imagined they would think rather more of their consequence. Your uncle was a very proud man as I recall, though generous.'

'Yes, he had his good points,' Drew agreed. 'He seemed very remote to me as a child. As for my consequence, what does that mean? I have inherited a title and a fortune, which ought never to have been mine—and which I never expected. I find it more of a burden than a pleasure and might have pre-rred the army career I had chosen for myself. Had my cousin

lived, I should have been quite happy to continue as Captai
Beck.'

'So that was your real name then?'

'Did you think I had lied to you?'

'You did not tell me you were a marquis.' Her eye
accused him.

'No, for obvious reasons.' They had reached a prett
village and Drew halted his horses at the edge of a larg
green. He got down, the rascal having jumped ahead of hi
to take the horses, and then gave his hand to Marianne. H
offered her his arm and they began to walk across the gra
to a picturesque pond where ducks swam and there was
wooden bench under a chestnut tree. 'I thought you unde
stood that I was in difficulty, Marianne. I used my fami
name, because I wanted to avoid the visitors and invitatio
I would have received had it been known Marlbeck wa
staying in the area.'

'Is that why you left so hurriedly last night?'

'I did have another appointment. I came to the Assembl
because Lady Edgeworthy told me you were there when
called on her. It is a sad fact, but true, my dear one. Since I i
herited the title I have been hunted by a succession of dete
mined mothers, all hoping that I will make their daughters
marchioness. It is not me, you understand, but the title and t
fortune that makes me such a prize. At least in the eyes
some.'

He had called her his *dear one!* All the rest went over h
head. She looked at him uncertainly.

'Do you think that Mama thinks of you as a matrim
nial prize?'

'Mrs Horne has more sense,' Drew said. 'She told me th

he does not care much for worldly things and wants only
our happiness.'

'Mama married for love and was happy until the day
apa died.'

'She was fortunate,' Drew said and frowned. 'This is what
wanted to speak to you of, Marianne. I believe you must
now that I have strong feelings for you—and I think you
ay have similar feelings towards me?'

Marianne nodded, but could not trust herself to answer.
rew took her hand as they sat down on the bench, looking
t each other.

'To understand what I am about to say, you must know that
oth my parents died when I was a small child. I hardly
member them. I was left to the care of a nursemaid, who
njoyed smacking troublesome boys, and I believe I must have
ied her patience sorely, for I was always a little wild. When
was old enough, my uncle put me in the charge of a tutor, who
ok not the slightest interest in my welfare for years and then
was sent away to school, because I spent my time in the
oods rather than studying. My uncle had a son of his own and
think he could not be bothered with his brother's child.'

'Oh, Drew,' Marianne said, and her heart felt for him.
ow alone you must have been. I always had the love of my
other and sisters—and especially Papa. He was so wonder-
l, Drew. I wish you could have known him.'

'I did meet him once,' Drew said, surprising her. 'I was
me on leave after Salamanca and, as I may have told you
fore, I was near mad with grief and anger. One morning I
alked into a church. I stood there and the anger must have
en in my face for a man came up to me. He asked me why I
as so bitter and I told him that I no longer believed in God.

Instead of raging at me for being a blasphemer, he invited me into the vestry and we sat and talked. I do not recall what either of us said, but I know that something about him seemed to reach into me and take away the pain...' He smiled at her. 'It was the beginning of my recovery. He was your father, Marianne.'

'Oh, Drew,' she whispered and tears hovered in her lovely eyes. 'I am so glad that you knew him...that he helped you. He was like that, everyone said it.'

'I did not know he was your father then,' Drew said. 'I have since realised it, but I did not know then.' He reached out and touched her cheek. 'I wanted you from the first moment I saw you, and though I tried to put you from my mind, you never quite left me. I think you must know that I have wanted to make love to you several times, but...'

'But you do not wish to marry?'

'No, that is not what I meant to say,' Drew said. 'I shall be honoured and happy if you will consent to be my wife, Marianne—but I have hesitated, because I am afraid of hurting you. I have not always been a good man or a sensible one. There is a wild streak in me, which I have tried to control, but I cannot say it has been tamed—and though I care for you, need you in my life, I am not sure that I can give you the kind of love you deserve. I am not sure that I know how to love a girl like you, my dearest. I want you, need you...desperately, but I fear that I may hurt you one day.'

'Oh, Drew...' Marianne's breath caught in her throat. She wanted to weep, but she also wanted to laugh, because she felt happy. He did care for her, he did want her. She reached out and took his hand. 'I love you, Drew. I think I fell in love with you the first time you kissed me, though I did not dare to think it then. Since then that love has become stronger and eeper, and I think I should never have married had you not sked me.' She smiled at him. 'Yes, I shall marry you, Drew, hough I must ask you if Lucy may come and stay with us ften, for it upsets her to be parted from me.'

'She may live with us if it pleases you,' he said gruffly and eached for her, drawing her into his arms to kiss her with uch tenderness and sweetness that any lingering doubts disppeared. 'Teach me how to love and be loved,' Drew said in humble tone that made her smile. 'I don't want to hurt you, ny darling, and I am so afraid that I shall.'

'If you hurt me unintentionally, it will mend,' Marianne aid. 'Papa told me once that human beings are frail creatures nd we cannot help hurting each other sometimes, but if a uarrel is made up before the day is finished it will be forotten by the next.'

'Your papa was a wise man,' Drew said and kissed her oftly. 'I think we should go back now, my dearest one. The ascal is watching everything we do and I think perhaps your nama should be told of our intention to marry.'

'Yes, that would be a good thing,' Marianne said and stood p. They strolled back across the grass to the curricle and rew helped her up.

The rascal grinned as he gave the reins to his master and opped up at the back. 'All settled then, milord,' he said. 'I've on me bet, for 'Arry said as you weren't the marryin' kind, nd I bet him a shilling that you would be wed afore Christmas.'

'As for that, it depends on Miss Marianne,' Drew said and ossed him a florin from his pocket. 'Watch your tongue, scal. I shall expect some respect for my wife in future.'

'Right you are, milord,' the rascal said, his grin becoming ven wider as he looked at Marianne. 'Robbie told me you

were a real beauty. He said that if milord let you go, he woul[d]
be a bigger fool than he thought.'

Marianne laughed as Drew gave him an awful look. If th[e]
rascal and the pirate were representative of Drew's servant[s]
it must be an unusual household.

'I cannot wait to meet the rest of your servants,' she said i[n]
a low voice to Drew. He smiled at her, but made no commen[t.]
Marianne thought that perhaps she understood. Having n[o]
family, he had taken the rascal under his wing, treating him wit[h]
careless affection, and no doubt, it was a similar feeling th[at]
made his friendship with Robbie what it was, but perhaps th[at]
was the limit of his indulgence, for the servants at Marlbec[k]
would have served his uncle and be of a very different ilk.

'I cannot wait to take you home,' he said. 'But first we mu[st]
settle the wedding—shall it be here or at Lady Edgeworthy[']
home? I understand that your mama and sisters are to mak[e]
their home with her.'

'Yes, that is so,' Marianne said. 'We must ask Mama and m[y]
great-aunt what they think would be best. For myself, I think [I]
should like it to be at Sawlebridge House, but we must as[k]
them.'

'I am sure they will be happy to do as you wish,' Drew sai[d]
'If they agree, I shall return to Cornwall and make the a[r-]
rangements at the end of the week.'

In the event it was decided that they would all return [to]
Sawlebridge at the end of that week. Lady Edgeworthy w[as]
delighted that Marianne thought of it as her home and w[as]
eager to make her wedding a happy occasion. She told the[m]
that she had enjoyed her stay in Bath, but would prefer to li[ve]
at Sawlebridge House now that she had company.

'You will be living with me, Cynthia,' she said, looking ery content. 'And Jo will come to us after her visit with Lady ainwright—and, of course, dear Lucy will be with us for me years yet.'

'Jo has written to say that the visit to Bath has been ferred yet again,' Mrs Horne said. 'She must come for your edding, Marianne, and my sister may come with her if she ishes. They may travel to Bath from there.'

'Yes, for I should love to see Jo again,' Marianne said. Her es were glowing with happiness as she looked at her mother d aunt. 'It is all so very wonderful. I thought that Drew had rgotten me—but he was ill. He went out in a storm and bbie had to nurse him through an illness, but he came raight here as soon as he was well enough.'

'Yes, he told me that he had been unwell for a few days. pparently it was a fever that he contracted while fighting th the army overseas, and it returns now and then, though assures me it is not serious,' Mrs Horne said. 'So every-ing is just as you would like, my dear?'

'Yes, Mama,' Marianne said. 'Of course it is. I love Drew ry much and I want to be his wife.'

If a little voice in her head told her that she wanted him to clare his love, she quashed it ruthlessly. Her heart told her at he did love her, but as he had confessed, he did not know nat loving meant. She was sure that when they had been arried for a while he would come to understand that what felt for her was love.

Henriette looked at the ring on Marianne's left hand when ey attended her dance. She frowned for the news had tered through, as it always did in small communities.

'You did not tell me that you were to marry Lord Mar' beck?'

'I did not know it myself until yesterday,' Marianne said. 'We knew that we liked each other very well, but h had not proposed.'

'Oh…' Henriette sighed, but did her best to hide her di appointment. 'He is very handsome—and Mama says rich but I do not care for that part of it. I hope that I meet someon as interesting as Lord Marlbeck one day, for at the momen I do not wish to marry any of the gentlemen I have met.'

'I am sure you will one day,' Marianne said. 'Perhaps ne year when you have your Season in London.'

'Yes, perhaps,' Henriette said, but she looked wistful as sh saw Drew approaching. 'You are so lucky, Marianne…'

'Yes, I am,' Marianne said and smiled as he came up to he 'I have saved three dances for you, Drew—though you are little late.'

'Yes, I am sorry for it,' he said. 'A friend of mine came see me and I was delayed.' He frowned and she sensed th he was bothered by something. 'I must leave in the morni early. I had meant to accompany you home, as you know but something has happened.'

'Is something wrong, Drew?'

'Nothing that need concern us this evening,' he said a smiled at her. 'They are playing a waltz—I trust this is o of my dances?'

'Yes, it is,' she said and went into his arms.

'Oh, it was such fun last night,' Lucy said as she sat on t edge of Marianne's bed the next morning and stole the swe biscuits from her plate. It was a ritual they had got into sin they had come to Bath and both of them enjoyed it. 'I am looking forward to your wedding, Marianne, but I shall miss you so much when you go away.'

'You will soon make friends,' Marianne told her. 'Aunt Bertha told me that she knows of one or two girls of your age that live not far from her. She will invite them and their mamas to tea and you will get to know them.'

'It isn't like having you and Jo,' Lucy said. 'I like Henriette, of course, and she says that she shall write to me, but she isn't you, Marianne.'

'Well, you may come and stay with us when we are married,' Marianne said. 'Drew says that you are welcome to stay as often as you like.'

'Oh…' Lucy's face lit up. 'Then perhaps I don't mind you getting married after all!' Lucy took her hand, examining the beautiful sapphire and diamond ring on Marianne's third finger. 'This is so pretty. You will have lots of jewels when you are married, I expect.'

'Perhaps, but I already have the pearls that Aunt Bertha gave me. I have returned Mama's pearls now that I have my own, for Jo may wish to wear them.'

Lucy looked thoughtful. 'Henriette said that I shall have to curtsy to you when you are the Marchioness of Marlbeck.'

'Henriette talks a lot of nonsense,' Marianne said and smiled as she leaned forward to kiss her sister's cheek. 'Drew does not expect you to curtsy to him, does he?'

'Oh, no,' Lucy said and giggled at the idea. 'He wouldn't, of course, because he is such a tease. I like him. He makes me laugh—and he gave me a guinea the other day, but said not to tell anyone.'

'Just like Papa,' Marianne said and laughed. 'He used to

give us a shilling and warn us not to tell Mama—do you remember?'

'Yes.' Lucy nodded. 'He gave money to the village children as well—do you suppose Drew does that, too?'

'I should not be surprised,' Marianne said, because she was discovering that there were many sides to the man she loved. 'Go and get dressed now, my dearest. We have a long journey ahead of us and Aunt Bertha wants to start by ten o'clock.'

'Yes, I hadn't forgotten,' Lucy said and snatched another biscuit before she left.

Marianne threw back the bedcovers and got up. She was glad to be returning to Sawlebridge, which had become her home these past weeks. In another few weeks she would be married, and then she would have to make her home at Marlbeck, as Drew's wife.

She began to sing as she dressed, feeling the happiness wash over her. It seemed odd to remember that when they came to Bath she had been close to despair.

They had been home for two days now, and each day had been wet, dull and dark. The rascal had delivered a note to Marianne on the second day. Drew had sent his apologies, but said that he would not be able to call that day, because he was busy, but would come the next day unless something happened to delay him.

Marianne had given the rascal a shilling and asked him if everything was well at the cliff house.

'The food ain't much good,' the rascal said, ''cause Robbie ain't much of a cook. But I've 'ad worse. His lordship has a friend stayin', see, and he's out all the time. They're searchin for some geezer what is gonna be in trouble when they get 'im—but I dunno more than that, 'cause his lordship told me to mind me own business.'

'Oh, I see,' Marianne said and frowned as she returned to the house. She had almost forgotten about Mr Hambleton, and the smugglers in the cove seemed a distant dream. She was sure it must be him that Drew and his friend were searching for, though she would have thought he would have gone long ago.

On the third morning the sun shone and it was much warmer than of late. Marianne spent the morning writing wedding invitations and opening some gifts, which had already begun to arrive. At a little before noon she went out into the garden to cut some flowers. There were still quite a few roses and some lilies, besides a pretty tall-stemmed daisy that would look well in her aunt's parlour.

She was smiling as she laid the blooms one by one in her basket, feeling the warmth of the sun on the back of her neck. She hoped that it would be fine on the day of her wedding, but it would be late October then and she could hardly expect it to be as warm as this. Not that it mattered. She would be happy to be married whatever the weather.

'So…' a harsh voice said behind her, making her jump. 'Nothing changes with you, except that I have heard that you are to marry that devil Marlbeck…if I don't make you a widow before you're a wife.'

Marianne swirled round, her face draining of colour as she saw Joshua Hambleton standing there. He looked different—he had not shaved and his beard had grown untidily, his hair looking as if it had not been combed for a long time. Her hand went to her throat, fear shafting through her.

'What are you doing here? Why have you come?'

'I am tired of living rough,' Joshua said, his eyes glinting with anger. 'All this would have been mine had it not been for you. Now I have nothing. I am ruined. There is nowhere for me to go, because they are looking for me everywhere.'

'You are a traitor to your country,' Marianne said, raising her head proudly. 'You betrayed men who were your comrades for money—and you passed information to a French spy. You brought your ruin on yourself, sir. Besides, I do not think that you are who you say.'

He moved closer. 'I have been many people,' he said. 'But I could have been a gentleman if you had not come here and ruined it all.'

Marianne took a step backwards, because she sensed the festering hatred in him and knew that he meant to harm her. 'You had no right to anything—but if you had behaved differently, my aunt would not have disinherited you.'

'But she did because of you.' Joshua took out a little pistol and pointed it at Marianne, making her give a little cry of fear. He laughed evilly. 'Oh, I don't mean to kill you yet. I want revenge on that devil Marlbeck—and I want money. I am taking you with me, Miss Horne, and he can pay to get you back, if he wants you.'

'No!' Marianne backed away. Her gaze was fixed on his face, meeting his look of menace with pride and courage. 'I shall not come with you. You cannot make me.'

'Maybe it would please me to see you dead,' Joshua said. He reached out and made a grab for her wrist, but she avoided him, retreating slowly but steadily towards the house. 'Do as you are told, damn you! If you resist, I shall kill you now rather than later.'

'Pull that trigger and you're a dead man,' a voice said from behind Joshua, causing him to spin round, his pistol now pointing at Drew. 'Shoot me and you will hang. I'm not alone. There are fifty men on this estate searching for you. You were seen making your way here earlier. We know that you met with Raoul Viera at the mine last night, and we know that you fell out with him. He refused to pay you for your losses and you killed him. We found his body this morning, though you had thrown it into the mine shaft. You are finished, Hambleton, or whatever you call yourself now.'

'Then I might as well take you with me and her!' Joshua cried, his finger coming down on the hammer. At that precise moment, Marianne threw herself at his back, knocking him forward and causing his shot to misfire. In the next instant, Drew was on him, and her heart was in her mouth as they struggled for Joshua's pistol, and then, suddenly it went spinning from his hand. 'Damn you!' Joshua swore as he struck out at Drew with such ferocity that for a moment he staggered and let go of his arm. Instantly, Joshua started to run.

Drew took aim at his retreating back, but then as Marianne came to him, touching his arm, he looked at her and lowered his pistol.

'Yes, you are right,' he agreed. 'He won't go far. Jack and five of the militia are only minutes behind me. It is best that he hangs. Besides, he may have information to give them.'

'You said he killed the French spy? Did he escape?'

'They let him go for reasons of their own,' Drew said and frowned. 'Some grand scheme of planting false information with the enemy, which came to nothing. Raoul Viera was seen making his way here and he was seen meeting someone at the mine. We believe it was Hambleton. A shot was fired, but when the men following him got there he had disappeared and the Frenchie's body—though they found that this morning. Hambleton must have known that area well, and he found somewhere to hide that none of our men could find. We think he has been hiding out here all the time, even though he has been searched for time and time again.'

'It must be the tunnel that leads under this house,' Marianne said. 'If Mr Hambleton came here and couldn't get through, he must have been angry. I shouldn't be surprised if you find the entrance somewhere in the mine itself.'

'Yes, I had begun to think on those lines myself,' Drew said. 'Because I now know that there are several different entrances to the mine. I had only looked at the recent workings, but they go on for some distance and some must be hundreds of years old. It is a maze of passages and tunnels down there, but someone ought to find it and make sure it is blocked, though it will probably happen when the mine is opened up again, for I believe it is Lady Edgeworthy's intention to start work there next spring.'

'Yes, I think so,' Marianne said and smiled. She heard a gunshot and her smile vanished for a moment, but then it was back in place as she picked up the basket she had dropped when Joshua surprised her. 'I must take these in for Lucy to arrange. Shall you take nuncheon with us—or must you find out what is happening?'

'Jack is coming now,' Drew said, nodding to indicate a man striding towards them. 'He is one of my closest friends, Marianne. I've asked him to be best man at my wedding.'

'Then he must stay for nuncheon, too, if he wishes,' she said and smiled as an attractive man came up to them.

'Captain Harcourt, Marianne Horne—the lady I have asked to be my wife.'

Jack inclined his head to her, his eyes narrowing. 'Drew always had good taste—and he was always a lucky devil,' he said with a grin at his friend. 'I wish you every happiness, Miss Horne. He is the best of fellows, though a little headstrong. I told him to wait for us, but he would not.'

'Had he not come, I might not have been here to greet you, sir,' Marianne said and smiled at Drew. 'Mr Hambleton was trying to kidnap me, perhaps to bargain for his freedom and more.'

'You've got him?' Drew asked, a grim expression in his eyes.

'Yes, we have him, alive, though wounded in the leg—but he will survive and stand trial,' Jack replied. 'We know that he took his employer's identity after the real Joshua Hambleton died of a fever. We also know that he has killed at least twice, and perhaps more—and that is besides charges of treason and theft. If he doesn't hang, I shall be very surprised.'

Marianne shivered and Drew put his arm about her. 'Don't feel sorry for him,' he said. 'He was an evil man and we may never know the true extent of his crimes.'

'I wasn't feeling sorry for him,' she replied, lifting her head proudly. 'But the sun has gone in and it is time for nuncheon. Will you stay, Captain Harcourt?'

'Willingly,' Jack told her with a look of approval. 'I shall stand up with this fellow here in church for your wedding, and I can tell you that it is a day none of his friends ever expected to see—but it is a good one.'

Marianne nodded, turning to lead the way inside. Drew's life was still a mystery to her, but she was getting to know more of him little by little. She thought that it might take a lifetime to really know him.

'When I saw you struggling with him, I was terrified that I might be too late,' Drew said when they were alone together later that afternoon. Jack had gone and Lucy was upstairs unpacking a trunk that had come for her from the attics at the Lodge. Lady Edgeworthy and Mrs Horne had gone out visiting in the carriage, leaving them to amuse themselves. 'If he had harmed you, I do not know what I should have done, Marianne. I do not think I could bear it if I lost you now.'

'It was a little frightening,' she admitted with a smile. They were standing together, looking out of the parlour window, his arm about her waist. 'But you came when I needed you, and he cannot harm me now.'

'Thank God for Jack and his scheme to have the Frenchie followed,' Drew said. 'Had he not been followed here to his meeting with Hambleton, we might not have known where he was hiding and…' He shook his head. 'No, we shall not speak of it again. It is over and we have better things to think about, my love.'

'Our wedding,' Marianne said, gazing up at him now. 'You must give me a list of the guests you would like to invite so that we can send out the invitations.'

'Jack, of course, and a handful of close friends. I have a distant cousin who might wish to attend, but I have no desire to invite the whole of society—unless you hoped for a big wedding?'

'No, not at all,' Marianne said. 'My Aunt and Uncle Wainwright, and Papa's cousin Toby, Jane and Dr Thompson perhaps Major Barr and a few of my great-aunt's close friends.'

'We shall of course hold a large social event when we go up to London next spring,' Drew told her. 'Do not think I mean to keep you in that great mausoleum of my uncle's, though we must spend some time there—but I have a smaller house in Hampshire that I like and I have had the London house refurbished in a more comfortable style.'

'I think the late marquis was a very grand person,' Marianne said, 'but perhaps we do not need to be quite so grand as he was?'

'You may be as grand or as ordinary as you please, my love,' Drew promised her. 'Though I believe when I take you to London you will find that you are invited everywhere and you may enjoy the social whirl.'

'Yes, I am sure I shall,' Marianne said and leaned up to kiss his cheek. 'And if your friends are all as charming as Jack Harcourt, I am sure I shall like them, too.'

'Hal is younger than either Jack or I,' Drew said. 'He is what you might think of as an irreverent gentleman.'

'I shall look forward to—' Marianne broke off as a travelling coach pulled up outside the house. Almost as soon as it stopped the door opened and a pretty girl jumped down, followed more slowly by an older woman and a gentleman with his arm in a sling. 'Oh, it is my sister Jo and my aunt and uncle. We had not expected them until tomorrow.'

Drew saw the pleasure in her face. 'Go and meet them, dearest,' he said. 'I shall stay to meet them and then I must leave. I have sent for some of my staff from Marlbeck, because I must entertain a few people before the wedding.'

Even as he finished speaking, Jo burst into the room, calling for her sister. She stopped short as she saw Drew, her eyes drawn immediately to his face and wide with curiosity.

'Dearest Jo,' Marianne said. 'This is Lord Marlbeck..
Drew, my sister Jo.'

Jo came towards him, her hand outstretched. 'It is good to
meet you, sir,' she said. 'Yes, I can see why my sister like
you so much. I wasn't sure that you would suit her, for I had
always seen her as the wife of a vicar—but I think you will
do very well.'

'I am flattered by your approval,' Drew said, a look of
unholy glee in his eyes, for he liked Jo's frankness and her
manner. 'I shall try to be worthy of her.'

'You had better be or you will answer to me,' Jo said and
went to embrace Marianne. 'You look lovely, dearest. Being
in love must suit you—though you never had time for aristocrats and I cannot think how you came to decide to marry
one.'

'Jo! That is unpardonably rude of you!' Lady Wainwright
said, entering the room at that precise moment and hearing
only the last few words. 'You must apologise to Lord
Marlbeck immediately.' She put on a simpering smile. '
believe we met earlier this year when you were in town, sir
It was at my daughter's coming-out ball…'

'Ah, yes, I seem to remember,' Drew said and took the
hand she offered, lifting it to air kiss her fingers. 'But you
must not scold Jo—she was merely speaking her mind, you
know. And she will never offend me if she tells me the truth
He grinned at Jo, who shot a look of triumph at her sister.

Fortunately, Lord Wainwright came in at that moment
'Ah, Marlbeck,' he said and went to shake hands with Drew
'Delighted to hear the news, sir. You will do very well for my
niece. She is a lovely girl in every way and I hope she mean
to ask me to give her away.' He smiled at Marianne. 'I have

missed your visits, young lady, and shall be glad to have you as a neighbour in the future. Especially as your mama tells me she is thinking of making her home here.' He glanced at his wife and frowned. 'The Lodge was never meant as a permanent home for her, Marianne. I have found a better house for her if she would like to reconsider.'

'I think Lady Edgeworthy needs her here, and Lucy has settled well,' Marianne said with an apologetic smile. 'But I am sure you will be welcome to visit—and she may visit me sometimes and you will meet her then.'

'Yes, well…as long as she is comfortable,' Lord Wainwright said and sent a look of annoyance in his wife's direction, which clearly indicated to the sisters what they had suspected all along—that it was their aunt who had decided on the Lodge, not their uncle.

'Oh, yes, I think she must be very happy, for my great-aunt is very kind and they get on so well,' Marianne said. 'Your rooms are ready, Aunt Wainwright. Would you like me to take you up—or would you prefer some refreshment first?'

'I should like to rest after that terrible journey,' Lady Wainwright said with a shudder. 'These Cornish roads are disgraceful! You may show me the room, Marianne, and I shall come down in an hour or so.'

'And I must take my leave of you, for I have things to do,' Drew said. He smiled at Marianne. 'Until this evening, my dearest.'

'Yes, we expect you for dinner,' Marianne said. 'Please come with me, Aunt, for I am sure you must be very tired.'

Lord Wainwright looked at Drew as they went out. 'My wife is an indifferent traveller, I fear, but she will be in a better frame when she has rested. I shall look forward to speaking to you later, Marlbeck. I stand as a father to Marianne, of course, and I dare say we have things to discuss.'

'The settlement, of course,' Drew said. 'I have not had time to instruct my lawyer as yet, but I believe you will find I shall be generous.' He nodded his head to Jo and went out, leaving uncle and niece together in the small parlour.

'Well, I dare say he will look after her,' Lord Wainwright said. 'Lady Wainwright refused to believe it at first, for she had settled in her mind that your sister would not do better than a baronet, but she is reconciled to the idea now. She may have to revise her ideas in the matter of your marriage now, miss.'

'Oh, no,' Jo said and grinned at him, for she liked her uncle far more than her aunt. 'Marianne is the beauty of the family, though I think Lucy may rival her in a few years. Besides, I am not sure that I wish to marry at all.'

'Well, I dare say your mother and great-aunt would be happy enough to have you live with them for a while,' he said. 'But you won't let your aunt down, Jo? She is counting on you to accompany her to Bath.'

'Lady Wainwright has been generous with my clothes, sir,' Jo told him. 'It would be unkind in me to refuse her now. But she must not mind too much if I do not find myself a husband.'

At that moment Lucy came running into the room, and after greeting her uncle, the sisters embraced, hugging each other and exchanging stories. Lucy then dragged Jo off to see her room, which she said was next to her own, and then Marianne came back into the parlour.

'You are alone, sir,' she said. 'Would you care for some of Aunt Bertha's Madeira? I believe it is very good.'

'I need nothing for the moment,' he said. 'Come and talk to me. I have wished that I had let your mama and sisters stay at the Vicarage until a decent house was found. Agatha…I believed the Lodge might suit, but I was very distressed when poor little Lucy was ill.'

'Yes, it was upsetting for Mama, but Lucy is better now, as I dare say you saw just now.'

'Indeed, she was her old self, and I am much relieved. You must know that I am very fond of you all…' He looked so uncomfortable that Marianne took pity on him. She went to him and kissed his cheek, smiling up at him as he responded in kind. 'There now, I see you don't bear grudges.'

'Why should I?' she asked. 'You have always been kind to us, Uncle.'

'And might have been kinder…' He shook his head. 'I've a special gift for you in my trunk, Marianne. Marlbeck is filled with treasures of all kinds, and so I settled on a diamond necklace for you—your husband has quite enough money and property as it is.'

'Yes, I suppose he is quite wealthy.'

'One of the richest men in England,' her uncle said and then laughed. 'Money is nothing unless you have someone to share it with, my dear. I believe you will give him as much and more than he has to give you.'

Marianne smiled, but was saved from answering by the arrival of her mama and Lady Edgeworthy. There was a flurry of greetings and the tea tray was sent for just as Lady Wainwright came down, and it was more than an hour later that Marianne was able to slip away to her room.

Jo followed her up, her eyes bright with mischief. 'I have been longing to be alone with you,' she cried. 'It seems ages since you came down here, though it is not so very long, of course—but now you are to be married!'

'Yes, I am,' Marianne agreed, her face alight with happiness. 'I can hardly believe it, Jo. I am so lucky!'

'Well, as to that, I think he is the lucky one,' Jo said. 'But if you are happy, that is all that matters.'

'I have never been happier. I can hardly wait for my wedding day.'

Chapter Twelve

It was a fine crisp morning when Marianne awoke to the realisation that it was the day of her wedding. The sun was shining, though there was a cool breeze out, because it was late October now. At least it was not raining, which it had done for some days the previous week, keeping all three girls in the house. However, it had been just like the days they had so often spent together at the Vicarage and they had been happy enough in their own company.

Drew had spent three days with Marianne and her sisters, apparently content to enjoy their company, until he was obliged to return to Marlbeck on some business for the estate.

He had taken his leave of her in private in the small parlour, her sisters tactfully taking themselves off to allow them a few moments alone.

Drew had kissed her lingeringly, a hint of regret in his face. I am glad we had these few days. I have enjoyed seeing you with your sisters, my dearest one. It has revealed to me a side of life that I have never known and I wish I did not have to leave—but there are things that must be done if we are to have our wedding trip to Italy.'

'Yes, of course you must go,' Marianne had told him, gazing up at him with such love in her eyes that he felt his throat constrict. 'It will not be long until our wedding.'

And now the days had passed and she was to be wed that morning.

'Oh, you do look beautiful,' Lucy said, coming in when Marianne was almost finished dressing. 'I brought you this— it is my own present to you, darling Marianne.' She gave her sister a garter of blue ribbon that she had made herself. 'I hope it brings you lots of luck!'

'I am sure it will,' Marianne said and kissed her.

Jo was the next to arrive with her gift. She had bought a journal of good-quality vellum, bound with leather. Into it she had pasted dried flowers and poems that she loved, also receipts for lotions and creams that their mama had taught them, and a lock of Papa's hair twisted and plated into the letter M.

'Oh, Jo,' Marianne said with tears in her eyes. 'What a wonderful gift. I shall treasure it always.'

'Well, Drew will give you all the clothes and trinkets you wish for,' Jo said. 'But something like this will remind you of us when we were all together as a family.'

'Yes, it will,' Marianne agreed. 'But you know that Drew has said that he will always welcome my family whenever they care to come and stay with us.'

'Yes—' Jo sniffed hard '—it isn't quite the same, though is it?'

Marianne agreed that it wasn't, of course. 'I was blessed with the best of childhoods,' she said. 'I shall never forget how fortunate I have been.'

'But now you have someone else to love,' Jo said. 'I know and I don't mind, truly I don't—but I wanted you to remember.'

After that, Mama and Aunt Bertha had come up to see her and to bring their own small gifts. Downstairs in the back parlour a table had been set with all the expensive gifts that had been showered on Marianne and her marquis, many more than she had expected, especially as some were from people she did not know and who had not been invited to the wedding.

'Do not let it alarm you,' Drew said when an impressive silver tea-and-coffee set arrived from the Earl and Countess of Sawston. 'Those we have not invited will be thanked and invited to our ball next year.'

Jane had come to see her, bringing a gift of lace handkerchiefs she had sewn herself, for which Marianne was as grateful as she had been for the massive silver tea service. They embraced, and Jane confided the welcome news that she thought she was already increasing.

And then it was time for everyone to leave for the church. Marianne's heart was beating wildly as she walked down the aisle to the sound of organ music, and then Drew turned his head to watch her and the look in his eyes sent a thrill of happiness winging through her, because it was the look of love.

She smiled at him as she took her place at his side, listening and responding to the Vicar's words, but truly aware only of the man at her side. In no time at all the Vicar had pronounced them man and wife and they were walking outside to the sound of joyful bells.

'You look beautiful, my darling,' Drew whispered as they were showered with rose petals and good wishes from the villagers who had gathered outside to press tokens and flowers on the bride. 'I missed you.'

'Did you?' She looked into his eyes and her heart raced as she saw the smouldering passion. 'I love you so much, Drew.'

'Keep saying that to me,' he whispered as he took her hand and they ran for the carriage. 'Tell me it every day, for I shall never tire of hearing it.'

'I will,' she promised.

When they were alone in the carriage he kissed her, tenderly at first and then with a deepening passion that made her body feel as if it would melt in the heat of their mutual desire.

'I have some presents for your mama and sisters,' he told her after he released her. 'Also both your aunts and Wainwright. They should have been delivered by the time we get back. I hope they will like them.'

'Oh, Drew,' she said, her throat tight. 'How good it is of you to think of them.' He had already showered her with numerous gifts of jewellery, lace and costly trinkets, but to bring presents for her family was something that pleased her even more.

'They are my family now,' he said and something in his voice made her look at him.

'Yes,' she said softly. 'They are your family now.' She could only guess at what that must mean to him.

The reception was a small one by the standards of society, but Lady Edgeworthy's house overflowed with happy guests. Drew's elderly cousin had come and presented them both with generous gifts. He told Marianne of his pleasure in his cousin's marriage and said that he hoped to visit them at Marlbeck one day.

Marianne could not have been happier than to welcome

him to their extended family, for Drew seemed at home amongst her sisters and aunts, and even Lady Wainwright was seen to smile on him with approval.

'I never expected you to marry so well,' she told Marianne and touched the magnificent diamond star brooch at her throat, which had been his gift to her. 'Marlbeck is a generous man. I believe you have done well for yourself.'

'I am in love with him, Aunt,' Marianne told her serenely. 'I married him for that reason alone.'

'Well!' Lady Wainwright looked slightly annoyed, but said no more as she sailed off in Lord Harcourt's direction to harangue him about something the government had done, with which she heartily disagreed.

The afternoon sped by and then Marianne was changing into her travelling gown, saying goodbye to her sisters and her mama, and accompanying Drew out to the coach that was waiting to take them on the first stage of their honeymoon. She gave him her hand and he helped her into the coach, watching her as she enthusiastically waved farewell to everyone who had come out to see her leave. When she could no longer see them, she turned to see the enigmatic look in his eyes and raised her brows.

'What?'

'I was just thinking how much my life has changed in a few short weeks. I had settled for second best and then you came and turned it all upside down.'

'I am not sure what you mean?'

'I was thinking of making a marriage of convenience simply to secure an heir for the title, but that all became lost when I kissed you. I knew that it had to be you or no one.'

Marianne dimpled at him. 'We shall be alone in Italy Drew,' she said. 'My family are very possessive, but they will not be with us on our honeymoon.'

'Oh, I do not resent them,' Drew said. 'I enjoy seeing you all together—and being part of your family. It is just that feel I have somehow got caught up in a whirlwind.'

Marianne saw that his eyes were filled with laughter. 'Yes I have a similar feeling,' she confessed. 'We have not known each other long, Drew. I hope you will not regret making m your wife.'

'Oh, no, I shall not regret it,' he said. 'Not for one instant I promise. There was a time when life seemed empty. I d not think it will feel that way in the future. But you never ha the chance for a Season in town. I hope that one day you wi not wish that you had waited.'

'I shall never feel that way,' Marianne promised him. ' love you, my dearest husband, and I always shall.'

'And I think…' Drew said, reaching out to draw her close His hand moved over the softness of her full breasts, caress ing them gently through the thin silk of her gown, as h placed a kiss at the pulse spot just at the base of her throa 'I believe that this hunger, this tenderness, this aching nee I feel whenever I see or touch you, must be this thing you ca love.'

'Yes, of course it is,' Marianne said and lifted her face f his kiss. His finger smoothed the line where her dress dippe showing the sweetness of her creamy flesh. She knew that h longed for the moment when they were alone in their bed, a she did. 'What else could it be?'

Gazing down into her eyes, seeing the innocence, the tru and belief reflected there, he knew that he would strive all h

ife to keep her faith in him as bright and shiny as it was on
heir wedding day.

As their lips touched, she felt herself drowning in the over-
vhelming surge of love and need that united them as one. His
iss promised so much, and she knew that she would find her
eaven in his arms that night.

Later that night, as she lay pressed against him, limbs
ntwined, their hunger satiated for the moment, Marianne
nderstood that she had been even luckier than she knew. He
ad loved her tenderly, sweetly, drawing her slowly along the
ath to the fulfilment of their mutual desire so that when he
ntered her the slight pain was as nothing and she was swept
way on a tide of rising passion.

'Nothing will ever part us now,' he vowed. 'I know that I
ave been fortunate beyond my deserts,' Drew told her
oarsely as the desire rose hotly in him again. 'I was alone,
ut now I have you and the world is no longer the empty place
thought it.'

'I love you, Drew,' she whispered. 'I shall love you for
ll my life.'

'And I love you,' he said, accepting that it was true, for she
ad shown him the meaning of love and he knew that at last
e could leave the loneliness of his past behind him.

Afterword

Marianne had gone and both sisters were already missing her. Lucy was sitting on the edge of Jo's bed, listening as she read a page of her story aloud.

'*As Mary looked round the large comfortable parlour a the Vicarage, she knew that she had made the right choice,* Jo read, a little frown creasing her brow. '*Had she accepte the earl, she would now have been living in an empty, echoin house with no hope of finding any kind of fulfilment. At leas as the wife of a good man like the Reverend Thornton sh could look forward to filling her days with good works.*'

Jo laid the page down with a sigh and looked at her siste 'It isn't very good, is it?'

'I'm not sure,' Lucy said truthfully. 'I quite liked the earl– why didn't you let her marry him instead?'

'Because I thought it was too unlikely to be true,' Jo sai and laughed. 'I wrote the story about a girl like us. I wa thinking of Marianne, for I always believed that she woul marry someone like Papa.'

'Drew isn't a bit like Papa,' Lucy said and smiled. 'In fac

I think he must be exactly opposite. But he is very nice. I like him and I think he will make Marianne happy, because he adores her.'

'Yes, he does,' Jo agreed. 'You can see it in his eyes when he looks at her.' She shook her head. 'But he isn't like most aristocrats—they are all so proud and they don't care about people.'

'How do you know that?' Lucy asked. 'You haven't met very many. If you are speaking of Aunt Wainwright, then I must agree that she doesn't care about anyone very much—but Aunt Bertha is so kind, and Uncle Wainwright is really nice when you talk to him on his own.' Lucy leaned forward to kiss her sister's cheek. 'I liked the earl. If you let Mary marry him instead of the Reverend, it would be much more exciting, don't you think?'

She smiled at Jo and left her in favour of her own bed, where, Jo imagined, she would curl up with one of her fairy stories. It was all very well for Lucy to say that Mary should have married the earl, and, indeed, Jo had developed a sneaking liking for him, despite the fact that he had done dreadful things and deserved to be cast into despair when he was spurned by the heroine—but life wasn't all roses.

Jo had seen so many cases of wives being cruelly treated by their husbands when she visited the village with her gifts of food and toys for the children. It had always seemed so unfair to her that the wealthy landowners should have so much while others had nothing. Her papa had been such a loving man, so kind and generous to others, though he had little to spare, and she had seen him as a hero, championing the cause of the poor.

Lucy was right, though, Jo admitted as she blew out her candle and settled down to sleep. Marianne's marquis was rather lovely, and she was glad that her sister was so happy.

For herself, Jo thought that she would still rather remain unwed, though she wasn't sure that her desire to become an author would come to anything. Her first story was certainly not the sweeping masterpiece she had hoped it might be.

A sigh escaped her as she thought about the morning. It was her Aunt Wainwright's intention to go straight to Bath from here. Lord Wainwright was to escort them there and stay one night, before returning home. He did not care much for taking the waters or insipid balls, as he called them, though he had given his niece twenty pounds for her pin money.

'Don't tell your aunt,' he had told her with a wink. 'Let her provide for you, Jo—but keep this in case you need it.'

'Thank you, Uncle,' Jo said and kissed his cheek. 'I shall keep it for emergencies.'

Having promised her aunt that she would go on this long anticipated visit, Jo could not change her mind, even though she would have much preferred to stay here. Like Marianne she enjoyed walking and it was lovely here, especially on the cliffs.

Oh, well, the visit to Bath could not last for ever, and when it was over, she would be able to return here. Jo buried herself deep in the softness of her feather bed and closed her eyes. Before very long she was dreaming, and this time Mar had married the earl and Lucy was right—it was more exciting....

Medieval
LORDS & LADIES
COLLECTION

When courageous knights risked all to win the hand of their lady!

Volume 1: Conquest Brides – July 2007
Gentle Conqueror by Julia Byrne
Madselin's Choice by Elizabeth Henshall

Volume 2: Blackmail & Betrayal – August 2007
A Knight in Waiting by Juliet Landon
Betrayed Hearts by Elizabeth Henshall

Volume 3: The War of the Roses – September 2007
Loyal Hearts by Sarah Westleigh
The Traitor's Daughter by Joanna Makepeace

6 volumes in all to collect!

Medieval
LORDS & LADIES
COLLECTION

VOLUME THREE
THE WAR OF THE ROSES
Bold fighters, courtly lovers

Loyal Hearts by Sarah Westleigh

Lady Pippa d'Alban was in turmoil. Her betrothed had returned to England with Henry Bolingbroke. Sir Giles d'Evreux had been in no hurry to wed her five years ago, so how could the contract be honoured now? Especially when her family supported the rightful king! Astounded at her blossoming, Giles meant to wed her, with or without her consent!

The Traitor's Daughter by Joanna Makepeace

Lady Philippa is tainted by her father's politics. Sir Rhys Griffiths has the power of life and death over her family. Yet he seems a man of honour, a man who has appointed himself her protector. Could it be that he seeks her father for quite a different reason – to ask for her hand in marriage?

Available 7th September 2007

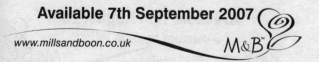

www.millsandboon.co.uk

M&B

FREE

2 BOOKS AND A SURPRISE GIFT

We would like to take this opportunity to thank you for reading th
Mills & Boon® book by offering you the chance to take TWO mo
specially selected titles from the Historical series absolutely FRE
We're also making this offer to introduce you to the benefits of th
Mills & Boon® Reader Service™—

- ★ FREE home delivery
- ★ FREE gifts and competitions
- ★ FREE monthly Newsletter
- ★ Books available before they're in the shops
- ★ Exclusive Reader Service offers

Accepting these FREE books and gift places you under no obligatic
to buy; you may cancel at any time, even after receiving your fr
shipment. Simply complete your details below and return the enti
page to the address below. You don't even need a stamp!

YES! Please send me 2 free Historical books and a surprise gift.
understand that unless you hear from me, I will receive
superb new titles every month for just £3.69 each, postage and packi
free. I am under no obligation to purchase any books and may canc
my subscription at any time. The free books and gift will be mine
keep in any case.

H7ZE

Ms/Mrs/Miss/Mr...Initials ....
BLOCK CAPITALS PLE.

Surname ....

Address ....

....

....Postcode ....

Send this whole page to:
The Reader Service, FREEPOST CN81, Croydon, CR9 3WZ